Books by Kay Boyle

Novels

THE SEAGULL ON THE STEP *(1955)*
HIS HUMAN MAJESTY *(1949)*
"1939" *(1948)*
A FRENCHMAN MUST DIE *(1946)*
AVALANCHE *(1944)*
PRIMER FOR COMBAT *(1942)*
MONDAY NIGHT *(1938)*
DEATH OF A MAN *(1936)*
MY NEXT BRIDE *(1934)*
GENTLEMEN, I ADDRESS YOU PRIVATELY *(1933)*
YEAR BEFORE LAST *(1932)*
PLAGUED BY THE NIGHTINGALE *(1931)*

Short Stories and Novelettes

THE SMOKING MOUNTAIN *(1951)*
THIRTY STORIES *(1946)*
THE CRAZY HUNTER *(1940)*
THE WHITE HORSES OF VIENNA *(1936)*
THE FIRST LOVER *(1933)*
WEDDING DAY *(1929, 1930)*

Poetry

AMERICAN CITIZEN *(1944)*
A GLAD DAY *(1938)*

For Children

THE YOUNGEST CAMEL *(1939)*

The Seagull on the Step

Kay Boyle

THE

EAGULL

ON

THE TEP

NEW YORK

 ALFRED A KNOPF

1955

THIS IS A BORZOI BOOK, PUBLISHED BY ALFRED A. KNOPF, INC.

L. C. catalog card number: *55-5604*
© Kay Boyle, *1955*

FIRST EDITION

THIS BOOK IS DEDICATED IN LOVE TO

those young people who are the flesh and spirit

of the new France (and who have, in consequence,

no time or need to read these pages), among

them my children who are there.

The Seagull on the Step

ONE AFTERNOON IN LATE JUNE A young woman none of the passengers had ever seen before got on the bus, and the bus-driver behind the wheel set his soiled white sea-captain's beaked cap at a jauntier angle as she mounted the step and put her suitcase down. From the look of her glossy chestnut hair, and her green linen hat, like an American sailor's trim, starched cap, pushed up off her brow, she seemed to be an American, and the French people sitting there on the cracked, imitation leather of the seats looked in censure at her, believing they knew so much about Americans that there was nothing left to know. The newspaper she carried under one arm was the evening paper of this shipbuilding place on the Mediterranean Sea, and in the newspaper were the stories they all had read, or others like them, the same stories, with only the names of the principals differing, but never the nationalities. Here an American army truck had caused the death of three French cyclists the night before, an item on the front page went—three more deaths in the endless roster of them, said the paper, due to the blinding white headlights which American army vehicles and American private cars continued to use in violation of the French road law. And here a brawl had taken place in a café between American soldiers and the French proprietor over the price of drinks, and the proprietor was quoted as saying from his hospital bed:

"If they stayed in America where they belong, the American army, they'd be paying twice as much for their drinks as what I asked them! I don't know what they wanted to start fighting for!"

Twice a day the bus left from under the plane trees in the main square of this seaport to which the girl had come, and passed out of the city and up the road along the cliffs, bearing shoppers and workers back to the fishing-villages that lay scattered along the bays of the wild, irregular southern coast. Once in the morning, and once in the late afternoon, it would move out of the frame of trees and café terraces, with twenty or thirty passengers crowded onto the seats, and another twenty packed upright in the center aisle. Those who stood kept their balance by holding to the racks above their heads, where soft deep baskets, woven in Italy, and black cord *filets*, packed with artichokes, and new potatoes as small and clean as pigeon eggs, and zucchini, and golden melons, had been placed with care. So it was worth the price of the bus fare, thought the girl glancing at the racks, to come from the fishing-villages to the shipbuilding town to buy for the week, for the women who rode the bus, and the men as well, were simple people, wearing rope-soled *espadrilles* and dark cotton clothes, with their forearms sunburned and their heads bare.

"I want to get off at Abelin," the girl said in fair enough French to the bus-driver, standing there in her pale-green linen dress, and taking her money out. Because of the singular guilelessness of her face, she might have been taken for a schoolgirl, perhaps no older than sixteen

4

or seventeen; and because her slender arms and legs were white, she could not have been long in this part of the country, where the sun rose at five in the summer months and, day after day, in the fourteen hours of its span, darkened the skin to rich mahogany. "Is it the first village or the second along the coast?" she asked.

"That depends on which way you're going," said the bus-driver in his loud, southern speech. He sat behind the wheel, the singlet he wore a faded pink, his cotton trousers a washed-out blue, the ticket pouch slung, as large as a handbag, on a strap around his neck. "If you were coming on foot from Italy," he said, peeling the strip of ticket off with his thumb, "the answer wouldn't be the same as if you were arriving by jet or rocket from New York," and, listening to him, the others began to laugh. He was an olive-skinned, tough-jawed young man, with a bull-like throat, and a high, full chest, and muscular, bronzed arms and shoulders springing with black hair. "As a military objective, Abelin isn't very interesting," he said, the look in his bold eyes partly sardonic, partly loving, as he shook his head in mock regret. To the passengers, this was the best thing he had said, and they laughed outright, for talk of this sort to an American was music to their ears.

"Well, from here, then, how far is it to Abelin?" the girl said, speaking quietly but stubbornly. She knew it well, the bated speech and the guarded eye of a people's hostile presence. She had known it more than once in Paris in the past year, but not in the cafés of the Champs-Elysées, and not in the shops of the avenue de l'Opéra, but in humbler districts, where men and women waited in endless lines for transportation, and where armies of cyclists wheeled homeward from the factories at the end of the day. But this town was stranger than Paris had ever been, and the voices

5

were louder, and she felt a tremor of uneasiness pass through her heart as she stood alone before its presence in the bus.

"What are you in such a hurry for?" the bus-driver said. "Certain people and certain countries are always in a hurry to get somewhere they haven't been yet. Why, I read every day about some countries that want to go jumping into a war, any war, just like that!" he said, and he snapped his second finger loudly on the hard, dark cushion of his thumb. "They're in such a hurry that they want to drag everyone along, top-speed, forcing guns in their hands whether they want to take them or not, and digging up other people's back yards for airfields! We'll get to Abelin just like we do every evening, and when we get there I'll stop the bus long enough to take the *apéritif* and play a round of *boules* on the square, just like I always do. Life's short, mademoiselle, and whatever bus we take, we're all going the same place in the end, so you might as well take it easy," he said, and the passengers still laughed.

"Yes, yes, I know," said the girl, but now the color had come into her face, and her young eyes meeting his had the same copper in them as gave life to her hair. "But there are times—certain moments in life—when one has to do things quickly, very quickly," she said, and she thought if she could find the courage to tell them why she was here, even the men and women sitting in the bus would listen and not laugh. She turned her head for a moment to look at their faces, at the Italian gold of their skins, and the women's richly oiled hair, and the men's warm, meridional eyes, but she could not bring herself to say to them that in the handbag she carried under her arm was a letter written in Abelin last week, and that it was in answer to this letter she had come. *If I were brave instead of merely being stubborn*

6

as a mule, she thought, looking away, *I would take the letter out and read it to the woman with the brass hoops in her ears over there, and to the man in the straw helmet by the window, and to the two soldiers, and to the man with the pointed beard, and to all the rest of them.*

But, instead, she leaned to pick her suitcase up, and the bus-driver got to his feet, as if reluctantly, but as he took the suitcase from her, his dark, urgent fingers touched her hand. He followed behind her, and lifted the mono-grammed suitcase onto the rack, fitting it in between the woven baskets and the *filets* packed with melons and lettuce heads and papery necklaces of garlic, where it rested like an emissary from a more luxurious world. Beneath it were the only two vacant seats, and the girl slipped into the one by the open window, and turned in uneasiness from the judgment of the bus to the strong, still presence of the plane trees, their trunks leprous-white, their leaves hang-ing dark and quiet in the breathless square. Behind her sat the man in the straw helmet, and beside him, as if delicately carved from seasoned wood, an old and in-finitely wrinkled peasant woman wrapped in a black, fringed shawl. On the twin seats before the girl were the young recruits, their necks shaved close, their ears flushed with the heat, their bodies sweltering in the cheap, shaggy khaki of the French infantry.

"It's a hot day for you to be dressed up in your winter flannels," the bus-driver said to the two soldiers as he passed them.

"It's going to be hotter where we're going!" said one soldier, his hoarse young voice raised in instant abuse. "And all we're paid for this dress rehearsal for the real performance is thirty francs a day!"

"Thirty francs wouldn't buy you an air-mail stamp for a

7

letter to Eisenhower telling him we could do with a lot less armament over here, and that we don't need Coca-Cola!" said the bus-driver, calling the words back over his shoulder as he sat down behind the wheel again.

"We've got three weeks of maneuvers coming up!" the second soldier cried out, and his blunt-fingered red hand shoved his khaki cap backward and forward on his close-cropped skull. "They figure they'll sweat the neutrality out of us up there in the *maquis!*"

"At that, it's cooler than Indo-China!" the bus-driver shouted as he started the motor, and he manipulated the lever of the folding-door until the panels of it sighed slowly closed. "Me, I'll take my war cold! We've all got a chance until they start shooting!" he roared above the clamor of the motor, and his eyes sought the reflection of the girl's face in the windshield mirror as the bus moved out of the shade of the plane trees and out of the square. In any northern place it would have been taken for anger, the violence with which he and the soldiers bawled their conversation out; but here, with Italy just down the coast, and North Africa nearly visible across the strip of Mediterranean Sea, it seemed no more than the way each man protested the interrupted tenor of his life, his voice raised in abuse against the heat, and against the price of postage, with the same emotion as against the single, bitter syllable of war. "Maybe she's just come over from Washington and can give you the right answer!" the bus-driver shouted, and he jerked his head back toward the girl as he took the bus down the avenue of blinding sun. "Ask her when they're thinking of dropping the first H-bomb in Europe, and where they're thinking of dropping it!"

The faces turned toward the girl again, even the soilders turning to look at her for answer, as if the mere fact of being an American invested her with a knowledge of what was to come. And she thought: *Now I should open my bag and take this one Frenchman's letter out, and pass it through the bus from hand to hand. I should say: "Here is a letter from a man called Vaillant, Michel Vaillant, who lives in Abelin, and perhaps you know him, or perhaps he's sitting listening as I speak."* But when she looked up at the two recruits, their faces close and flushed with heat, and across at the doe-eyed lady with brass hoops in her ears, and behind at the man in the straw helmet and the old lady carved delicately from wood, she could not bring herself to take the letter out.

The bus had passed the glinting waters of the harbor and turned from the sight of the islands lying out to sea, and the driver maneuvered its width and length now through the cobbled streets of the old part of the town. He swung it between fish-stalls, and fruit-carts, and trucks halted for loading and unloading, leaning from his seat to shout through the open window at the truckmen, and the pushcart vendors, and the fish-women behind their stalls. It may have been that he spoke of nothing more violent than the weather, but his accent was strong and foreign, and his voice was loud, and the girl could not always understand his speech. He might have been asking the fish-women nothing more than the price of sea-urchin or eel, and they shouted their answers back in loving insult to him, knowing that he, like the rest of them, would like to stretch out on the ancient stones of the port in the shade and eat fresh figs and drink wine from the coastal vine-yards without computing the number of francs per kilo or per bottle that fruit and wine would cost.

"How much are the mussels?" he shouted, and in Paris, the girl thought as she watched the street, the mere fury of his utterance would have stopped all traffic and started the whistles of the police crying shrilly through the air.

But now he had set the pace of it, and all around her in the bus came the chorus of voices speaking of prices: the price of butter, and the price of lard, and the price of lettuce that should grow like a weed in your own garden, the women said, if you lived in a part of the country where enough rain fell. The price of potatoes, and the price of fruit, and bread, and eggs, was the story the passengers told one another, while the bus-driver manipulated the bus unerringly and roared his questions over the harbor-clamor of the street.

"Nine hundred francs the kilo for sole? Throw it back in the sea!" he would roar through the open window as the smell of fish rose in a salty tide.

"Well, what about some lobster instead? Lobster's only two thousand francs, and we throw the shell in free of charge!" the fishwives would shout, their voices like rusted metal, their eyes pressed narrow against the sun. "What about octopus, have some octopus!" they would cry out, and they would lift up the lobster and octopus from the trays of vine leaves, and, with fish scales glaucous on their arms and hands, they would wave the sea-beasts at him in bold, savage humor as he passed. He would swing the bus among the parked trucks, the moving carts, the stalls, as if in hot impatience, but knowing to a hair's breadth the margin allowed. "What about salmon at three hundred francs the quarter-pound?" they would cry out, slapping the firm sides of the fish with the palms of their open hands.

But even shouting out to them for the price of sea-spider and crab, he would seek the girl's reflection in the mirror tilted above the windshield glass. And once, when their eyes met in it, she saw a look of sentiment live sorely, briefly, in his urgent eyes.

"Maybe there're one or two Americans worth saving from America," he began saying, and then he saw the lady who signaled from the curb, and the sentiment died in his voice.

She was a lady of sixty or more, perched like a bird of prey on the curb, her nose high-boned, her eye wearily-lidded and circled like a vulture's eye, her hair beneath her stiff three-cornered hat tinted a cold blue. The suit she wore was striped lilac and gray, and she raised her furled gray parasol in signal in the bright, encumbered street.

"Halt, halt!" she cried, pointing her parasol at the bus, but it passed her by, and the raised parasol fluctuated behind it, like a weathervane seeking wildly for the wind. "Halt!" she cried out still, and the passengers turned, laughing, in their seats to watch her run. "Stop! Will you stop?" she cried out, coming even faster in pursuit as the bus slowed down to let a donkey cart go past, and these women with no hats on their heads, and *espadrilles* on their naked feet, laughed shamelessly in their pleasure at the sight of conventionality, of class, of aristocracy, it might have been, so flagrantly defied.

"Watch out! She's gaining on you!" bawled one of the recruits, and the other guffawed.

"She's got one more pushcart of bananas to go, and then she'll be up with you!" called a man's voice from the rear.

"An artichoke fell out of her basket! Now she's stopping to pick it up!" a woman cried in shrill delight.

"Now she's behind a fish-stall, and she can't get by!" another voice went on with it uproariously.

The bus was moving faster now, and as the girl turned

too it seemed to her the laughter that filled it took on another sound. For an instant she believed that the voices were not convulsed with ridicule for a fleeing woman, but convulsed with grief for all that France had lost through war and through dissension, and now they were crying out in disillusionment and pain. She saw the strangely distorted mouths, and the eyes squeezed small with laughing, and in that instant it did not seem like laughter to her, but like the wild shuddering of sobbing, and then the moment passed.

It was only the bus-driver who did not laugh, having perhaps come one step beyond these others in despair, and already fixed the source of blame. He maneuvered the bus between a pushcart laden with green figs and another piled with rabbit hides, and he brought it to a stop beside the curb. His eyes were on the reflection of the girl's face as he reached to pull the lever of the folding-door, as if asking now that some sign of recognition of what he had done be given him by her beauty and her youth and her nationality.

"So I suppose you didn't see me! Is that it?" gasped the lady in the striped suit as she clambered up the step at last, her accent as different from the others as if she spoke another tongue. She put down the neat little basket she carried, and laid her parasol across it, and with one agitated white-gloved hand she set her hat straight on her head. "If General Marceau had lived another year, there'd be a second bus service on the coast road!" she cried, straining for breath as she fumbled in her handbag and brought her money out. "Competition! That would put some manners into you! What is France coming to when a bus-driver can choose whom he'll take on to ride with him and whom he won't?"

"Well, now that you've got on, Madame Marceau," said the bus-driver, his voice ringing through the halted bus; "now that you've made it, I can tell you my side of the story, and it's up to you to take it or leave it alone! This looks like a bus to you, doesn't it?" he said, his eyes bold and dark and hot as he peeled the ticket savagely off and put it in her hand. "Well, maybe it isn't a bus, no matter what it looks like, and maybe I'm not a bus-driver! And maybe because of what this vehicle is it seemed best to keep you out! You belong with the mayor of Abelin, and the others like him, and the rest of us sitting here, we're on the other side!"

"Well, now, what side are you putting us on without asking us first if we want to be there?" said the patient, half-humorous voice of the man in the straw helmet, his words and his gulp of laughter leaving the smell of garlic on the air.

"If Frenchmen had any respect left for their municipal officers, the country wouldn't be in the state it's in today!" said Madame Marceau, and the neat white neckband at her throat, such as French ladies of a certain age and of definite distinction wear, seemed on the point of throttling her.

"Maybe this bus is France, and maybe I'm premier!" the bus-driver shouted, jerking the lever of the door until the panels closed behind her, and then flinging the motor into gear.

As the bus began to move, Madame Marceau held to the back of his seat to keep her balance, fixing him with her sharp, censorious eye.

"Premier!" she cried. "The country's in trouble enough without giving it to a Corsican to run!"

"Who's a Corsican?" the bus-driver shouted, and with

13

his strong brown hands gripping the wheel, he swung the bus so savagely that the Frenchwoman lurched and nearly fell.

"There're enough Corsicans around to fill a jail!" she said, her face as scarlet as a turkey's comb as she leaned in agitation to retrieve her basket and her parasol. Then she came staggering up the aisle, with basket and handbag and parasol as impediment, grasping the backs of the seats to steady her on her way. There was one place left, the seat beside the girl, and the girl reached out and took the basket from her as she swayed. "Just because there was one literate Corsican once, just one, they'll never get over it, the island of them," she was saying. "They talk about history as if they'd made it, singlehanded, and they give the name of Bonaparte to every bandit's son!"

"Who's a bandit?" the bus-driver cried out, turning in his seat as he drove. But Madame Marceau had fallen into the seat beside the girl, and now she reached out and took the basket from her, and set it on her own knees.

"If you're not familiar with this part of the world, then I don't know what you make of all this play-acting!" she said, and her trembling, gloved fingers smoothed the blue waves of her hair. "These people have an etiquette of their own, baked into them by the climate. When the streetcar fare was raised last week, the fishwives and the dockhands and the shipyard workers went out and lifted the streetcars off the tracks and turned them over in the streets. I doubt if you ever saw anything like that where you come from!" she said, appraising the girl as fowls appraise, with a single, glassy eye.

"I've been living in Paris for a year and a half. I've been studying painting there," the girl said.

"Ah, Paris! The Parisians are civilized people!" said

Madame Marceau. "But, let me tell you, it isn't the French who do these things. It's the foreigners. We can't keep them out of these port towns. There are the Algerians and all the other riff-raff, swarming like flies along the waterfront. General Marceau always said that the first step to be taken to put France on her feet again was to clean the foreign element out."

"Who's a foreigner?" the bus-driver shouted, his hot, rueful eyes seeking to find their faces in the mirror as he drove.

"I'm a foreigner too. I come from Columbus, Ohio," the girl said in a low voice.

"But one can see you come from nice people. The well-bred of any country have a great deal in common," Madame Marceau said, and she folded her hands in satisfaction on the basket on her knees.

"If any other Frenchman can deal with the extremes better than I'm dealing with them, I'll step down and give him my place!" the bus-driver cried out grievously. "I've got the anti-clericals on the five back rows where they can't argue with the priests who get on at the Abbey School, and I've got the colonials on one side of the aisle, and the anti-colonials on the other! At the *carrefour* there'll be the shipyard workers getting on, and that will give me a labor majority!"

"Ignorance and shiftlessness characterize these people of the south," Madame Marceau was saying, her hawklike eye still fixed in cold dissection on the girl. "They've got too much Italian blood in their veins. It turns them wily. They'll chew American chewing-gum and smoke American cigarettes, but they won't say a good word about the Americans. I come from Paris. I have a more enlightened point of view. But bear this in mind," she said severely,

15

"the women and men who carry the market baskets in any country have no effect upon its foreign policy." As she said this, she and the girl both glanced at the basket bearing artichokes and tomatoes and lettuce heads that she held on her knees, with her gloved hands folded in complacency across the top. "I do this once a week. I'm not a regular basket-carrier," she hastened to say. "General Marceau would never have tolerated it when he was alive."

"Foreigner!" the bus-driver roared again, his wounded voice as if shadow-boxing with the woman's voice behind him which he could hardly hear. "You're leading the opposition, Madame Marceau, you and the tourist from America, and the military clique!"; and at this designation of themselves the two recruits guffawed and slapped their thighs. "Don't try to make any secret agreements with anyone in uniform! We've been sold out once too often by the people with country houses and city houses, who keep their military decorations under glass!"

"If I hadn't known him for ten years, I'd say he was a Communist," said Madame Marceau to the girl. "But that's the trouble with France now, everyone in the country, including the royalists, talks like a Communist, so you don't know where you are."

"Who's a Communist?" roared the bus-driver in his pain.

"If you look in the artichokes you buy," said the woman with the brass hoops in her ears, and she leaned across the aisle to say it, "you'll find a message printed small on a thin little strip of paper, stuck down between the leaves."

"I found one yesterday," another woman said. "It wasn't the first time."

"Sometimes they say: 'French housewife, I was paid forty francs the kilo for these artichokes! What are they asking you?' " the first woman said, her voice tense, the earrings trembling. "Or they'll say: 'It isn't the man who planted me who is asking the price you had to pay!' "

"I found one last week that read: 'Frenchmen, this is inflation! Where does inflation end?' " said the other woman. "It was signed 'The Producer.' He's the one who's been paid forty francs a kilo for the artichokes, and we're asked three hundred when they get this far!"

"Or else it's the Communists who slip in the messages once the artichokes are on their way," said the man in the straw helmet, and one of the soldiers turned quickly in his seat.

"*B'en*, the trouble with the Communists is that sometimes they're right!" he said.

"Communists or not, we've got inflation," said the other soldier, and he rubbed his cap up and down with the palm of his thick, square hand.

"My advice to you is not to listen to anyone," said Madame Marceau to the girl.

"But I've come all the way from Paris to listen," the girl said.

"Then take the next train back to your family, and go on painting," said Madame Marceau. "The surrealists are easier to understand than the state of mind of the average Frenchman today."

"I haven't any family," the girl said. "My mother died so long ago that I don't remember her, and my father died last year. I've come to find someone in Abelin," she said, and her hand moved in uncertainty, as if she would take the letter from her bag, but she did not take it out. "If you live in Abelin, perhaps you know a man called Vaillant, Michel Vaillant?" she said, and she looked in question at Madame Marceau's face.

17

At once, then, the man in the straw helmet leaned over the back of their seats, and his breath came, pungent with garlic, between the woman and the girl.

"I know Vaillant. I know him well," he said, one big-knuckled hand holding fast to the back of Madame Marceau's seat as the bus swung free of the town.

"Don't be an imbecile, Raffio. Everybody knows Vaillant," said Madame Marceau.

"At this time of day, he might be starting out with the fishermen," Raffio said, his *r*'s rolling under his faded gray mustaches, and the smell of garlic lingering on the air.

"Nothing of the sort," said Madame Marceau sharply. "He'll be correcting his English assignments at the Café du Port while he waits for the Paris newspapers to come. He's always in town for the evening bus. Monsieur Raffio owns the pharmacy on the square, but he's not always accurate about the habits of his customers."

"I don't keep watching them from behind the bottles in the show-window! No, that I don't!" said Monsieur Raffio with a guffaw.

"There are some who might bear watching," said Madame Marceau, and then she turned her acid tongue, her speculating eye, upon the girl. "Your father," she said. "I suppose he wasn't in trade?"

"He was a doctor. Perhaps you've heard of Dr. Wayne Farrant?" the girl said in modest pride. "He won two national awards for the work he did."

"Your hat, Monsieur Raffio," said Madame Marceau testily, "is continuously catching in my hair."

The bus rushed onward, its klaxon blaring out in warning, pressing hard through the stream of slower cars and of oncoming traffic, as if the man who drove it sought to spend his soreness and his passion in the intensity of its advance. Now the road was flanked on the land side by low garden walls, behind which fancy terra-cotta or lime-yellow villas were scattered like dollhouses, and as temporal, among the tall black cypress trees and the cactus plants like monuments in stone.

"On the left, *messieurs*, '*dames*," came the bus-driver's loud, sardonic voice, "you have houses with running water in them, and gas, and electricity! On the right, just this side of the sea, you have the shipyards! Now, you and me, we might think that the houses over there with their nice little gardens had something to do with the men who work in the shipyards. But we'd be wrong! In France they don't work things out that way." It was the end of the working-day, and the men were coming from the yards, knots of them moving on both sides of the street now, pushing their bicycles beside them, their shoulders weary, their lined faces stern, as they waited for the traffic to pass. Behind them, on the coast side, the shipyards could be seen, with the timber skeletons of ships, and the sky above the yards laced intricately with rigging and with masts. "Or, you and me, we might think in our simplicity that the men coming out of the shipyards had something to do with the nice little homes over there!" the bus-driver shouted, venting his spleen by keeping the flat of his hand on the klaxon and driving the bus ever harder through the two-way, impeding cars. "But we'd be wrong again, for the men, some of them, have an hour's ride still on their bicycles before they're home, and the home they get to was modern a couple of hundred years ago! So what do they do, if they have any money in their jeans, but sit down in a *bistro* before going home, and have a drink, and read the paper about what the government's going to do next year, or the year after that, about building houses for them. And when they come to the part about the bathtub with running hot water, they take another drink, and you ought to hear them laugh!"

"The papers were saying the government's going to put up three-room houses, with kitchen and shower, all over France next spring!" one of the soldiers called out.

"Sure! They're for the American air force!" the bus-driver roared.

"Give a French workingman a bathtub and he'd keep rabbits in it!" snapped Madame Marceau.

And now the man with the pointed beard who sat two seats behind them reading the evening paper, lowered the trimly folded sheets of it and, for the first time, spoke.

"Real estate is a science. Greek to the uninitiated," he said, speaking with precision, his red lip trembling moistly in the frail hairs of his beard. "Keeping prices stable safeguards the national economy. Bring the price of a modern villa down to the workingman's salary, and your villa wouldn't be worth the ground you built it on."

"That is the house-agent of Abelin. He buried the family silver somewhere on his property one night before the Germans walked in," said Madame Marceau under her breath, "and he's never been able to find it again. He thinks the Americans took it when they came in, but he isn't sure. So every Sunday afternoon for ten years now he's spent digging for it underneath his cactuses," she said, and the paper was raised again before the pointed beard, the scarlet underlip, the foxlike nose.

"The ground of France worth nothing!" the bus-driver cried out in sudden pain. "That's a house-agent's estimate! It's never a Frenchman's!" he said.

He brought the bus to a stop at the *carrefour*, and he left his place behind the wheel, and, with the sea-captain's soiled cap pushed off his brow and the ticket pouch hanging from his neck, he went out the folding-door. At the rear, he swung himself agilely up the iron ladder to the roof, and there he clung by one muscular bare arm while with the other he hauled the shipyard workers' bicycles up, taking them one by one, with no apparent effort, from their raised hands, and stacking them across the top. When this was done, he jumped lightly down and came back by the street side of the bus, and as he passed the open window where the girl sat he jerked up his dark, strong, bull-like head.

"Do you want to get off here? You still have time. Or do you want to ride the rest of the way with us?" he said, and his eyes were on her with the same hot, rueful look of sentiment that she had seen in them before. "We're French. You're American," he might have been saying to her. "Maybe you can't take the lingo we talk."

"No, I'll stay on. I have to see someone in Abelin," the girl said.

"What's his business?" he asked, and behind him the traffic roared past on the highroad, but he seemed to hear nothing but the sound of her voice, and see nothing but her mouth, and eyes, and hair.

"I'm going to ask for him at the Town Hall. I think he's in politics," she said.

"When we get to Abelin, wait," said the bus-driver, his voice gone confidential now. Had he stood close to her, it seemed to her then that he might have laid one arm across the seat-back in bold, belligerent defense of woman and of woman's vulnerability. "These men getting on have another half-hour's pedaling beyond Abelin before they're

2I

home. While I get their bicycles down, you wait. I'll skip my game of *boules* and find him for you before I go on along the coast."

"Now, why in the world should she need your help?" said Madame Marceau, leaning forward over the basket on her knees and speaking through the window to him. "I'm taking care of her. You go back to driving your bus!" she said, dismissing him who was servant and underling, as was her people's long-inherited right.

His eye was black with ire, and he would not have turned away without the last word then if the men from the shipyards had not called from the bus across the empty driver's seat to him.

"We're late enough getting home as it is!" one called; and another cried out: "We want to see our wives and kids before it's dark!" And a third leaned the flat of his palm on the klaxon, and it blared loudly, shamelessly, as if calling the bus-driver's name.

"The principal thing wrong with him," said Madame Marceau when he had turned away, "is that his grandfather came from Corsica once. Like all men with island blood in their veins, he doesn't trust any place bigger than a peninsula. What has he got against the Americans except that America happens to be a continent?"

Then he was at the wheel again, and the men in their faded cottons and their *espadrilles* paid him their fare, and some among them shook his hand in greeting as they passed. They were moving, step by step now, two-deep down the aisle, their faces weary, retreating backward as others and still others crowded in.

"You're letting too many on!" Madame Marceau cried out in impatience with the press of their bodies in the narrow space. "There's standing-room for ten passengers!

22

It's printed up over the door! The Minister of Public Safety will hear of this! I'll make a complaint to the authorities!"

"The French government fell last night!" the bus-driver shouted back as the last of them pressed in, and he closed the door with difficulty behind them. "There isn't any Minister of Public Safety! There isn't any more authority!"

At once the bus was off again on the coast road, and as it gathered speed, it swung out from its side of the road to pass vehicle after vehicle, facing the oncoming traffic for a perilous instant and then returning, with a hair's breadth of space allowed, to the safety of its own lane. And now the house-agent called down the aisle in a voice gone shrill as a woman's in his fear.

"Keep your mind on the road instead of talking politics! You'll drive like this once too often, and then we'll all be dead!" he cried, the terror in his voice so sharp that for a moment it pierced their hearts with premonition as cold as a steel blade.

Here the look of the landscape abruptly changed, and civilization, without any warning being given, was inexplicably wiped away. Now the wild, mountainous land descended in steep walls on either side, the cast-out boulders of it white, and the dry soil veined by countless paths. Here and there in the desolation pine trees, stunted by wind and shriveled from the heat, rose derelict, like the mastheads of long-foundered ships, above the static surf of the brush that Frenchmen of the south call the *maquis*.

"Who are you building boats for now?" the bus-driver called out to the men behind him who swayed upright with the motion of the racing bus.

"Why, for the Germans, poor devils!" one man shouted in irony. "They're the only ones who had no luck with invasion by water in the last war!"

"If we want bread, we've got to do what the Americans tell us," said the shipyard worker who stood in the aisle by Madame Marceau's seat, his bare arms raised, his strong hands closed upon the rack above his head, his voice sardonic, "and the Americans say we've got to help a fellow member of the European community!"

The soldier seated by the open window turned his head to it, then, and the girl saw his neat red nostril dilate above the golden stubble on his lip.

"Fire. I can smell fire," he said, and the soldier beside him leaned too toward the fleeing air.

"*B'en*, I don't smell anything. I don't see any smoke," he said.

"You have to come from the *midi* to smell it," the first soldier said, looking out on this land on which the receding sea had left its salt-bleached boulders and vegetation that may have flowered once in reefs below the water line. "You have to have fought fires since you were a kid in the *maquis*."

"I've done enough fighting," said the other soldier, his blunt fingers scratching the back of his head. "They can fight their war in Indo-China without me being there."

"I've never seen you do any fighting," said the first soldier.

"*B'en, mon vieux*, there's been enough fighting in my family," the other soldier said. "The Boches killed my grandfather in '18, and they got my father and brother in 1940. If anyone starts shooting now, I'm neutral. Anybody wants the country bad enough, they can have it," he said, and he shoved his cap up and down on his cropped head, his eyes seeking over his shoulder for approbation from the others in the aisle. "Look at the books they're writing about Mahatma Gandhi! They call him 'the conqueror without a gun' on the national radio!"

"You have to be a dead Hindu before they'll let you stay out of war!" the bus-driver said.

"It's the brush burning," said the soldier by the window, and his nostrils lipped the smell of it.

"The other day in the pharmacy, fellow tried to sell me a fire-extinguisher," said Monsieur Raffio, beginning to laugh under his mustaches.

"Must have been American-made," said the man who stood by Madame Marceau's seat. "We know the deal. They'll forgive us the percentage due on the 1914–1918 war debt, the Americans will, if we buy everything they have to sell."

And this gibe at the affluent and the powerful seemed to the others as good as, or even better than, anything they had heard that day, and while they laughed their weariness was shed.

"Don't be a fool, Raffio!" said Madame Marceau sharply. "A fire-extinguisher is a very useful thing, if you know how to use it. Ask this child here. I'm sure every American has one in his home."

"But I'm not a child," the girl said in her low, stubborn voice. "I'm going to be married in two weeks."

"To a Frenchman?" asked Madame Marceau, her eye turned sharp as a fowl's eye on the girl.

"To an American," the girl said quietly. "To an American working in Paris," she went on saying, and she had her handbag open at last, and her fingers trembled as she took out the letter she had clipped from a Paris newspaper five days before. "Peter, his name is Peter, and he works for

25

the government, the American government, but he doesn't know how to tell the French about America," she said. "I come from the Middlewest, and my family worked hard, and we believed in the people of other countries, but Peter isn't that way. He says the French are a nation of parasites, who ask and ask and never give. I cut this letter out of the newspaper, and I wanted him to come down here and see there's a France he doesn't know."

Madame Marceau ran her pince-nez to the end of the gold chain pinned to her lapel, and placed it on the high bridge of her nose, and then took the letter in her hand.

"This is written to an American, but I do not know if the American I write it to will ever see it," were the words Madame Marceau read in avid silence, her eyes jerking rapidly from word to word, from line to line, while, over her shoulder, Monsieur Raffio leaned to read as well. "I am no more certain of an answer than if I put this letter into a bottle and trusted it would be carried to America by the tide. I followed the harvest through the midwest once, and I hitch-hiked from New York to California, so I know the American to whom I write. I went to college in Illinois for a year with him, and others like him, and I want to find him again now. I was young during the war in France, but still I served as one link in that clandestine chain of Frenchmen who stretched across the country, getting downed American fliers to safety. For three years I walked the roads at night with them, and in the dark we talked together, and maybe in danger and darkness, when neither sees the other's face, men come to know each other better than by day. It is to the American I walked the roads with that I write. I want him to come to my village and see what I am trying to do. I'm trying to make this one small place a testing-ground, and I need as much of

26

one American's time, and his experience, as he could give."

"First Jeanne d'Arc, and then de Gaulle, and now Michel Vaillant," said Madame Marceau tartly. "Does he think some hard-drinking Texas flier is going to read this and come down from Orléans and keep on mineral water long enough for Vaillant to explain the situation of France to him?"

"I tried to make Peter come," the girl said in a low voice, "and because he wouldn't, I came instead."

Now the light was changing, for the brilliance of the sun was draining from the southern sky, but there was no approach of twilight in the air. The way grew steeper, and the motor throbbed like a living heart in the confines of the bus with them, and the bus-driver talked still, but the words he and the others spoke were scarcely to be distinguished now, for the motor hammered steadily at the shape of them until no meaning reached the ear. A wall of white, eroded rock followed outside the window, a natural wall broken by the narrow, perpendicular troughs of long-dried streams which ran full with water perhaps no more than fifty months every century, a fortnight out of every year. The gutter flowered with asters burned paper-dry, and roots of heather and arbutus writhed in the earth, parched to the quality of stone. Because of the men who rode crowded upright in the aisle, the girl could not see the other side, but she knew that there the cliff must drop away to the sea that glittered, silent and vast and motion-less, below. And then the straining of the motor abruptly ceased, and the bus came to a halt and held precariously to the incline, and the girl saw that, a stone's throw ahead, the road entered the dark mouth of a tunnel and was gone as finally as if a door had closed.

"Abbey School!" the bus-driver bellowed. "All dis-believers get off here!" But even as he shouted the words, he raised his head as though hearing some warning the others had not heard. "I can taste smoke," he said. "I can taste the burning *maquis*."

The woman with brass hoops in her ears was the only one who had risen here to go, and she made her way with difficulty into the aisle, struggling through those who stood to reach down her black cord *filet* from the rack. Then she had it in her hands, laced full with artichokes and lettuce heads and horny-hided cantaloupe, and she pushed for-ward up the incline to the door.

"Shall I put a stone behind the wheel so you won't roll back down the hill?" she cried out in mockery to the bus-driver, her voice disembodied now that she could no longer be seen, but filled with singular beauty as she laughed.

"I checked the brakes this morning! They're strong enough to hold even if every man of the Abelin fishing-fleet, and the town officials and their wives, decided to climb on and take a ride!" he shouted, and then he slammed the flat of his hand on the klaxon, and it brayed, lingering and strident, across the high, soft air. "This is the first time in two years the curé's been late!" he said.

"When were you last in church that you need the curé so badly now?" a voice cried out from the back of the bus as it waited in the heat, and those standing in the aisle guffawed.

"I'm not thinking of myself, I'm thinking of the coun-try now!" said the bus-driver, his voice loud and ag-grieved. "I'm thinking if this bus is France, and I'm trying to form a government, it's a queer sign if the curé lets us down! Last night when he got on, we were talking to-

28

gether about the trouble they give the French over getting
into Heaven now. They've got even Paradise on relief, the
Americans have, either I was saying to him or he was
saying to me, and if you don't fill out their questionnaires
you haven't got a chance! An inspector climbs right up
on the hearse when you're on your way to the graveyard,
and you answer his questions about your past affiliations,
or you know where you can go! Your baptism certificate
used to be enough to get you past the French, the curé
was saying, or, anyway, I was saying to him, but now we
have NATO, and once you're dead, your widow submits
six copies of your military record, and your employer's
notarized recommendation in triplicate, and a sworn statement that you've never been out on strike, and then maybe
they'll let you in!"

"The first time he went into church," said the faint
thread of a voice behind the girl, "I carried him in my own
arms," and, turning, the girl saw that the wrinkled,
shrunken little woman who sat beside Monsieur Raffio
had been roused from sleep by the cessation of the bus's
movement as a child will wake when the wheels of the
carriage in which it rides no longer turn. "He didn't like
the water they sprinkled on him!" she said, her voice
fluting, birdlike, in her throat, her ancient fingers seeking
to set aside her shawl.

"Unless water has a shot of something else in it, *grand'-
mère*," said the bus-driver, turning his head, "I still don't
like it now."

When the girl looked through the open window, she
could see a flight of stone steps mounting through the
desiccated brush, and the woman with brass earrings had
started the long way up these steps, her head lowered, her

filet swinging, laden, from her hand. And now, as the bus-driver struck the klaxon savagely, and over and over, with his open palm, the woman turned and waved to them.

"*Adieu, adieu!*" she called; *adieu*, as if forever, to the faces at the windows of the bus, and to the eyes that watched her as she climbed. Afterward, when the girl reconstructed, instant by instant, the day, she remembered the finality in the woman's strangely sorrowing voice, and the clarity of the light that touched the rocks, the roots, the flowers by the road.

"Was it possibly the Abbey School that burned?" said Madame Marceau, sniffing the air. "God's vengeance, perhaps, on *monsieur le curé* for redeeming Communists up there."

"It's the brush burning. I know the smell," said the soldier by the window.

"Even an ex-Communist might give off a familiar odor," Madame Marceau said.

And now, as the klaxon blared, a man came running down the steep, uneven flight of steps, a young man, running quickly, with a bicycle carried easily across his shoulders as he came. He was black-haired, black-browed, and heavy, and his cotton trousers and shirt were torn and streaked, and his face and his strong forearms were branded with soot, as if by the grease of a mechanic's trade. When he reached the road, he swung the bicycle down, and, pushing it beside him, he passed quickly under the bus windows to the lowered pane by the driver's seat, and the bus-driver ceased sounding the klaxon and reached out and shook the young man's hand.

"Since ten this morning we've been fighting the brush fire on the other slope," the young man said, and there was a liveliness in his speech, and in his eyes, a quick, confident intelligence, as in a thoroughbred animal, and his head well-cast and heroic like an archaic statue's head. "The fire companies were up from Abelin and Bandulu, and it looked as if the vineyards and the Abbey School might go. It's out now, but an area maybe six kilometers square was razed, and it's smoldering still, so the curé's staying the night up there. He's giving the firemen a glass of wine before they go."

"For three francs fifty I'd go up and have a drink with them!" the bus-driver said, but the shipyard workers called out in impatience, and the bus-driver started the motor instead. "Put your bicycle up!" he shouted through the window, and the young man in the road drew the back of his soiled hand across his forehead and shook his big, dark head.

"I'll coast down and cool off in the breeze," he said, and as the bus-driver flung the motor into gear, and the fiercely throbbing heart came alive in the bus with them again, the young man looked at the faces at the windows, first at the bus-driver's, and then at the faces of the two recruits behind him, and his eyes moved on, and halted suddenly on the girl. "Welcome to southern France!" he called out in mockery, perhaps speaking to nothing more than the whiteness of her skin, or to the linen hat, like an American sailor's round-brimmed hat, pushed off her brow. "The playground of the world!" he called, and dimples cut deep as scars in his firm cheeks when he smiled.

He stepped back from the bus and swung one leg across the saddle of his bicycle, but he did not go, for now the sound of a violin being scraped for music arose as if from the molten tar of the road. Whatever sound it achieved, it was not music, but a whining, puny cry that missed all keys and, in its haste, outstripped all tunes, becoming a jig

31

for the halt and the blind to dance to, and then screeching in macabre humor at the spectacle they made.

"It's old Marrakech!" the bus-driver shouted through the window, and, outside on the road, the young man set his bicycle aside and squatted down on his strong legs by the wheel.

"This time he's riding under the bus," he said, and the bus-driver quieted the motor again, and those who sat, and those who stood, leaned forward to watch the young man draw the strange musician out. "That's no way to get from one place to another," he said, and the instant he set the musician on his feet it could be seen that he was an emaciated, gnome-small Algerian, in rags and broken *espadrilles*, whose wizened mask leaned to his violin, and whose bony arm still fiddled as he spun in the circles of his senseless dance.

"Another two minutes and I'd have run over him!" the bus-driver shouted through the open window. "Put him into the bus and he'll act as representative from the colonies! This is France on four wheels, and it can't be France without him here!"

But the Algerian had begun to move sideways, crablike, on his crooked legs, and when he reached the stone steps in his dance, he climbed them, spinning and scraping the violin still, and the men and women watching from the windows laughed; except for the house-agent, sitting erect, with his newspaper folded under his arm, who turned his pointed beard, his foxy nose, from the ludicrous sight of the waltzing gnome and the smell of the scorched air.

"They carry the pest on them," the house-agent said, and he might have been stating the final figures on real estate, and no bargaining allowed. "Algerians, they carry the plague under their fingernails," he said, and the pin-points of his eyes darted first to one and then to another of the men and women held captive with him in the bus called France. "Madame Marceau, you've lived a good part of your life in the colonies. I think you can speak with authority of these natives of North Africa, part man, part vermin, certainly not French, who spread the pest," his voice came down the aisle.

"Marrakech has been five years dancing on these roads, and we haven't caught anything from him yet," snapped Madame Marceau.

"Once he came into the pharmacy with his foot cut nearly in two," Monsieur Raffio said as he watched him through the glass. "I got Dr. Angelo to sew it together and give him a shot against tetanus, and all the time we had to hold him down to keep him from dancing, just dancing that way, like a fool."

"He sleeps on the beach," said the shipyard worker who hung to the rack above Madame Marceau. "He eats from the gutter. What's he got to dance and fiddle about?"

"Because he's free as the wind of real-estate agents!" shouted the bus-driver, and he jerked the motor savagely into gear.

In the perilous instant before the bus began to climb, the wheels appeared to refuse the impossible burden put upon them, and then the heart of the motor strained until it seemed that it must break with its own wild anguish, and the wheels gripped the nearly liquid surface of the road, and the bus mounted anew. Beyond, the fiddler waltzed up the steps to the Abbey School, playing as he went, and the young man on the bicycle passed under the bus windows, standing almost upright on the pedals because of the steepness of the climb. And then Monsieur Raffio leaned suddenly above the girl and called out through the open window:

"*Hé*, Vaillant? There's a young lady here who wants to talk to you!"

And instantly the visual presence of the bus, the men and women riding in it, the perpendicular road, the dead-white rock, the young man pedaling, were obliterated as the bus roared into the tunnel's open mouth. Now it was absolutely dark, and the girl turned quickly in her seat.

"Vaillant!" she said. "Was that Vaillant? Ah, Madame Marceau, why didn't you tell me that when the bus stopped back there?"

"You're a nicely bred girl," said Madame Marceau's voice, hushed now in admonition in the darkness. "I didn't want you making a spectacle of yourself for everyone to see!"

"But if that was Vaillant, I must get off! I have only a few days here!" the girl said, and she groped her way past Madame Marceau's knees, with the basket on them, and through the swaying press of people toward the door. "I must get off right away!" she said to the bus-driver when she had come to his seat.

"Get off here? This is nothing! This isn't a stop!" the bus-driver shouted above the tumult of the motor that echoed even louder against the tunnel's hollow stone. Then he reached to switch the headlights on, and their illumination brought to life the dripping roof and walls. "You paid your fare to Abelin, and that's where I'll take you!" he cried, while ahead, set high at the long cavern's end, was a small round aperture of light that waited like a fixed, unblinking eye. "The people from some countries are as unreliable as the winds along this coast," he said in loud, abusive grief. "First the sirocco from Sicily, and then the sirocco from the Adriatic, and then the bora off the mountains, and when you think you know where you are, the mistral starts to blow! Look at the Americans over in Germany, how they change their minds!" he went on saying. "First they hang a dozen German generals for starting the war, and put the rest of them in jail where they can't start another, and five years later they take them out, and measure them for uniforms, and ask them how many divisions they'd like to have! And you, *mademoiselle l'Américaine*, first you want to go to Abelin, and you can't wait until you get there, and then you decide you'll get out and start climbing up through the *maquis!*"

"Because the man I came to see is riding a bicycle down behind us!" the girl cried softly out. "Will you stop so I can get off here?"

"Not for Vaillant or any other man!" the bus-driver shouted. "If Vaillant is advertising for a wife, if that's what he's doing now, then he could specify that no member of the occupation forces need apply! He can do what he's running around like crazy trying to do: start a school of his own, run for mayor, get a newspaper out, and we're with him as long as he does it like a Frenchman, without American aid!"

"But I'm not bringing him money! I have no money!" the girl cried out, and, standing there among the unseen strangers, she felt the weakness of crying tightening in her throat.

"I'm not married myself," the bus-driver said, speaking less bitterly, and they might have been riding alone in the bus, the girl and the man behind the wheel, with his eyes watching the way ahead. "I'm not married, but if I'd advertised for a wife, and you came along, I'd consider getting married, provided we came to certain agreements about nationality. I don't say I'd do it, but I'd consider it. I wouldn't make any promises, but I'd tell the others to hold off." As they rocked on through the darkness, no other voices could be heard. "So if I'm not married, and you're not married, then if you sat down and had the *apéritif* with me at the Café du Commerce on the port, it wouldn't be hurting anyone," he said.

"Yes, yes, I will! I'll meet you tomorrow, or the day after that," the girl said. "But let me out here, so that I can talk to Vaillant on the way!"

"He's never the man for you, mademoiselle!" the bus-driver cried, his voice gone loud again in ire. "He's a teacher, and his teaching will come before any woman for him all his life! He won't take you dancing, Vaillant won't, and he never sets foot inside a moving-picture theater! You'd sit home at night writing his campaign speeches for him! Do you think I'll stop the bus for that?"

His voice had not quite ceased when the girl turned quickly and groped her way back through the swaying men to Madame Marceau's seat. There she held to the metal of the frame and leaned into the aura of garlic, speaking to Madame Marceau in the dark.

"It's just about my suitcase," she said. "When the bus stops at the pass to let the soldiers off, I'll get out too. So if you'd take care of my suitcase for me when the bus gets to Abelin, I'd be grateful. Just leave it for me in a café."

"So you've made your choice!" the bus-driver cried out in loud bereavement, having perceived she no longer stood beside him as he drove. "So you've taken sides with the opposition against the rest of us who make the heart of the country beat, *mademoiselle l'Américaine!* I'll tell you this: if you've thrown in your lot with the colonials, and the royalists, and the house-agents, and the other museum pieces of France, then honest men like me are through!"

And then the little peasant woman who sat behind Madame Marceau spoke in the dark.

"He's good, my grandson," the fluting voice said. "He was six years old when he first started bringing home fish for the soup. We lived in Corsica. He was always out in the boats, helping the men." At the end of the tunnel, the far aperture of light opened wider and wider as they rode, and the darkness was thinning, and the girl could see the old woman's eyes, with the iris of them clouded as if filmed over by her memories. "And afterwards, when we came here to the coast, he was always providing, providing for others," she said, and her smile folded and unfolded in love in the complex parchment of cheek and mouth and chin. Then she started back, as the others did, when the daylight struck a blow across her eyes.

"He may be a good provider, but he drives too fast!" said Monsieur Raffio beside her as the bus roared out on the open pass. The soldiers had risen from their seats to go, and the girl would have followed them as they pushed their way forward, but Madame Marceau held her arm.

"I have just one question," the Frenchwoman said. "What does the young man you're going to marry have to say about you running all over the country after another man?"

"He's busy dining in expensive restaurants with expensive people," the girl said, speaking almost in bitterness. "He doesn't know that I've come here."

"So he has money," said Madame Marceau, and her nostrils dilated as if to the cold, metallic odor of it, and she released the girl's arm to rub the end of her nose. "Don't ever play fast and loose with a young man with money. Marry him first, and then pick flaws in him," she said.

"Now we're beginning the descent, *messieurs*, *'dames!*" the bus-driver shouted out ahead, but, instead of slowing, the bus was gathering speed. "On the right there's a drop to a shelf of sheep-growing land, and after that come the cliffs, and the Mediterranean, two kilometers and a half below! And as long as I'm premier still, and before I lose the majority, I'm letting foreign aid and the military go!"

"On the left," called one of the soldiers in hoarse, high mimicry, "is the road to camp where we get off! Slow down!"

"*B'en*, you've passed it!" the other soldier shouted.

"Stop the bus! Stop it instantly!" the house-agent screamed down the aisle, the request as preposterous as if it had been demanded that time recede, that the bus stand halted at the Abbey School again; as unavailing as if he had cried upon all Frenchmen to stop economic disaster or the course of history.

Through the open window, the girl saw the rocks, the bush, the tilted desert passing fast, and she held to the back of Madame Marceau's seat for strength, for the blood had turned to water in her veins.

"On the right—" the bus-driver began again, and then his altered voice made the wild, final statement of their doom. "The brakes!" he shouted, his right foot pumping savagely at the pedal, his right hand jerking the useless lever by the wheel. "There's nothing there! The brakes are gone!" came the voice that was no longer his, no longer foolhardy or irate or brave.

"Let us out! Let us out!" cried the passengers, and they stampeded toward the open door. But they could not reach it before the bus shattered the low, crumbling barricade on the cliff side of the road and flung itself forward into the deep blue bowl of space.

In that last instant, only the little peasant woman spoke in modest complaint.

"Ah, not death, not death," she beseeched the others, as if in humiliation that she must meet it here in the open, without ceremony, in her old black shawl.

 THERE WAS A PERIOD OF DARK
non-being, and then, like the tentative flicker-
ing of life in the woods and fields in the gray
of early morning, faint threads of memory
and pain began to stir. A long time passed
before a lagoon of quiet opened, and the
presence of light pressed heavy on the eye-
balls that ached for sight in the sockets of the
skull. When this weight lifted, the vision of a
room came with difficulty into focus: green
curtains drawn across a window, a white
plaster wall, a green bedspread with the
shape of a body and long, slender legs molded
in it. Then the lens shifted, and on the bright
white screen of consciousness the picture
blurred again. Once Madame Marceau's face
emerged, like the face of one long-drowned,
floating, discolored, bloated, in the current of
the passing nights and days.

"Are we alive?" the girl whispered as it
passed her.

"I presume we are," said Madame Marceau's swollen mouth. "With labor asking the
prices it does today, I doubt if the authorities
would have undertaken to have my villa
transferred, garden and all, into Eternity."

The girl drifted will-lessly, floating from
day to night, out of sleep into waking, and

into sleep again, as if in a gondola, with her fingers trail-ing in the water at the side. And then, one afternoon it was not memory, but the insistence of voices that, roused her to a knowledge of the room again.

"I know all about concussion, Dr. Angelo," Madame Marceau was saying, and the girl moved her eyes care-fully. "The General had it every time he fell off a horse. Once, in Martinique, it lasted over a month. The doctors had him up and around, but he didn't know one rank from another, so for weeks we couldn't let him out of the house for fear he'd ask an enlisted man for a drink in the Officers' Club. He was perfectly lucid in every other way."

"When logic is wiped from the mind by the force of a blow, we call it concussion," said the doctor's voice. "At times, symptoms of temporary insanity may be observed, as in the General's case you have just described. But it is nine days now that your niece is ill. I would still advise removing her to my clinic for observation," he said.

"Not as long as she's better! She's taking liquids now," said Madame Marceau. "*Merci, cher ami*, I'm keeping my niece here!"

"But I'm not your niece!" said the girl, startled into speech. On one side of the flickering screen she could see Madame Marceau's face, bruised yellow and blue, and the mouth and nose gone thick. On the other side was the doctor's face, firm-jowled, fresh-skinned, a white mus-tache clipped evenly along his clean pink lip.

"You see?" said Madame Marceau, her eyes cocked at him.

"Her speech is clearing," said Dr. Angelo, leaning above her in his gray silk suit. His fingertips, the nails immacu-late, closed on her wrist, and the girl lay looking at the cold blue marbles of his eyes. "The pulse is good," he said, and he bared the two rows of his porcelain teeth close to her face.

"She's still confused as to her identity," said Madame Marceau.

"May I say that I am too?" said Dr. Angelo, his teeth still bared.

"I'm Mary Farrant!" the girl cried out, speaking French because they spoke it, and suddenly the tears came down her face.

"She's been living six years in America," said Madame Marceau. "My sister always worried about the effect it would have on her accent. You can hear it for yourself. It's a catastrophe."

The next time the girl roused, the curtains were drawn aside at the long window opposite the bed, and she saw the papery green fronds of the palm-tree tops in the garden, and, beyond them, the heat-misted half-circle of the sea. On the table below the window a vase of mint sprigs had been placed, the odor of them fresh and tender in the room as she sat up against the soft, square pillows and, once seated, she knew that she had drifted clear of the deep current of dreams, for the thoughts moved singly now, without confusion, in her head. She pushed the green cover back, and saw her own feet, miraculously familiar, and she slipped free of the linen sheets. Standing on the oval of woven straw beside the bed, she looked in wonder at the long white gown she wore. It was soft as a handkerchief from years of careful laundering, and it had been buttoned neatly at her throat and wrists, this out-moded habiliment of an alien century's propriety.

To be beautiful in this, one's bones would have to be very small and delicate, and mine are certainly not small enough, she thought, and she touched the bones of her own wrist. On the front of the nightgown, above the heart, was a hand-done monogram, an elegant "M" with its spider-thin legs clamped viciously down upon a helpless "C." "*M*" *for Marceau, and "C" for Charlotte, or Christiane, or Claire,* she thought. *I am the General's widow now. I have changed my identity.* She turned to look for a mirror in the cool, faintly fragrant room, thinking to walk fearlessly to it and to look at what had become of her face, but there was no mirror, and she lifted one hand and tentatively felt her nose, her brow, her hair. The hard bone of her skull above the temples was sensitive to the touch, and her forehead was tender. *But it is good to be living again,* she thought. *It is good to feel the strength coming back, and to know I do not have to die.* Her hair was neatly brushed and braided, and the tips of the braids moved lightly across the shoulders of the nightgown as she tried shaking her head.

Then she saw the vase of mint leaves on the table beneath the window, as fresh and dark as leaves found in a forest, and she made the long excursion to them across the terra-cotta tiles. For a trembling instant she leaned to the mint sprays, looking into their many-leafed darkness as into the woods of childhood, the fragrance of them not a flower's ephemeral perfume, but the cool, deep breath of sap and shadow and wet bark that came to life with every American spring and did not die until the snow. She touched them separately, softly, with her lips, those that stood taller than the others on the dark-green stalks, and, leaning to them, she saw that the window looked down upon a garden so thickly grown with vegetation of the semi-tropics that pathways could barely be discerned in it, and the mint leaves against her mouth seemed to have come from the soil of another continent. Beyond the garden wall, other gardens, other villas, descended in spiked, hirsute, vine-like profusion on both sides of the steep, winding lane, and, except for a young man who had thrown his leg across a bicycle and was about to go, no life stirred in the heat. And then she recognized the head, the hand on the curved bar, the movement of the leg, and she straightened suddenly. She could not place these things in time or circumstance, and it was like searching the memory for the name of a piece of music, or seeking the continuity of a dream, and no clue given, nothing re-called to label him stranger or friend, except for a spray of mint behind his ear.

When he was gone, she saw that the newspaper lying on the table had been opened out and read, and the front page folded inside now, and the date in the righthand corner was meaningless.

"It was a Friday. It says here Friday, June 25," she said half aloud, feeling weariness and uncertainty sub-merging her again. "So that was two days after I left Paris. But how do I know how long ago in days and weeks—" And her voice ceased, and she felt a chill hand of foreboding close on her heart.

She picked the paper up, and it shook in her hands as she turned the pages, and then she had found the front page, and folded it over, and—as startling as if she had come upon her own obituary, outlined in black—the photograph was there. It was placed mid-page, and above it the blaring headline read: TWENTY-FIVE KILLED AS BUS FALLS 200 FEET FROM COAST ROAD—a retouched picture with a line of hyphens and an arrowhead marking the scrub-hindered path of its descent. The bodies of passen-gers were circled in white where they lay among the olive trees and the grazing sheep, and the bus itself lay on its side on the shelf of land, its nose overhanging the

44

final cliff, the individual life it had borne strewn care-
lessly about it, as an airliner, in the instant of its thun-
derous, untidy end, disposes of the splinters of humanity
which have paid so exorbitant a price to be carried from
the earth for a little, merely to be callously flung back to
earth again.

"Twenty-five. Twenty-five dead," the girl repeated in a
whisper, and her eyes moved down the list of names of
those who had perished, moved over the foreign syllables
of Allegro, and Ponzi, and Picard, and Raffio, her mind
gone blank in panic lest she find her own name there.
"Raffio!" she cried out in sudden comprehension, and
there was the straw helmet behind her, and the gray mustaches, and the smell of garlic instead of mint in the quiet
room. "The woman who got off at the Abbey School, she
called farewell to us! Why didn't we get off then, all of us?
Ah, Raffio, Raffio!" she cried in senseless grief. "And the
little old woman beside him? Did she too have to die?"

She was shuddering with sobs, as if shaken by the cold
of winter, when Madame Marceau came up the stairs
and crossed the hall, and came into the room, bare-armed
in a dress as blue as her corrugated hair.

"You are not strong enough to be up," said Madame
Marceau. "Come," she said. "Come," but the girl held
to the table, crying, shaking her head.

"If it had not been for me," she said, "they would none
of them have died!"

"You? Why you?" said Madame Marceau. The colors
of violence done her had faded in some measure from her
face, but her eyes were circled with purple like a vulture's
hungry eyes.

"Because he was enraged with me, the bus-driver!" the
girl cried out. "I was my country to him! I was every-

45

thing he believed my country to be! Simply by being American, I killed them all! How can I live now, knowing that is true?"

"Hush, you must rest," said Madame Marceau, as softly as a mother might have said it, and she took the girl's hand as though taking a lost child's hand and led her, weeping, to the bed. There she drew the sheet and the green spread up over the girl's long, slender legs, and over her body in the soft white gown. For a moment her eyes rested on the embroidered monogram of her own name above the heart, and it might have been some facet of herself, her own past youth, her own lost tenderness, that she covered now as if covering the dead. "They're gone, the bus-driver, the soldiers, and the rest of them, but there are other voices left to speak for France," she said, and she sat down by the bed, her pure-white, crêpy-skinned arms in the lap of her blue dress, voluptuous strangers to her high, bony beak and her bleak, ravenous eye. "It was I who got you through the window of the bus, not the others. It is never the others. In every country it is the people who have been bred as you have been who will always take your part."

"But I'm nothing to you! I don't belong in this house!" the girl cried.

"Yes, you belong here," said Madame Marceau, speaking in singular gentleness, "because I got you through the window while the others died. They were six hours carrying the living up to the ambulances that night, and I claimed you, niece or not. I had the right to." Her white-skinned arm reached out, and she picked up a length of rose-colored knitting, with long steel needles run through it, from the commode that stood against the wall. "I

46

wanted to keep you out of a public hospital, and your name out of the papers. You are a girl of gentle breeding. I knew that from our talk together in the bus, and well-bred people don't let their own kind down. I took care of your handbag with your money and passport in it, so nobody here knows your name or your nationality," she said, the knitting-needles moving fast.

"But what am I doing here in this place?" the girl said, and she lifted her hand and covered her eyes, as if by closing out the present she could see more clearly what had gone before. "I'm from the Middlewest. I was studying in Paris. I remember packing a suitcase. Perhaps in the suitcase there's some explanation of why I came," she said.

"Your suitcase went over into the sea," said Madame Marceau. "So I've hung some clothes in the wardrobe for you to wear in the garden when you're strong enough to walk."

"I was studying in Paris, learning to paint. I've been a year there, living alone. Since my father died, I've no one left," she said, retracing the outline of her own life, slowly, meticulously. "My father was a veterinary, a specialist in cattle, a man who should have lived forever," she said.

"In cattle?" said Madame Marceau, and the sound of the needles suddenly ceased.

"Dr. Wayne Farrant. He won two awards for his work in hoof-and-mouth disease. I've always been proud of everything he's ever done. He killed himself working," she said, stating the final total of it behind her shaded eyes. "He was given a government grant. Dr. Wayne Farrant. All this I'm sure of. All this is absolutely true."

47

"Killed himself for a herd of cows?" said Madame Marceau, but the girl was looking into the past, and did not hear her speak.

"So I came to Paris to study," she went on with the re-construction of her own life. "My father had always put money aside for it, but he wanted me to wait a year or two. But after he died, I didn't wait. I closed the house up right away. I was seventeen, and I'd always done things for myself, so that part of it wasn't hard. It was thinking of the years ahead, of finding the kind of people to make my life with. But my father had thought even of that. He left me letters to all the friends he'd had when he'd done re-search over here."

"All veterinaries, I presume?" said Madame Marceau acidly, the needles clicking fast again.

"No, painters and writers and their sons and daugh-ters," the girl said, her hand still keeping the afternoon light, and the venom in Madame Marceau's voice, and the sight of the present, out. "They were French people, and they knew my father had wanted to be a painter once, so they accepted me. We all worked hard, and we didn't have very much money, and our nationalities never seemed to get in the way. And then I met Peter, the son of one of my father's scientific friends. They'd gone through university together, and my father wanted me to know his son. Once my father had taken us to the circus together. Peter was ten and I was three, but I don't re-member that. Peter works in Paris with the government. He was the only American among the rest of us, and after I met him everything changed."

"What changed, may I ask?" said Madame Marceau, knitting still.

48

"He had no time for the students I liked or the things I liked," the girl said, and she took her hand down from her eyes. "You know, there's one thing that's kept coming back to me all the days and nights I've been lying here. It's a queer, guilty thing about wanting to be happy, foolishly, crazily happy, and about how one hasn't any right to be. I think of my father, and I want him alive, and I think of Peter, and the way he feels about the French, and it breaks my heart." And then her face was masked suddenly with bewilderment. "Do you think I was running away from Peter, Madame Marceau?" she said. "Is that why I came here?"

"I never heard of anything so absurd!" said Madame Marceau, and her hands manipulated the long, cold needles furiously. "Why should you be running away from the man you're going to marry? Now what would be the sense in that?"

"Perhaps because I'm afraid of what he's going to become," the girl said. "He has to decide about money, government money, where it should go, and it's made him pompous about things. My friends thought that he spoke for America, and so they decided they didn't like America. He was the real America, they thought, sent over here to speak officially."

"We'll send a wire off to him in Paris, and tell him where you are," said Madame Marceau, putting a stop to the foolish sound of this complaint. "A wire will cost three hundred francs, if we word it properly. No more than that. Three hundred francs is not excessive when your entire future is at stake." Her lips went on moving even after she had ceased to speak, perhaps computing the cost per word of the message that would go.

49

"My future," the girl repeated grievously. "What good is my future if the bus is always there with me, and the deaths of those people who didn't have to die?"

"I was your age once," said Madame Marceau, huddled over the length of wool and the needles like a long-beaked, blue-feathered bird. "And I was alone in Brittany for one afternoon one summer the way you are alone in France. I made the kind of a fool of myself that I don't want you to do. Give me the name and address of your young man now, and I'll send a telegram to him. He'll come right down, and when you can travel, he'll take you back."

"His name and address," said the girl, and her voice was troubled. "I can't remember his name and address. I remember the name Peter, and the way he looked, but everything tightens in my head if I try to remember more."

"The General's concussions took weeks to clear up," said Madame Marceau, and she went on, saying: "You had thirty thousand francs in your purse, and I've kept an account of every centime that I've spent. What's left will take care of you for a little while. As my niece, I kept you out of Angelo's clinic. He would have charged you a fine price for that!" But it might have been that she was thinking still of that other time, that summer afternoon in Brittany. "As soon as we'd buried the General, Dr. Angelo started chasing me around the palms. Ah, not for myself, not for love, but for what I was worth! The gay Lothario!" she said in bitterness, and then she told the story of her youth that she had wanted to tell. "That summer in Brittany, I met a young Count. My aunt had been to school with his mother, so that part of it was perfectly proper, but I was engaged to the General then. The Count's

50

people were really quite nice, but almost penniless. They didn't have a country place, so they had to spend their summers in a hotel, like tourists, which is always awkward for anyone well-bred. One afternoon the Countess asked my aunt and me to tea on the hotel terrace with her and her son," said Madame Marceau, knitting steadily. "My aunt never forgave herself that she accepted for the two of us."

"And you fell in love?" the girl said. "You know, I think I've never been in love," she added quietly.

"Love had nothing to do with it!" snapped Madame Marceau. "You are far from your own people, and I am speaking to you as if I were one of your own kin. I was eighteen then. The Count was a little older. We met in broad daylight, in a public place, and we acted like fools. You can scarcely call that love!" she said. In the near dark of the room she ceased to speak, and the needles ceased to move in her hands, and she seemed to be asking in silence the favor of mercy from the girl. "I have never told anyone this," she said in a whisper, "and if it were not that we have been near death together, you and I, perhaps I could not say this to you now. The Count and I walked down from the terrace after tea, and we sat down on the rocks, and we took our shoes and stockings off. Ever since that summer—forty-five years ago it must be now!—and all the scandal and heartache it caused, I've hardly dared think of it even, but the shame was always there."

"I will understand if you don't wish to tell me any more," the girl said.

"I must tell you all of it," said Madame Marceau, "for you are in my care. The Count and I ran barefoot, holding hands, the whole length of the beach," she said, her voice as breathless as if she had just ceased to run; "in

51

front of all the people, in full view of the hotels. He had white teeth, but he laughed too loud, and his hair was much too long. We ran for half an hour, hand in hand, into the water and out of it, and both of us laughing, laughing, and laughing, as I've never laughed again."

And *Ah, that is it*, the girl thought; *the laughter that goes silent, and you listen and listen, but too much has happened, and your own laughter is really done. That is why men look at my face, coming close to stare at it, watching my eyes and my mouth for the sign, because they are thinking: She is young. She won't have forgotten how to laugh.* "And then what happened?" she said aloud.

"Then my aunt came down from the hotel terrace, holding her parasol in one hand, and her skirt up with the other," said Madame Marceau, "and she handed the Count the parasol to hold so that she could slap my face. My mother and aunt both cried their eyes blind in fear that the story might get to my fiancé in North Africa. There was some kind of native uprising, and he was stationed there. This century, there's been one thing after another for people in our walk of life: the natives making trouble all during my girlhood, just when I began going out to dances, and then, right after my marriage, along came the First World War." Beyond her, the window was filling with the deep blue of the Mediterranean night, and, as she went on talking, the sound of the needles began again in the dark. "I never saw the Count again. He was killed at the Marne, without acquiring any rank to speak of. I believe he was only a captain when he got his head blown off, and it doesn't surprise me. I know his hair was too long that summer I knew him, and he was too light-hearted for responsibility. But I've never seen such white teeth in my life," she said through the darkness, "or heard anyone laugh the way he laughed the afternoon we ran on the sand."

"Did the General have a happy laugh?" the girl asked.

"The General was a public figure, a very distinguished man. He laughed like a public figure," said Madame Marceau, and her voice was strangely muted now with sorrow, with regret, as if it had come to her finally, and without drama, in the quiet room, that everything life had promised had added up to nothing in the end. For a while there was no sound except the ticking of the needles, and then the frogs' voices began to throb, heavy and myriad and deep, in the sultry jungle of the garden below.

"But why did I come to Abelin?" the girl said at last. "What was I running away from? What was I trying to find?" And the answer seemed almost there, almost ready to be given, and then it slipped like a silk thread through her fingers, and she could not find it in the dark.

"I want to know what made me come to Abelin," she said the next day to Dr. Angelo, watching him as eagerly as if he brought the answer to her as he came across the terra-cotta tiles. He set his black bag on the polished wood of the commode and drew a chair up by the bed, and under the clipped line of his mustache his even teeth were bared.

"You came to visit your aunt. That would seem to be reason enough," he said, and he shook his shirt-cuff down inside his gray silk jacket sleeve, and placed his fingertips on the soft skin of her wrist. "A little uncertain still, like the breast of a dove—this wrist with the life quivering in it," he said his fingers on the quickly springing pulse. "And now that you're here, you'll stay and keep your aunt company. You'll stay and come to know the rest of us, and you'll see, living here with her, how much we have

53

her interests at heart. Your aunt is a rich woman, very rich, but poor in personal relationships. She has led a lonely life here since the General died."

"How can I stay?" the girl said, and she would have moved away from him, but she could not, for under the nightgown's long, buttoned sleeve he held her wrist, and she lay, transfixed, before him, watching his cold, translucent eyes. "I have to go back and try to find my friends, the place where I lived in Paris, even try to find myself," she said, the words coming uneasily, and the doctor shifted closer to the bed.

"You've given *madame la générale* a heart," he said, his voice scarcely louder than a whisper. "I've seen her crying in this room when she thought that you might die. You must stay here a few months with her. You must stay and eat our good food, drink our good southern wine, swim in our warm, gentle sea. You are too thin, too severe, like a little stone saint on a church portal, as beautiful as a saint, and your flesh as cold," he said, his lips drawn back in singular grimace. "Stay here for a little while," he murmured, and his hand reached out as if to smooth her hair.

"I am nearly well," the girl said, moving before he touched her. "I want to go down and walk in the garden today."

"Not in this heat, mademoiselle!" he said, and his fingers released her wrist. "You must let me prescribe for you a little longer. You don't know the south! A man learns to adapt himself to the south, as to a woman. The peasants of this coast are up at four in the morning to work in the vineyards, outwitting the sun, and they take their goats into the house during the five hottest hours of the twenty-four. You are still not well. You must listen to me for a little longer, and do exactly as I say."

"I haven't seen my face in a mirror yet," the girl said. "I am afraid of what I shall see."

"Then let me be the mirror," said the doctor. "Look into my eyes, and do not be afraid, and I shall tell you what to do. When your aunt comes in, you will have a talk with her, suggest going through her papers with her, show an interest in her future, for she is a lonely woman now. When the time comes for you to return to Paris, persuade her to go back with you, and to rent her villa through the house-agent here."

"But this is her home!" the girl said quickly.

"Ah, home!" said the doctor, stirring in impatience on his chair. "You have perhaps heard of the Englishman who accused the Frenchman of having no word for 'home,' and the Frenchman retorted that the Englishman had no word for '*patrie*'! Now, take my case. I own six villas here in Abelin, all quite nice properties, and they are rented for me by the house-agent, whose business it is to get the highest prices he can. This not only increases the value of the property, but keeps the wrong people out of the residential quarter of the town. I make my home, as you call it, in whichever one the house-agent hasn't rented for me, and when they're all occupied, I sleep on a couch in my office temporarily! At a hundred thousand francs per month per villa, in the season, I haven't the least objection to calling my doctor's office 'home'!"

"But six times a hundred thousand francs a month is a fortune!" the girl said in wonder.

"A modest fortune," the doctor said pleasantly. "The mayor, the house-agent, and I, we run things here as Frenchmen, without any need of foreign subsidies." As he leaned back in the chair, he spread his fingers and laid the tips of the fingers of one hand lightly against the fingers of the other, letting them touch, and then lightly spring away. "We've been colleagues for over twenty years, and we feel confident that measures such as we've put into effect in Abelin, if practiced throughout France, would stabilize our currency. In the matter of rents, and in property sales, the mayor, who is also our notary public, follows the custom of declaring on paper a lower figure than the one actually involved. This has proven to be a very salutary measure for the general economy. Money which would otherwise be immobilized by taxation is put into circulation, and it keeps property and income taxes down."

"But the house-agent. He was in the bus," the girl said, the picture of his foxlike face, the sound of his high voice, suddenly coming clear.

"That was not prearranged," the doctor said quickly. "His car broke down, so he caught the bus home that afternoon, the first time in five years. He fractured an arm and a leg and was badly bruised, but I got him in plaster and had him hopping around the village on crutches the third day. Death was selective that afternoon. You were spared, and Madame Marceau, and a handful of others," said the doctor, and he studied the nails of his right hand a moment before he went on saying: "It is interesting, however, to consider the death of Madame Marceau, hypothetically. If she had died and you survived her, you, as her niece, would have had a legal claim on all she owns. You might have inherited the General's fortune, and this villa, and the General's medals, the family silver, the Marceau heirlooms," he said, counting the items off on his fingers as he spoke. "Provided you were the sole heir," he said, and he cocked one eyebrow in inquiry at her, "the house-agent would then have rented the villa for you at an interesting figure, the mayor would have drawn up a contract showing a lower one, and within half a year you would have been enjoying a five-zero income, with only the fraction of it that appeared on the public files subject to taxation. Provided—" he began again, but the girl said in a low voice:

"There's enough on my conscience without adding Madame Marceau's death to the others who died!"

"You could atone by staying here among us, mademoiselle," the doctor said, and he leaned forward again, and drew one forefinger, in tentative caress, across the back of her small, motionless hand. "Besides the rent from my villas, I have my medical practice without competition here. That's understood in Abelin. The mayor wouldn't tolerate any inexperienced young doctor trying to get a foothold in the place. I'm a widower," he said, his eyes as cold as money on the texture of her hair. "And, let me tell you, the Frenchman is not the tough proposition the Americans they send over here to do business with us have all turned out to be! Don't let any American misinform you about that! The Frenchman is loyal to his friends, sentimental almost. Our mayor, for instance, would never make a decision of any consequence concerning Abelin without first conferring with the house-agent and me!"

"And for twenty years it has been like that in Abelin?" said the girl, and she could not move from under the bright, cold compulsion of his eyes.

"For twenty years, and each of us indispensable to the other, just as the English, the French, the Americans, with a little imagination, could also be," the doctor said. "But the Americans and the English have no imagination, and the French cannot be expected to supply it for the rest!"

"But twenty years. That is too long. I think Madame

Marceau should head the opposition," said the girl, and she sat up against the pillows, breaking free of the coercion of his eyes and hand. "She should rent her villa by herself, or else not rent it at all, exactly as she wishes."

"Opposition to us?" said the doctor, and he leaned back in the chair again, and laid his fingertips together, and then lightly took them away. "Opposition to measures that maintain the *status quo?* If this is your opinion, you have made a mistake in your analysis of the situation here, a very serious mistake. And I must add that when I took your part against my colleagues I did not think that your defiance would be my reward."

"But why should you have to take my part?" the girl said softly.

"But you forget the house-agent was there in the bus!" said the doctor, his voice half-jocular. "He saw why and how the accident took place. Because of my long friendship with Madame Marceau, I persuaded the mayor not to make the whole thing public. I protected you as Madame Marceau's niece," he said, shifting forward on the chair again, "and because I was drawn to you, strangely drawn to you. I would like to be your friend."

"But from what have you tried to protect me?" the girl cried in a low voice.

"There's a law in France," said the doctor, speaking slowly, sharply, accentuating every word, "a law against engaging a man in conversation when he's driving a public vehicle. And you talked to the driver of that bus, made promises to him, agreed to take a drink with him, urged him to stop and let you out in the middle of a public highway. You led him on until he was driving with his eyes on nothing but the reflection of your face in the glass! The house-agent saw it coming, even called out in warning to

58

him, to that man who'd never had an accident before, never so much as scratched a fender, in all the years of driving over these steep roads! You'd driven the man out of his mind," said the doctor, the words coming sharply through his teeth. "Because you're young, with a face like a little stone saint, he wanted to take you in his arms, hold you against him, make you come alive! And because you came as a tourist, with an American sailor's hat on your head, and an accent acquired from six years in the U.S.A., he wanted to throw you off the bus and never have to see you again, or anyone like you! That's the way he felt about Americans. You had him driving the bus at a hundred kilometers the hour, they say!"

The girl dropped her slim legs in the long white gown quickly over the far side of the bed, and she stood barefoot on the polished tiles, facing the doctor across the barrier of the green bedspread. *And now*, she thought fiercely, *he is waiting for me to laugh, as a young person laughs, but I shall never, never, never laugh again!*

"Now I am well, and I shall be going back to Paris," she said, holding herself tight in her own arms to still the trembling of her flesh. "So you may go. You need not come to see me any more," she said to the blue ice of his eyes; and then Madame Marceau's voice could be heard from below in the garden, cawing in reprimand to housemaid or gardener, in the harsh cry of a bird of prey.

"I would not be in a hurry to go," said the doctor, and he seemed another, gentler man now as he got to his feet and spoke. "In cases of nervous shock, relapses often occur, and even now there are blank gaps in your memory. I would give some thought to the suggestions I've made, and discuss Madame Marceau's future plans with her. It might be embarrassing if the city councilors detained you for a session of questioning. But there's no reason why they should, if you responded with courtesy to those who have offered you the hand of friendship here."

When Madame Marceau came into the room, they were standing so, one on either side of the bed, the blue-eyed man with the white-thatched head and the girl in the long-sleeved gown.

"Ah, you again, *mon cher!*" Madame Marceau said to the doctor, her breath coming short because of the two flights she had climbed. *At eight hundred francs the visit*, she did not add, but the sound of it was in her voice, and the look of calculation in her eye. "What heat!" she said, and she lifted the big, black, finely woven hat from her head, standing, her shapely, soft arms raised, outlined an instant against the window which held the motionless palm spears of the garden and the glittering hemisphere of sea. "Hat-pins! What an anachronism!" she said, and she held the big-brimmed hat as if it were a living thing, and stabbed the jet-studded pins back through the crown of it, and tossed it over to the empty bed. "Until the General died, I always had a topknot of hair on my head. He didn't approve of short hair. And now, out of habit, I keep on wearing the hatpins, and have to stick them through my skull!"

"Dr. Angelo has been talking to me about Abelin," the girl said, speaking quickly and ruefully because her heart was sore, "and now I see things differently. I had thought of Abelin as a simple fishing-village, but now I see it is divided, as the bus-driver said the whole country is divided, and everyone coming to it must decide on which side he belongs. Down there around the harbor," she said, and she lifted her head as if to see the houses from where she stood barefoot on the tiles in the long, white, modest gown, "down there is where the fishermen and the shipyard workers live. And if you live up here above the port, the game you play is to get a number of villas. The game is to outbid all the other players, and ruin them in the end, like in 'Monopoly.' The coast should belong to the fishermen. For centuries it's been theirs," she said, "and yet they would never be able to own a house up here the way the others do."

"Ho, the fishermen!" Madame Marceau cried out. "We're paupers, we villa-owners, compared with them! Every time they haul in their nets, they're filled with solid gold!"

"Maybe it's only the gold of the sun on the water, the way it looks now," the girl said, wanting this one thing to be true.

"Oh, no! It's the kind of gold they put in the toes of their socks, all right!" said the doctor, laughing pleasantly.

"It's the custom in France," said Madame Marceau, with her eye on Dr. Angelo. "I'm told that even the president of the republic does it when he thinks nobody's looking his way."

It was nearly noon, and Dr. Angelo had picked up his little black bag and gone, and Madame Marceau was changing for lunch on the floor below, when the girl went barefoot down the stairs. She had put on a sleeveless cotton dress of faded blue that Madame Marceau had hung in the wardrobe for her, saying: "When you are strong enough to walk down to the garden, this will be cool to wear." Once down the stairs, she moved tentatively across the smooth tiles of the lower hall, and in the shadows she saw another figure move, but when she had paused she recognized her own reflection in a full-length glass. There were the wide blue dress, the coral ribbon at her waist, the silver bracelets at her wrists, and she crossed on tiptoe to the wall on which the mirror hung. For a moment she held her breath, in fear of seeing a strange, mutilated face, but in the half-light the face was hers, small, stubborn-lipped, unaltered, except that the cheeks were thinner and the look of health was drained out of the skin. *I'm older, five years older*, she thought, and she looked at her hair, brushed glossy and dark behind her ears, and the eyebrows arched, black, silky, and narrow, above her hollow eyes. *I look at least twenty-two. I look as if my teen-age self had died.* Before she turned and moved on bare silent feet to the threshold, she listened for voices in the garden, and then she stepped out onto the pebbles, warm still from the morning sun, although the shadows of the palms had fallen on the path. Through the multiple greens of the jungle vegetation she saw a door in the garden wall, and she hastened, head lowered, toward it. When she had reached it, she pressed the iron latch down, slipped through the door, closed it again, and leaned against the stones of the wall to still the agitation of her heart.

"There, in that house, they will not tell me why I came to Abelin," she whispered. "Perhaps in the village someone will speak to me, something will happen, to make me know."

There was no one coming up or down the steeply tilted lane in the heat, and the girl went quickly, feeling the flat stones in comfort under her feet. She walked between ancient garden walls, bleached dry by the sun, and far older than the villas they enclosed, and over their antiquity hung the silvery branches of olive and mimosa trees. Below the villas the wild coast stretched like a great, slumbering beast, and the girl thought of the transformation if the land should rouse and stir beneath this brac-a-brac of bright-blue houses and red-tiled terraces and stretch its sultry length from cliff to cliff along the sea. The villas would crumble, their plaster disintegrate in dust, she thought, and only the timeless lanes remain as footpaths veining the wilderness. The garden walls, with the salamanders flicking across them faster than light, and the sinuous roots of palm and cactus, the tough ropes of the vines, these would survive, if only the land would stir and cast away the things that man had made.

Now the lane made a sudden turn between the garden walls, and the orange and olive trees were gone, and the frayed paper fans of the palms and the long horns of the yucca had vanished, and the girl descended the cobbles of a precipitous village street. Here, simple, narrow houses leaned on either side, like people who have gathered slowly, one by one, standing patient, incurious, each with its own plain, humble-featured face, as the houses of the European poor have always stood. Clotheslines were strung from window to window overhead, and seamen's striped cotton sweaters hung drying on them, and infants' ruffled dresses in mauve and yellow sleazy silk, and salmon-colored underwear, and the bronze of sailcloth dungarees. But in the street there was no stir of human life, no children were playing on the cobbles, and no old people sitting on the rush-bottomed chairs by the doors in which the beaded strings of fly-curtains hung. There were only the lean dogs, the sly-eyed cats, of these southern parts, searching the gutters for fish-heads, their skeletons visible through their sun-dried hides.

It is like a ghost town, a town of the dead, the girl thought, and in spite of the warmth of the stones and the leaning houses her palms were wet and cold. "Because of me," she whispered. "A street without the sound of voices because

63

of me." And in the silence the memory of the bus racing wildly to destruction was even sharper, more living, than it had been before.

And then from the harbor below came the alternating waves of voices laughing and voices crying out in uproar, the timbre of them reverberant, as if they rang against four walls of stone. First there would be the far, rippling music of an accordion that played, the delicate notes of it coming up the steep stone alley of the street; and then would come the shout of a single voice, sun-drenched and light and male, and singularly dimensional, as the voices of bathers will echo across water; and then the deep wave of multiple voices would rise.

"*Ah-h-h-h-h-h-h-!*" the voices would breathe aloud, as if witnessing great beauty; or they would cry out: "*Ah, non, ah, non, ah, non!*" in protest, or else their laughter would roar aloud. "*Ah-h-h-h-h-h-h!*" they would say to the marvelous presence of the sea and sky; and then, when this had subsided, it seemed to the girl that a thousand voices spoke out in grief because their kin had died.

Then she had come past the houses that concealed the waterfront, and she stepped into the noon heat of the quay. And here were the village people, a hot, dense wall of them, with their attention fixed upon the harbor waters, some with children held up in their arms to see, or seated on their shoulders, or children running like quicksilver between their legs. Here were the men and women of Abelin, their backs turned to the land, and death forgotten now behind them. Beneath the beaks of their canvas caps, or the gaudy silk straw of their hat-brims, or under their lifted, shielding hands, their eyes looked out across the harbor, watching the drama that was enacted there.

From an open window above the port came the quick, sweet music of the accordion, and, as the girl turned to make her way through the people, the composite roar, this time of laughter, echoed across the water and the quays.

Almost immediately, then, a man halted before her in the crowd, a young man whose presence was solid as a wall, and if he had just finished laughing with the others, his eyes had sobered now, and his brows went like a stroke of paint, single and black, across his face.

"Hello," he said, his accent like an Englishman's, and he did not move aside.

"Hello," she said, and she waited uncertainly before him, not knowing whether it was in painting or photograph or in the flesh, this year or last, in this country or another, that she had seen the dark, lively eyes, the heavy, heroic head.

"It was two weeks ago," he said, speaking English to her, and speaking it well, but with an alien care for the shape and value of the words. "Once you looked at me, once you didn't. The second time, you couldn't because your eyes were closed."

"I don't remember. You see, I don't remember," the girl said in a low voice. "I don't even know why I came to Abelin," she said, and she waited there in helplessness, his face, his voice, the look in his eyes almost familiar, the syllables of his name nearly recalled.

"I had my bicycle. You were riding on the bus. That was the first time," he said. "I followed down behind you from the Abbey School."

"I remember we stopped at the Abbey School," she said, "and then everything is wiped away. The bus. The whole thing happened because of me. You knew that,

65

didn't you?" she whispered, and the brilliance of noon came hot off the sea, hot off the stones, and she reached out to save herself from drowning in its tide.

"Because of you?" the young man said, and he took her hand, and held it absolutely still. "Stop talking that way. Stop it at once," he was saying. "We'll go over there to the cafés and find a place to sit down out of the sun. They'll be calling me to my boat in half a minute, but I've got to talk to you before I go." He pulled her quickly, almost impatiently, against him, turning her so that she faced the houses with him, his arm fitted under her arm so as to hold her upright like a lifeless doll as they moved through the crowd. "You had nothing to do with it. Don't go around saying things like that. Don't let them think you're a frightened girl." He laid his arm around her shoulders to guide her as they walked, and she felt a portion of the burden lifted from her heart. "You wanted to take the blame for it, perhaps because there was talk and feeling against your country in the bus and an American takes censure of his country as his own particular responsibility. This time it was something different," he said.

"It's good to be speaking English again," the girl said, and, walking with him, she saw that beneath their feet there were letters painted, tall as a man, on the cobbles of the quay. First came a *U* painted large enough and black enough for a passing airplane to read it, and beyond this outsized magnet of the *U* a giant *S* was visible for an instant before the rope-soled *espadrilles* and the bare brown feet of the people effaced it momentarily with the rest of what was written out. "Wait," she said to the young man as they walked, for now the shape of the other letters could be seen, then lost, then seen again. "Wait," she said, and she read it under her breath. " 'U.S. Go Home,' it says."

"Be proud," the young man said, and, as if in impatience with her, his hand tightened on her shoulder as they walked. "You'll see it written on garden walls, and across the cliffs, and on the macadam of the highways. It has nothing to do with what you are," he said, and then they heard the voices behind them speaking together in the musical, quick cadence of the south.

"There was another fire in the *maquis*, this time near Bandulu," said a man's voice. "You could see the flames all night across the hills."

"They say it was an American soldier who started it," a woman said. "He was driving up the back road, drunk, and he threw his lighted cigarette away."

"Not his country, eh?" said the man. "Nothing to him if the olive groves and the vineyards burn. Once I saw an American soldier drink five *pastis* down, one right after another, in less than half an hour, and then start breaking the windows in the place!"

"This soldier at Bandulu, they say he didn't pay for the drinks he had," said the woman's voice, "and what did he do but kick the table over when they asked him to!"

"I knew there was a forest fire," a third voice said, "but I didn't hear about the American soldier starting it."

"You mean you think he didn't do it?" the woman cried out. "Even though Albert saw him drink five *pastis* down?"

"Be a woman. Don't be a frightened girl," the young man said in a voice of admonition as he walked with his arm around the girl's shoulders. "There are other things to say." Now they had come through the people to the terraces of the cafés at the fringe of them, and not only were the tables filled, but customers stood on the iron chairs to see across the heads of the crowd to the stage of the harbor waters, where the drama was still played. They

67

had come to the Café du Port, and he led her in among the tables, guiding her past them, under the awning, into the interior area of shade. Back, back, they went into the near-dark of the café's depths, and there, under the fly-specked mirror in the corner, he found a vacant table, the top of it still wet from the rings of the glasses that had stood there just before they came. He pulled out a chair for her, and she sat down, unaware of her weariness as she watched him sit down facing her and run his fingers through his hair. "You must understand what happened," he said, his dark eyes on her, his voice so low that no one else could hear the words he said. "The bus. It wasn't an accident. The air-tubes of the brakes were cut."

And then the waiter had come, a cloth in his hand, and he leaned between them to wipe the marks of the other people's glasses away.

"What will it be, *m'sieu*, *'dame?*" he said.

"Wine? White wine?" said the young man, looking at the girl.

"Yes. That. Anything," she said. When the waiter had gone, she said, watching the young man still: "It isn't possible. No one could have planned the horror of that."

"I was one of the first to get there," the young man said. "We saw it. There're half a dozen of us who know that it was done. But you—one might just as well say that the bus went over because an American soldier drank too much at Bandulu, or threw his burning cigarette away, or did any of the things that all Americans do. It's easy to blame an American passing through for the way the mistral or the sirocco or the bora blow."

"But who could have wanted the bus to go over?" the girl said, still not believing this thing was true.

"It could have been one way of murder," said the

68

young man, and his heavy, handsome statue's head, his lively eyes, seemed bolder than reality in the shadows of the place.

"But twenty-five people!" the girl cried softly.

"Whoever did it may have wanted only one. The others didn't matter. It could have been like that," the young man said, and as the waiter set the two glasses of white wine before them, the sound of English ceased, and he looked up at the waiter's lean, dyspeptic face. "I'll pay you now, Marius. They're waiting for me on my boat," he said, and he took his money out.

"There's a lot of talk going on in the back streets and along the port, Michel," said the waiter, and he picked the young man's money up and counted the change out on the table, bill by pastel-tinted bill. "There're a lot of questions being asked about the bus. What's the mayor up to," he asked, his eye gone baleful, "putting *la joute* on now when the whole town's mourning its dead?"

"Takes the minds of the people off the situation, national and local," said the young man, the French that he spoke now as much of the south as the waiter's, but the precision of it a thing none of the others shared. "I'm in the games myself for the same reason everyone else is: for the size of the purse they're offering this year."

"Ah, money, money," the waiter said, and he might have been sick to the depths of his being of the look and the feel of the delicate bills. "Men pushing each other into the water for money, when it used to be for a woman or the sport of the thing. Even *la joute* turned into a business so good they'll be coming over from Hollywood to film it to show Americans how the average Frenchman lives. Ah, money!" he groaned, with the pain of it griping in his flesh. "All right, Michel, get out there and play! Get out

69

there and win at *la joute*, and win the election for us too!"
he said, and he used the short form of the verb to him,
such as members of a family use. "Why do you think they
drink, the lot of them here, sitting swilling the green stuff
and the red stuff and the white stuff down? Because they
know there isn't any government in Abelin! You go to
sleep knowing that at night, and you wake up knowing it,
and you carry it around with you all day. It's like a kid
having a father and mother who don't care if he's out
shooting crap at the corner, because they're shooting crap
themselves behind the house!" Before he went, he picked
up the coins which the young man pushed toward him
across the table, and he dropped them, wearily, distaste-
fully, into the pocket of his vest. "Ah, money, money!" he
said, sick of his own hand that had reached out and
gathered the coins in, sick of the barter and exchange that
set the rhythm of their nights and days.

The girl was aware for the first time, then, of the clothes
the young man wore: his shirt a luminous, deep red, with
long, full sleeves buttoned at the wrists, and the material
of it the shiny satinette from which masquerade costumes
are made. He had crossed his strong legs beside the table,
and she saw that his trousers were of the same cheap cotton
stuff, but white, and cut like a Spanish dancer's, and his
feet, his hands, his muscular neck were as dark as leather
against these carnival clothes.

"Here's to *la joute*," he said, speaking English again, and
he lifted the glass of wine in his quick brown hand and held
it level with his mouth.

"But what is *la joute?*" the girl asked, and she went on,
saying: "If I drink, I'll be tipsy. I don't dare."

"It's a game left over from the time of the kings. Take
a little. You look tired," he said, and he waited a moment,

70

watching her wet her lips with wine. "It's the game that knights in armor used to play in tournaments, only now the players ride toward each other on boats instead of on horses. There's a big prize of money for the man who throws the greatest number of players into the sea. I need it for the things I want to do here," he said, his eyes, his mouth, his hair, so close to her, so richly colored, that the faces of the others in the café room seemed no more than the faded photographs of men, and their voices faint and far. "A school of my own, a newspaper of my own— they're taking shape. And this year the mayor decided to triple the purse as a means of buying the good will of the town. That's the money I want," he said, and he stood up, and the little glass was empty before his place. "Wait for me here, out of the sun—"

"No," said the girl, and she got up quickly. "I want to see you play." When she stood beside him, she thought: *I'm not afraid when I'm with him. He might be someone I've known a long time, gone to school with, talked about books and stars and music with; someone I've walked with through art galleries, and we both liked the same pictures without having to say why.* "But who was on the bus," she said in a low voice to him, "that anyone would want to kill?"

"No one, or else a half a dozen people," the young man said, and he put his hand under her arm to guide her through the tables toward the sun. "We'll talk about this. Not you, not Madame Marceau, not the house-agent, for you were three unexpected passengers that day, as far as anyone can tell. I like your Indian bracelets," he said.

"I got them in Arizona," said the girl, looking down at the silver cuffs on her narrow wrists. "I helped my father one summer when he was working there."

"I opened the passport in your handbag that after-

71

noon," the young man said, "so I knew you were American then. Before Madame Marceau claimed you I had read that it was requested of 'all whom it might concern to permit safely and freely to pass, and in case of need to give all lawful aid and protection to Mary Farrant,' of Columbus, Ohio, aged eighteen, hair chestnut, eyes blue, with no distinguishing features whatsoever." The long, deep dimples scarred his cheeks as he looked down at her, and his eyes went suddenly shy. "I loved you for being American," he said. "I wanted an American to come to Abelin, to come very simply, with one little bag, the way the English or the Irish come, not with a lot of air-weight luggage, I think they call it, and a car that won't fit into any French garage." Now he was guiding her through the crowded tables, past the chairs on which the onlookers still stood to see the harbor waters, and once they were free of the awning's shade the sunlight poured hot and bright across their brows. "I wanted an American to come," he said, bringing her through the moving people on the quay, "any American, even that American who kicks over tables and throws his burning cigarettes into the brush, so that I could say to him: 'Forget what they've told you about the French. Let me tell you what I'm trying to do.'" Now their feet passed over the giant letters of animosity written black on the cobbles, but the girl was listening to the things he said, and she did not see them there. "I want to win at *la joute* because I can use that money to win at the other thing too. I want the school, the newspaper, and I want to stop the construction of the casino out there on the mole. I want to build houses for the shipyard workers up there on the hill. So I've started an opposition party here. I want to be mayor of Abelin," he

72

said, as if he were saying: *I'd like to take the sun down and try another way of lighting for a while.*

They had come through the density of people to the edge of the port, and the immured waters of the harbor flashed so vibrantly, so richly, fiercely, blue, that the girl stood suddenly still in wonder and looked out to the bay. Ahead, at the single wharf, a pure-white yacht, with brasses shining, pulled gracefully at its ropes, and to the left, below the dusty village square, a row of pleasure launches, their fringed canopies spread like parasols above the flowered cushions of their seats, stirred with the lazy lapping of the sea. But in all the port there were only two boats that crossed the water, two motor-driven fishing-boats that maneuvered without haste, coming into position opposite each other, with a wide, glittering expanse of harbor lying in between. In the stern of each, a high, sloping runway had been fixed, a structure as temporary as the scaffolding of a float in a parade, and each runway topped by a platform on which one man could stand, and on each a man now stood, dressed in the white and red costume of *la joute* and armed with a gilded wooden shield, and a long spear balanced in his other hand. Because of these flying buttresses fixed in the stern, they were no longer merely weathered fishing-boats, nor were they Spanish galleons, but hybrid craft bred of the two, and as they advanced upon each other, they seemed to strive to rise from the water as the Winged Victory strives to rise from the confines of stone.

"The one on the right, that is my boat, my men," the young man said as they stood on the edge of the pressing people, his hand under her arm.

"Ah, they are beautiful!" the girl cried softly. "If anyone could get those colors onto canvas, it would make a whole room blaze with light!"

In each of the boats, below the warrior with his shield and spear, men in the same red shirts, the same white trousers with the flaring Spanish cut, leaned casually, pirate-like, against the gunwales, six or more to a boat, with sun-blacked faces, and red bandanas tied across their hair. And now the two boats came nearer and nearer to each other, until it seemed that they must strike, prow splintering prow. But the two men on their separate pinnacles braced their bare feet on the wood, braced their long spears against their hips, and each fixed the other in the eye. In the swift instant of boat passing boat, with scarcely a hair's breadth between, each flung his weight upon his spear and thrust it hard against the other's shield. One man toppled, then, from the high bridge of his galleon, flinging his shield and spear aside, and shouting his single word of capitulation as he fell. And "*Ah-h-h-h-h-h!*" the voices of the people breathed loudly in acclaim as he struck the water, and the other rode on in triumph while the galleons slowly turned. The boats maneuvered into position again, and a new player ran nimbly up the runway and took his place on the empty platform, bearing with him the other's wooden shield and spear.

"If you stayed here in Abelin," the young man said, his hand still under her arm as they watched the two men riding forward against the burning blue Italian sky, "you could help—help not in the debased meaning of the word, but help perhaps by nothing more than listening, just one person listening to another, the way that helps when a man, a country, is in trouble, helps to clarify the thing he's trying to do." Out on the water, the two boats advanced upon each other, the two men poised in readiness, while those below them leaned against the gunwales in the sun. "Mary Farrant, will you try to remember my name? You knew it once," he said, and he looked with singular urgency into her face. Beyond them, the two boats passed by their narrow margin, and both players braced their spears, and this time, as the spear points struck the shields, both players wavered and fell. The water broke into glittering pieces as their bodies struck it, and the people watching roared aloud, and for an instant the two men were gone beneath the surface, and then they emerged again, shaking the bright drops from their hair. "When both players fall," said the young man, and he and the girl watched them swimming toward each other in the sun, "they must kiss each other's cheeks before they swim to shore. It had a meaning once, but now the meaning has been lost, perhaps merely that, whatever the competition, once the weapons are gone, man is committed to man, victor to vanquished." Then the two men in the water kissed each other's faces, and turned, and with long, slow strokes came toward the quay. "Now it is my turn," the young man said.

But the girl said: "Wait," and she slipped the Indian bracelet from her left wrist. "This is the strongest one. Wear it. You see, it's open. You can make it any size."

"From the side nearest the heart," said the young man, and she saw that he was smiling as he forced the broad, etched silver band wide enough to pass his knuckles and the width of his dark hand. "Ladies of the court used to give tokens to their knights to wear in contest—"

"You say that almost flippantly," the girl said, standing before him, wounded, soft-haired, and young.

"Frenchmen are flippant. Didn't you know?" he said quickly, and the long dimples scarred his cheeks, and for a

75

moment it seemed there was something else, quite different, that he was about to say. And then the men's voices called: "*Hê*, Vaillant, Vaillant, come!" and he looked across the water to his boat drawn alongside the wharf now, and from it the costumed players called: "*Hê*, Vaillant! You're the next to play!"

"I'm on my way!" he called out in answer, but before he went, he turned back to the girl again, and he ran his fingers through his hair. "My name is Vaillant, Michel Vaillant," he said, and his eyes, moving from feature to feature of her face, found no sign of recognition of the name. "If you'd meet me at six, on the terrace of the Café du Port, we could talk," he said, and then he was gone, half running along the wall of the quay, moving quickly on his bare feet along the edge of people.

"*Vas-y*, Vaillant!" a voice rang out as he skirted the pleasure-boats with their softly blowing canvas canopies. "*Vas-y*, Vaillant!" shouted the same voice or another, or the composite voice of many people, and then he had passed the moored yacht, running, and swung himself into the galleon with the others in their bright, savage clothes.

THE SEA AIR CAME HOT OFF THE waters of the harbor, and the girl watched the two boats maneuver into position and turn to face each other across the glittering blue field. As they turned, Vaillant mounted the runway of his boat, with the gilded shield, the wooden spear, carried lightly; and then a hand in the crowd touched the girl's arm, and her name was spoken, sharply but wearily, and the girl looked back from the boats and the sun and the sea.

"Come with me at once," said Madame Marceau in a low, tense voice, and she stood there, sleek as a jay, under her parasol. "I've been running through the town like a fool, looking for you—and you down here in this heat, in that rag of a dress, with no shoes on!"

"Do you remember the day you ran barefoot on the sand?" the girl said softly, and Madame Marceau turned her head this way and that, like a big-beaked jay, for the sight or the smell of public censure, but the others were watching the boats advancing across the water, and they had no interest in the women standing there.

"Something has happened, something very grave," Madame Marceau whispered, her eye alert still for what the others in the crowd might see or overhear. "Come with me at

77

once. Walk with your head down. Keep your face concealed. Take my arm," she said. "We don't want anyone
to recognize you now."

"But the game!" said the girl, and she looked out at the
water where the two players rode against the background
of the sea-wall and the sky.

"There's no time for the game!" Madame Marceau
whispered almost savagely, and then she jerked her chin
toward the newspaper folded under her arm. "The police.
They're after you. The paper's just come out, so the others
haven't seen it yet." And her eye was on these others, on
the women with their black hair richly oiled, and lacy
blouses leaving their dark shoulders bare; on the children
they carried in their arms, with gold chain bracelets on
their doll-like wrists and earrings in the tiny petals of their
lobes; turned sharply on the men in cotton trousers and
striped sailor's shirts or in singlets from which their ma-
hogany-dark shoulders and arms swelled. "We must get
to the mayor at once," Madame Marceau said, drawing
the girl under the green shade of the parasol.

And now, as the voices of the people rang in acclaim
across the water, Madame Marceau's sharp, mesh-gloved
fingers closed on the girl's bare arm like the claws of a bird
upon its prey, and she moved quickly with her through the
crowd. Over their heads, the accordion played at the window still, and the composite laughter of the people sounded
upon the sunlit air, but now nothing was the same as it
had been before. It seemed to the girl that this was another
quay from the one she had crossed with Vaillant, and as
Madame Marceau hastened on with her over the cobbles,
she could not believe that the café where she and Vaillant
had sat together would still be there. But now Madame
Marceau drew her toward the village square, where white-

78

barked plane trees cast a wide canopy of shade upon the dust, and here, in sudden relief, they were free of the presence of the crowd, for even the *boules* players had gone to watch the drama of *la joute* being played. Here the town hotel stood on the corner of the square, with sleep lying heavy and hot on its deserted terrace, and three lean dogs were stretched, annihilated by slumber, in the dust in their reddish hides. Madame Marceau leaned against the plaster wall of the hotel to get her breath, and closed her parasol, and took the newspaper from under her arm, while beyond, on the waterfront, the people's voices rose in pleasure, and then in protest, and then in pleasure again, in comment upon the games which the two women could no longer see.

"Here! Look at this!" said Madame Marceau, and she opened the paper in agitation. "What have you to say to this?" she asked, and the girl stood looking at the page the Frenchwoman held open in both hands.

"But that's my passport photograph!" the girl said at last.

"Only ten times enlarged!" snapped Madame Marceau. "Your Peter, your Mr. Cornish, has put the police of Europe on your trail. He thinks you've been kidnapped, spirited away."

"Yes, Cornish! Yes, of course, Peter Cornish," the girl said, and now that the name had been established, she believed all the rest would suddenly come clear. She took the paper from Madame Marceau's mesh-gloved hands, and her eyes went intently from line to line of the column of print: ". . . left her Paris hotel, taking only a suitcase with her . . . American Consular offices throughout France alerted a week ago . . . the police of three countries called today . . . all passengers at airports and

79

making channel crossing checked . . . Peter Cornish, the missing girl's fiancé, said last night . . . Mary Farrant in good spirits the night before her disappearance . . . fears foul play. . . ."

"But I left the restaurant where we dined together crying! I ran out ahead of him. I remember that," the girl said, and for a moment the words of their argument were almost heard, the reason for crying almost recalled, and then Madame Marceau moved with such impatience that she seemed about to stab the paper with her parasol.

"But don't you see the position this puts me in?" she said. "I'm the criminal in the case! I'm the one who's been concealing your identity! I went down and registered you at the *mairie* of Abelin as French, as my sister's daughter, my only niece, whose papers had gone with the rest of the baggage into the Mediterranean. And now this picture comes out on the front of every newspaper on the continent—your face, the same name I gave, but you're an American, not French, who's been missing from Paris since two weeks, so I'm part of the conspiracy. Only the mayor can straighten it out with the police. But you've got to get some shoes on your feet. You've got to dress like a lady when you meet the mayor."

From the corner of the deeply sleeping square they could see three narrow streets winding upward behind the houses on the quay, three steeply tilted streets empty of people now, but lined with market stands on which were piled melons and plums, peaches and gourds, ripe figs, tomatoes, lettuce heads, green almonds, trays of grapes. Each street was divided, lengthwise, by shadow, so that one side of it lay in sunlight so brilliant that it seemed less a sidewalk than an illuminated stage, while the other lay in the area of shade which the houses cast upon the stones.

"Madame Marceau, I'm hungry. For the first time in weeks," the girl said, her voice faint with longing for all she saw. "I'd like to eat my way up one of those streets, cramming the fruit into my mouth, peaches, and grapes, and plums, and figs!"

"You wouldn't get very far," said Madame Marceau, and she folded the newspaper over, and forced open her parasol. "If they're down watching *la joute*, you can be sure they've left the grandmothers on guard behind the stalls. They'll be sitting just inside, in the dark, watching like cats," she went on saying, her leanness of leg and color of plumage more like that of an ostrich than a woman, the girl thought, and she felt her own mouth smile. "They counted each grape before they took off," said Madame Marceau, setting one foot before the other with ostrich-like care. "Come quickly now, Mary Farrant," she said, and she drew the girl under her parasol. "But as for eating anything as we climb, the General used to say that the custom of eating out of bags while circulating in the streets was peculiar to horses. We must get home without delay. I'll give you my new white linen suit to wear, and the blue kid slippers the mayor won't remember I wore at Easter, and he'll see at once that you're the kind of person he could ask to tea. Only don't bring up the topic of hoof-and-mouth disease, although the whole of the interior's crippled with it. There's no reason why he should know what your father did," she said. "If he's pleased, he'll certainly waive the registration I made concerning your nationality. He'll notify the *préfet* you've been found, and the *préfet* will inform the Paris police, and your young man will come down at once and take you back, and that will be the end of it."

"Only I'm not ready to go back," the girl said, and

beyond on the quay the voices breathed "*Ah-h-h-h-h-h-*"
as if those who watched had just witnessed a sight of great
beauty or great skill, and she thought of Vaillant on the
galleon, and of his words, and she believed with new
fervor in the things there were to say. "I want to find out
why I came down here alone, to a town I'd never heard
of," she began, but she did not finish it.

"Oh, there's no time for that!" said Madame Marceau
in impatience, her arm through the girl's arm, her head
jerking quickly to right and left with the pace of her
steps, tilted like a fowl's head to fix the worm, the bit of
grain, the fleeing frog, within its sight. "We'll go up by
the middle street. It's the steepest and quickest. Just look
what the natives do to their vegetables and fruit!" she
said as they stepped out of the shade. "Everything that
grows in the south is bleached of its color by the sun, or
else by whatever wind is blowing, either the mistral or the
bora or the sirocco or the bise, so what do the storekeepers
do? They pile up their stands with all this that could never
have come out of the ashes and lava of the coast, and
maybe they fool themselves and you, but certainly not
me! I know the oranges come from Spain, and the lettuce
and artichokes from the north, and the peaches and plums
from the interior, and the only tomatoes anyone can eat
are shipped from Italy. Oh, the south of France, I have no
faith in it!" she said, and she spoke as bitterly as if of a
lover whose mouth had kissed her mouth with passion
once, and who now had turned away.

But they had scarcely stepped into the avenue of sun
that lay between them and the mounting streets when the
girl brought Madame Marceau to a halt. Behind them
came the puny crying of a violin, and the girl turned

back to the sight of a warp-legged figure that waltzed through the dust of the abandoned square. Here was a man, a little man, with a fiddle under his chin, who scraped with an ancient bow at the strings of it as he spun, a stunted Algerian in ragged trousers and coat whose rope soles flapped loose from his *espadrilles* as he turned in the crazy circles of his dance. He waltzed to a stop before the women, and lowered his fiddle, and took the soiled cap from his head.

"It's only old Marrakech," said Madame Marceau, and she cocked her eye at his leathery mask. "No money, no money today, Marrakech!" she said, as if speaking to a man who was deaf, or who stood a great distance away. "No mon-ey, no mon-ey. Go a-way," she called across the chasm that lay, deep and eternal, unbridgeable forever, between his dark-skinned statelessness and her own color and established nationality.

"But I've seen him somewhere, perhaps on the stage, perhaps in a ballet, in *Petrouchka!*" the girl said, the pain of seeking to recall, and not recalling, almost physical in its intensity. He stood there, small as a child, his fiddle in one hand, the rag of his cap in the other, an iron-gray fuzz like the intricate scrub of the *maquis* growing out of the cavities, over the prominences of his skull. "How do I know him? Where have I seen him?" the girl asked, but there was no answer to it. His head was bowed, his mouth sucked closed over his empty gums, more monkey than man, he seemed to be, except for the beauty of his dark, long-fingered hands.

"No mon-ey, all poor peo-ple to-day!" cried Madame Marceau, and she moved her hand in its mesh glove back and forth in negation above him, as if to rub him out.

83

"But you can't do that," the girl said quickly. "Please give me some money. You can take it out of the francs of mine that you have."

"Five francs is far too much for him," said Madame Marceau under her breath as she searched through her bag.

"I'll give him ten," the girl said, and when he had it in his hand, he put the rag of a cap back on his head and the violin under his chin, and the wishbone of his legs began to turn in the steps of the senseless dance.

It had nothing to do with music, this wailing of catgut on the air. It was merely a tireless sawing away at silence, and when the saw stuck, then the bow chopped with staccato strokes at what was left of the peace and quiet. The sleeping dogs roused now to the macabre sound, and came from under the tables on the hotel terrace, their hair rising on their necks as they sniffed at the Algerian's flapping *espadrilles* and the rags and tatters of his clothes. And now children filtered back through the crowd upon the quay, coming into the shade as if into cool water, and laughing with pleasure at the sight of the little figure spinning there.

"Come! We must hurry, hurry!" said Madame Marceau to the girl.

But a fisherman had joined the children, a young man with the yoke of his shoulders bronze and bare in his faded singlet, and fish scales drying on his cotton trousers of workman's blue.

"Go to it, Marrakech!" he said, and he stood there laughing as the children laughed, a blue cap tipped so low on his golden brows that he must draw in his chin and stiffen his thick brown neck to see from under the visor of it. "There's ten francs in it for you if you waltz around each tree the length of the square and back!" he called out, and the little man danced toward the trees, his lips sealed over his toothless gums, his lean arm sawing faster, faster, as his feet spun through the dust. "Let's have it faster than that! Can't you do it faster, Marrakech?" the fisherman called after him, and he gave a straight, honest, good-natured look from under his blue cap at the women, and winked his eye at them, and caressed his strong young arms lingeringly in his palms. "Come on now, faster! Last week you had the plane trees spinning too!" he said, and Marrakech turned even faster on his crooked legs, with the children skipping and jumping behind him as he circled the first tree in the row.

Then one of the children picked up a nailhead-studded ball that the *boules* players had forgotten when they left, and threw it, and it hit the little dancer hard between the shoulder-blades.

"But they can't do that to him!" the girl cried, but the little man's arm did not slacken in its bowing, and his feet did not falter in the dance.

"He's touched in the head," the fisherman called out in explanation to the girl, and he twirled his forefinger just short of his own temple in indication of the state of Marrakech's brain.

"The fisherman," said Madame Marceau under her breath, shielding their faces from his sight with the green silk of her parasol, "he's got a newspaper there in his back pocket. Let's go quickly before he has the time to open it out."

And "Yes," said the girl. "Yes, yes. I know." Beyond them, Marrakech waltzed on, with the children behind him pulling the tail of his ragged coat and the strings of his *espadrilles*. He circled the second tree and the third,

85

and the children tripped him with their bare feet thrust out in the dust, and they laughed in high, sweet voices when he stumbled, and felt in his pockets for what he might have, and found the coins and took them for their own. "But how can we go now? We have to take care of him!" the girl said, and she saw that his face was wet with tears, but the black seam of his mouth did not split with his grief, and his feet danced steadily on. "Why doesn't he speak? Why does he take it silently?" she asked.

"Marrakech can't speak. He has never spoken," said Madame Marceau. "They say he lied once when he was a child and his father cut his tongue out. Now, come, let us hurry," she said.

Then out of the hotel door came a broad, tall, heavy man who had certainly eaten too well and drunk too well for thirty or forty years or more, the last meal taken perhaps an hour before, and his blood still surfeited with it, and his limbs still heavy with sleep. He paused on the terrace among the empty tables, and blinked at the sun, and hitched his ocher-colored linen trousers up over his swollen paunch, packed full, it might be, with richly creamed shrimps, or sea mussels steamed with onions and herbs, or snails stuffed with garlic and sweet butter and chives, completed with pancakes as thin as tissue paper, and varied cheese and fruits, and this washed down by, first, a carafe of white wine and then a carafe of red.

"*Hé, bon jour*, Madame M.!" he called from behind his black mustaches, the sound of it muffled as if he were just beginning, or just finishing, a yawn. And at the booming of his voice the lean dogs roused, and they looked at his heavy-jowled face in expectation, their russet tails fanning slowly at the air.

"*Bon jour*, Monsieur Antoinetti," said Madame Marceau, her eye on the newspaper under his arm. "We'll have to go quickly now," she whispered to the girl.

"Let's have it faster, faster, Marrakech!" the fisherman said once more, and then he slapped his leg, and the newspaper fell from his pocket, and he leaned, guffawing, to pick it up, and he saw the photograph on the front page of it, and his laughter died.

"If your ancestors sit eating dung for seven centuries, you end by trying to get some exercise for yourself," said the hotel proprietor, and he yawned again as he looked at Marrakech waltzing around the fifth tree in the row. "We pass a law to keep them out of the country, these dope-smuggling Algerians, these rug-and-heroin peddlers, but they get in just the same! We could pass ten laws, but still they'd infest the ports of France with their contraband carcasses, hiding like rats in the produce that's brought in. Every crime that's committed in France, there's a North African at the bottom of it, yet we give them the status of citizens and dress them up like men!" He might have gone on with more of it, but now he was looking at the girl's face, and the words he was saying against the dark men of Algeria came abruptly to an end. "Now, you, mademoiselle, I've been reading about you in the paper," he said, and across the dust the fisherman stood looking from the newspaper in his own hands to the girl and back at the newspaper again.

"There's no necessity to tell the whole town, my dear Antoinetti," said Madame Marceau, smiling grimly as she gathered together her bag, her newspaper, her parasol, the girl.

"And if we're to believe the Communists, mademoiselle," the hotel proprietor went on saying, "you Americans have your problem with the black man too. There's

87

a written law against killing him off, at least in your northern states, and an unwritten law against assimilating him. That's the way we see it from here. But read the story about the police of Europe looking for you," he said, and he seemed to be stifling a yawn as he offered the folded paper to her, and Madame Marceau reached out and struck it sharply with her hand.

"Put it away!" she said in a low voice. "We're on our way to the *mairie* now. We don't want a crowd of hoodlums following her. We want to do it nicely, quietly, through the intermediary of the mayor."

But already the crowds at the waterfront were breaking into separate currents, the men and women moving slowly toward the streets and square, lingering a little, like people leaving a theater once the performance is over, reluctant to exchange the shared unfamiliar vision for reality. Already the avenue of sun was filled with the drifting women and men, and the *boules* players were returning, and children came running, barefoot, to join the others who danced their dance of ridicule behind the Algerian who waltzed around the trees.

"I like the Americans," the hotel proprietor's voice boomed out, and he hitched his linen trousers up again, perhaps reflecting on the nation of tourists who brought their own cars with them when they came. "I've never had any trouble with the Americans. I'd like to see every table on the terrace filled with them, but you get a rabble of manual workers, like the crowd over there, who don't know how to run a business any more than they know how the economy of a country is run, and they'll swallow any story that's going around, provided it lets them vent their spleen," he said, looking at the girl. "Now take the casino out on the harbor that we wanted to get finished for the summer trade. I tell you, it's a symbol of the French Empire today. It's standing there half-built, and if it's still not finished by next year, that's the fault of the workingman of France, and don't let them tell you any differently. First the masons go out on strike, and when they've got what they wanted, then the carpenters walk out, one strike called by the Communist, and the other by the Catholic, trade unions, so you don't know whether to put the blame on Moscow or on Rome. If we had American aid to finish building it, we could get non-union labor in. I say we ought to call the army up, with fixed bayonets, to get the men back on the scaffoldings, and do it before the scaffoldings of France collapse and fall!" All this that he said was spoken not in the meridional speech of the coast, but in French of the north (he, a Parisian, perhaps, come to this beneficial warmth a long time back because of an irritable heart or the threat of apoplexy in the blood), and every word of it in contradiction to the things that, for a year now, she had listened to the youth of Paris say. "A casino," he said, hitching his trousers over his paunch, and no sound of slumber left in his voice, "it would put Abelin on the international map." *The French Empire, the French army, the place of one town on the international map*, the lingo of men long dead, and he, in his yellow linen trousers, his flesh surfeited with too-rich foods, with vintage wines, seeking to give the failures of another century a contemporary urgency. "We'd become a tourist center, with money moving from hand to hand. But the workingman, he's too shortsighted to see beyond his *pernod* glass. Let me give you a tip, mademoiselle," he went on saying, and he gestured with one hand toward the people coming slowly from the quay. "You'd better have your answers ready before you start back through that crowd. If they recognize you from the picture in the paper they're stopping to buy now, they'll want to know about germ warfare in Korea and how many states are still Jim Crow. And something else, mademoiselle," he said, lowering his voice, and the arch of a yawn beginning, and then dying, in his jaws; "if they think you're the girl who rode in the bus two weeks ago, they'll want to know why you were talking to the bus-driver and taking his mind off the road." The people were overflowing from the avenue, some moving up through the shade of the tilted streets and others advancing, bare-limbed, bare-shouldered, impregnable, upon the square. Each face in the crowd was drawn with singularly enduring clarity, the black curls under the sun hats of the women, their heavily rouged mouths, and the men's dark throats, their coarse-pored, weathered skins, their stubborn brows, the eyes of women and men alike putting the questions to her, and the odor of musk and sun-oil strong and alien on the dust and sunlight of the air. "Now I wouldn't know if you were that girl, but that girl was American too, and there were twenty-five people killed on that bus," he said. "Their relatives call it murder, and I don't know how you'll answer that. I'm telling you this as a friend of America." And then he roared in sudden fury across the square: "Let's stop this noise!" The blood went dark in his heavy jowls, but the children shouted in jubilation, for now they had got one *espadrille* off the Algerian's foot, and they tossed it up through the canopy of leaves. "No one will sit down for a drink on the terrace with this going on! Get the lot of them off the square!" he ordered the fisherman, and the fisherman looked from under the visor of his cap at the other man, the back of his head, his neck, his spine, like a straight, smooth piece of timber stained richly brown.

"You wouldn't do him out of his ten francs, would you, Monsieur Antoinetti?" he said in mock concern. "He has six more trees to go!"

"And last time he did it, you didn't pay up, and he was sniveling around all week for his sous! *Allez!*" the proprietor's voice boomed through his mustaches to the dogs, and he clapped his big palms, and the three of them went, heads lowered, mouths yelping, in the direction he gave them with his irate hand. "*Filez!*" he shouted to the children, and they broke apart before the dogs, and scattered, as fleet as minnows, through the green, untroubled shade. And then the girl too was running barefoot across the dust while the others stood watching, arrested within the confines of their own identities.

The dogs moved fast, and despite their emaciated bodies, their craven tails, their docile eyes, they seemed fearless as bloodhounds as they closed on the little man who had not ceased to dance. One seized the tail of his coat, and the other the rags of his trouser-leg, and the third snapped at his ankle-bones, until the waltz became, step by panic-stricken step, a wild stampede and the fiddle screamed out like a living thing, and then Marrakech went down. But the girl had come nearly as fast as the dogs; she was there at their heels when the crying of the catgut died.

"Stop it, now, stop!" she said fiercely through her teeth to them. "Let go of him now!" She was down on her knees in the dust with them, and she struck with her fists at the links of their spines in their coarse, reddish coats, at their flat, stubborn skulls, fighting them as she had once fought her father's dogs when they had cornered her pet Belgian hare. "I'll save you as I saved him, Marrakech!" she whispered savagely, and under the hammering of her fists the first beast, and then the second, released the stuff of the little man's clothing, and the two of them cowered before her within their mottled hides. But the third dog was the wildest, and he wanted the bones of the dark-skinned ankles and nothing else, perhaps to crack them like chicken-legs in his jaws and suck the marrow out. He was snapping and snarling, his lips drawn up from his strong, white teeth, when the girl closed both hands on the collar around his neck and flung him back. Then she kneeled down between the slinking dogs and the fallen man, who lay with his face pock-marked and wizened, his bluish cheeks sunken, his sealed lips like a black, disfiguring scar. "I will take care of you," she said, leaning above his almost incredible ugliness, and she searched his features for some sign of what he was. He lay there, thin as a spider, and his face as hideous, small, terrible, intent, but in his closed eyelids there was an unexpected beauty, as startling as if two smooth mauve tulip petals had been laid upon the leathery texture of his mask. His eyes did not open, his nostrils did not flicker with breath, and only his long, narrow hand seemed living still as it groped for his violin in the dust. Then the girl had the bow, the fiddle, and she gave them to him, and she stood up, her fingers closed over his, and helped him to his feet. "Don't be afraid. I will not leave you," she said as he looked in apprehension around him. "I will take you away from here."

But when she turned, she too saw the *boules* players gathering on the square, their studded balls cradled like weapons in their hands, and, behind the *boules* players, people filling the tables on the hotel terrace, and beyond these people, others moving steadily across the avenue of sun. The whole of Abelin seemed to be gathering behind them, with metallic balls in the palms of their hands, or with newspapers open, the accusation in their eyes, the questions to ask already on their tongues, and the girl drew back in fear. *You'd better have your answers ready*, said the memory of the proprietor's voice as clearly as if the sound of it had not yet died, and the girl thought in panic: *What can I answer? How can I tell them there are a thousand Americas and I can answer only for one?*

So the people gathered, like a dark storm gathering, and the girl and the Algerian went quickly together, almost running, crossing through sunlight toward the stretch of beach that ran from the harbor along the cliffs hemming the bay. And whether or not the dogs were after them, or whether voices called to them, they did not know, for they did not turn their heads to see, and their ears were deaf to everything except the beating of their own hearts as they fled. Marrakech took the lead, scuttling sideways over the breakwater to reach the sand, limping fast, with one *espadrille* off and one *espadrille* on, and his fiddle silent, fleeing as if the pack was at their heels. And deeper and deeper into the solitude of this territory that was his, she followed him down steps worn in the rock, feeling the sea-moss soft underfoot, hastening past miniature pools in which starfish and periwinkles and mussels, blue as grapes, lay in the water's unblemished clarity. All about them were boulders the high cliffs had cast down in other years, in stormy seasons, and the little man sidled crabwise through the labyrinth they formed, his bow and fiddle in his hand. And *Here, here, we are safe from the whole town of them*, the girl thought, following him through the maze of giant rock. *Here he is safe from what they can do to him, and*

93

I am safe from the questions they can ask. For here there was only the sound of the sea breaking against the stones, and the whisper of its withdrawal, and the only voices that were heard were those of the circling gulls.

Marrakech did not stop until they had come to the foot of the first soaring cliff, and there, in the blinding light of afternoon, he halted abruptly and glanced about him before making a sign to her to follow where he led. He held his fiddle and bow against his breast, with the rags of his coat drawn carefully across them, and then he slipped from sight between two segments of dark, porous rock that had fallen in another year, another season, from the cornice high above their heads. These boulders masked the dark mouth of a cave, and at its entrance Marrakech reached his own long hand back for the girl's hand and drew her with him into the obscurity. But step by step as they advanced, the darkness diluted, and the girl could see that seams of moisture ran bright as veins of ore in the stone of the corridor through which they passed. And then they had come into a courtyard, enclosed by massive rock, but standing open to the light of day.

This was a sort of garden, the girl saw, and she looked in wonder at the beauty of it, for although the center burned with heat, in the shade of the overhanging walls cool receptacles of stone had been arranged. Some stood on the packed, yellowish sand, and others were set in recesses hollowed in the rock, and species of alga and coral lived in the water that they held. Here Marrakech laid his fiddle and bow with care on a stone ledge, and he turned in the precarious shadow and lifted a tray of fresh fruit from a deep, stony cleft and carried it to where she stood.

"Oh, Marrakech, food! I'm dead with hunger! Did

you hear me say that back on the square?" she said, but
he shook his head. It was merely, said his humility before
her, that he must give her the things he had to give. The
figs were purple, and soft to the touch, and they opened
like flowers in her fingertips; and the peaches were as good
as honey to the taste, and the juices ran down her chin.
"It is good. I want to eat all of it," she said, and the scar
of his mouth did not alter, but he stood softened with
acquiescence before her, as if the blood was melting in his
veins.

First it was this he must give her, this fruit that he could
never have paid out money for, but had perhaps filched,
piece by piece, from the market stalls in the evening as
he waltzed and fiddled past. And when she had eaten the
fruit, it was the tray she must take, the curious tray that
was the bleached spine of a mammoth fish, perhaps por-
poise or dolphin, she thought as she touched the pointed
scallops of the bone. And there were other things he had
to give, for this was his garden and his aquarium, and he
smoothed the stones he had chiseled into shape as a sculp-
tor smooths the statues he has made. Here were sea-
anemone blooming as in a flower-bed, and shells assembled
in intricate mosaic, and, in deeper basins, seahorses and
starfish explored their captive pools for liberty. These
seahorses, with their stiff, armed crests, and the baby
octopi that swung, limb over limb, like miniature apes,
through the branches of the coral trees—these were hers,
said the eloquence of his open hands, and he lifted a starfish from the water and offered it to her, as red as orange-
peel, and as coarse, upon his bluish palm. And there was
something more he had to give, his sudden animation
cried out, and he scuttled before her across the courtyard,
past the basins of shells and sea-plants under water so still

that they seemed caught beneath panes of luminous blue glass.

The girl followed him through the chaos of rocks, and when they were free of them, they stood upon the beach again, perhaps half a mile from where they had been before. Once on its sand, the girl turned to look back the way they had come, and she saw only an avalanche of boulders, and the cliff wall rising sheer and high. So now his garden might be something she had dreamed, she thought, or something he himself had dreamed to offer her in homage, for there was no sign of it, and she followed him quickly as he ran fast down the beach toward the rocks that edged the sea. In a cove of rock was a fishing-boat, its boards streaked with peeling azure paint, and Marrakech stooped and pulled gently at the rope that moored it, and drew it close, caressing it as if it were a living thing that pulled at a halter rope to go.

"Is it your boat, Marrakech?" the girl asked, and the little man looked into her face, squatting there on the rock and looking for the first time into the eyes of this woman from another country, another people, whom he had allowed to violate his solitude. If she had thought to see cunning, or caution, or insanity in his, she was deceived, for instead there was hope and longing and sub-mission in their depths, so that her heart stirred in rebuke, and she leaned down and touched his shoulder with her hand. "I would like to go out in the boat. Could we do that? Is that what you would like to do?" she said, and Marrakech nodded, his lips sucked tight around his empty gums.

He held the boat quiet while she stepped down from the rock, and when she was seated in the stern, with her back turned to the sea, he unknotted the mooring-rope, and he waded out into the water, pushing the boat before him as he came. He slid on the sloping floor of rounded stones, and his second *espadrille* came loose, and he kicked it off, and the water rose now to his knees. When he had waded out so deeply that it came to his waist, he turned the boat, and the girl saw the wide blue arc of sea before them, and then he braced his hands on the gunwale, and he swung himself up over the side. As they drifted with the tide, he set the rudder for her, drawing the guide-strings below her armpits and putting the two ends in her hands. Then he pulled the tarpaulin from the boarding at the prow, and the oiled metal of a motor was there, a motor assembled with his own hands, it might be, for he turned to look at her with pride. He braced his feet on the planks, where the tarpaulin and a hand-net lay, and he leaned to jerk the motor into life, pulling the worn rope to spin the propeller once, then twice, before it caught, and as the quick, steady throbbing of its life began, he sat down on the cross-seat, facing the girl, his face almost fierce with courage as they headed out to sea.

When she pieced together the record of that journey after it was done, she thought it must have been three o'clock when they set out, and in the direction of Africa and Italy the sky was deep with color, but it seemed to fade as it soared above them, as if the sun drained it of its intensity. A wind was purling the surface of the water, but whether it was the sirocco, or the bora, or the mistral drawing its first breath, she did not know, and when she spoke these names to Marrakech, he shook his head, and this talk of the winds became a conversation between them as the boat moved on the sea. Was it the Etesian winds of the ancient Greeks that were said to blow from the northwest to the Mediterranean for forty days each summer, she asked, or the hot, dry sirocco that came from Sicily, or the humid sirocco from the Adriatic, and in answer he shook his head. And just before four, perhaps, when the shadows of the gulls on the water, and the vines of floating weed and sponge, and the wide, burning expanse, became monotonous, Marrakech halted the motor and let the rusty chain of the anchor run out. Then, with the bamboo pole of the fishnet in his hands, the gathering in of the sea things began. There were glassy jellyfish that glowed with the soft green light of their outrage as he brought them in, and sprays of pink sea-moss with jellyfish buds, like the buds of fruit trees, on their boughs. Once the net captured a passing sea-star, and dead-men's-fingers, soft as wax, and, in the end, a turtle that lay in the bottom of the boat, no larger than an avocado, and its shell as green. Perhaps at half past four, she reconstructed it, with the cliffs so far now that they were no more than a tracery between the water and the sky, she knew that the sun was too hot for human endurance, the sea too metallic for the eyes, and the rocking of the boat at anchor more sickening than she could bear.

"Marrakech, we must go back," she said, and he looked at her and quickly put the net down with his trophies on the wet boards of the floor, and then he rubbed the bones of his forearms with his open palms, his wizened mask raised to the sun. "Yes, burned," she said, "and my head is burning. I should have had a hat. I should have had more sense." Pulling the anchor in, he had looked at her in wonder that anyone should be harmed by the sun or the motion of the sea. "Only I'm afraid to go back, Marrakech," she had said as he leaned to the silent motor, and then he had ceased to move, but stooped there listening to her speak. "I'm afraid of the questions the people

98

of Abelin may ask me," she said, seeing the throng of them again, their dark, strong throats, their weathered skins, the women, the men, shouting the questions in menace across the hot, bright surface of the sea. "I know so well what I believe, but I can't make it clear to them. There isn't time. You see, it's this: the police are looking all over France for me." Marrekech's hands dropped from the motor, and he turned quickly on his heels. *The police!* said his eyes in apprehension. *The police! They're after Algerians too!* he was telling her, for he pointed fiercely to his own breast, and then he flung his wild arms out, describing a circle that closed slowly in upon himself, his forefingers the muzzles of their cocked revolvers, and the triggers his bent, hammering thumbs. *Because of the color of our skins*, he might have been saying, for he dropped the two revolvers of his hands and patted his cheekbones with his fingertips. *Because we haven't any money*, said the umbrage and eloquence in his eyes, and he made the national gesture for currency, rubbing the end of his forefinger against his thumb. "It's because I ran away from Paris. They have my photograph in the papers. They're looking for me," the girl said, and Marrakech listened as he crouched before her, his face covered with his dark, long-fingered hands. "First I ran away from Paris, and now I'm running away from Abelin," she said, and after a moment Marrakech raised his head from his hands in sudden hope, and he stood in the softly swaying boat and pointed a long way out to sea. At first the girl could see nothing in the haze of distance and heat, and then she perceived the far, dim shape of a lighthouse, and in that vapor which was neither wholly water nor wholly sky floated shadows that might have been islands or might have been rock, or else mirages of these. It had seemed to her then that it was not her own voice that spoke, but another, saying: *Be a woman. Don't be a frightened girl.* "We can't run away forever, Marrakech," she said then. "Start the motor. We must go back to whatever it is they want to do."

But he had not started the motor at once. Instead, he had come toward her across the drying jellyfish and the sprays of coral, savagely shaking his head. In his face was the history of old, familiar fears, old menaces, old indignities, and he halted to point again toward the islands and the semaphore, and then he took the guide-ropes of the rudder from her hands. It was he who would set the course now, and he motioned to her to change her seat, and she obeyed. But before he spun the motor, he opened the tarpaulin out so that she could use it as cover from the sun.

"And once at the lighthouse, what will we do?" she asked him gently. He sat in the stern, his face tense with the illusion of escape. *Never mind*, said his wisely nodding head as the boat moved again across the water. *The police at least will not be there*, said his calculating eye.

"So you were a woman, a good, brave woman, after all," said Michel Vaillant's voice, and the girl stirred under the tarpaulin that Marrakech had laid over her a long time ago. Now it was night, and the light of a lantern swung slowly with the movement of the boat, and she sat up in bewilderment. "Help them keep it steady while I lift her over, Marrakech," Vaillant said, speaking French to the Algerian. "Get in with us afterward, and tie your boat on, and we'll tow her in." Then the tarpaulin was gone, and Vaillant had put his arms under her, saying, half humorously, as a brother might have said it: "So you were a woman, a good, brave woman, starting out for North Africa with Marrakech."

"I was running away," the girl said. *If I look straight at the lantern in the other boat*, she thought, *I will not cry.* "He wanted to get me to the islands, and then, about six, it must have been, the motor stopped. The gas gave out."

"That was five hours ago," said Vaillant, and he stood holding her easily in his arms, as if she were a child. "Running away from what? From the slogans they write out on the stones? From the voices behind you in the crowd?"

"From the newspaper—" she began saying, and then she stopped, thinking: *Perhaps he hasn't seen the newspaper. Perhaps he still doesn't know.*

He passed her to the arms that waited in the other boat, and the smell of fish was on the sweater sleeves that took her in, and the viscous feel of scales on the hands that helped her to the rough plank of the seat. There were two men, and as they moved across the wet, folded nets on the boards of the floor, they kicked aside the flickering bodies of fish. The girl held fast to the plank beneath her to quiet the shaking of her flesh, seeing in the rocking lantern-light the great, slippery haul of fish, white-bellied, pal-pitant with life, that filled the prow. Then Vaillant came over the side, heavy and tall in his windbreaker and corduroys, and Marrakech followed after him, moving crablike, and weightless as a crab, across the nets to tie his own boat at the stern. Vaillant sat quickly down beside her, and took his wind-jacket off, and guided her bare arms into the sleeves of it, and even the touch of his fingers wounded her burned skin, but she gave no sign. Then he buttoned it at the neck with the kind, patient, half-exas-perated touch of an older brother's hands.

"And what would have happened if the fishing-fleet had not gone out tonight, and if three boats had not seen Marrakech's boat adrift and given the warning to the rest of us?" he said, and his eyes were moving gravely on her face. "Or if it had been the mistral or the bora blowing?"

"Which wind was it that blew?" the girl said, and her teeth were shaking still.

"It's a wind that comes from nowhere. We call it the bise. It would twist you in the current, but it would not take you out to sea," he said, but the girl wanted the answer to another thing.

"Did you win at *la joute?*" she said.

"Yes, I won at *la joute*, and now I can begin to do the things I want to do," said Vaillant, and he put his arm around her, the act petitioning nothing, preliminary to no sentiment, merely holding her against the fish smell of his corduroy. "You brought me luck. Either you or the American Indians who hammered the bracelet out," he said.

When he talks to me, I don't remember why I was afraid, she thought, wanting to tell him that one summer as a child she had swum too far in the Ohio River, and her father had gone after her in a canoe. Having been near to death, she had believed a lifetime had passed, and that she was a frail old woman when her father had taken her out, that her throat was wrinkled and her hair white, until she found a glass.

"Is my hair white now?" she said to Vaillant suddenly.

"It's brown," he said, and in the lantern-light he looked down at it growing away from her temple and springing back from the fine peak on her brow. "Brown, with a reddish light all over it, like a hunting-dog. It's the right color for hair to be." *In a moment, when I'm not shaking with the cold any more, I'll tell him about Peter and the police. I'll tell him about everything,* she thought, but she did not tell him. Instead, she sat quiet, listening to him say: "If I'm going to keep on winning, I'll need your bracelet at election time next year."

And now he took off the broad silver band that she had given him, and he found her wrist in the windbreaker's unbuttoned sleeve, and he slipped the bracelet over it, the etched metal still warm from his flesh.

"I think you will always win," said the girl, and she pressed the pliable silver tighter with her fingertips so that it fitted her again.

"Frenchmen are not very well suited to defeat," he said, and then, perhaps mistrusting the vainglorious sound of this, he went on saying: "I'm campaigning now. These are men of my constituency. For the fishermen, it's the question of the fishing-nets, and whether they can stop the casino from being finished on the mole. For the shipyard workers, the issues are something else." Now he spoke in French to the two fishermen who moved in the rocking lantern-light, men of perhaps forty, and therefore old men to the girl. They were dressed almost identically, as if in a uniform enjoined by tradition or circumstance, with their trousers rolled above their calves, the elbows of their sweaters raveling out, and visored caps low on their brows. Now that Marrakech's boat was fast, one fisherman took his seat behind them at the rudder, and the other squatted by the motor with a flexible, worn strap coiled in his hand. "They've been adrift five hours or more," said Vaillant. "Pass Marrakech something to put on." He sat below them, among the stray, quivering fish, small, tense, and alien, almost malevolent, with the mauve tulip petals drawn smoothly over his eyes. Whatever he had been in the afternoon was done with, and, having no gifts to offer in his open hands, he had drawn a dark cloak between them and his pride. His boat had failed him, and with it his strangely articulate power had seemed to die, and he did not turn his head, or acknowledge by any sign the garments that other men threw him to wear. "When we get in, will you see that Marrakech gets a pail of fish for himself?" said Vaillant to the man stooped by the motor.

"*B'en*, he's already slipped a couple inside his coat," said the fisherman at the rudder, and he and the other man, tautening the strap to flick the motor into life, looked out from under the visors of their caps and laughed at the sight of the Algerian sitting like a turtle, with head and all the other appendages withdrawn into his shell.

"Marrakech, do not listen to what they say," the girl said. She leaned forward to touch his shoulder. "We will walk on the beach tomorrow in the sun," she said, and in the dipping and rocking of light and shadow, shadow and light, he might have been turned to stone.

Now the quick, buoyant pulse-beat of the motor began, and the fisherman stood up with the strap hanging from his fingers, having heard the words the girl spoke as he propelled the motor into life.

"Are you English or American, mademoiselle?" he said, his ear sharp to the accent that gave the words another nationality.

"She's American," said Vaillant quickly, "but she doesn't own a car." The fishermen sought to laugh at this, but the laughter did not come with ease, and Vaillant held her closer in his arm, as if committing himself to what she was as the boat rode on through the dark. "These

104

constituents of mine, they're among the rich of Abelin," he said in English to her blowing hair. "They own their own houses; make no tax declarations; count their fish like currency. Every night and morning when they go out, each boat makes its separate soundings, for none of them trusts the other to say which way the current's moving or how the fish will go."

"And will they vote for you?" the girl asked.

"If I settle the question of where they can hang their nets. If I can keep the casino from being finished on the mole," he said. "These are the issues. The larger one, as to whether I'm a European or a Nationalist, they haven't the patience for. While we talk of the nets, I tell them we live on a continent called Europe as well as in that part of it called France, but they're not sure that they want it just that way. I can speak for the shipyard men, for they're like any men who want decent living-quarters and better wages and fireproof factories, and who'll fight like any American for the rights of the minorities. But the fishermen want the quays and the harbors to themselves, and the rights of man to them are the right to turn the fish to gold."

"I wanted them to be the best people in Abelin," said the girl.

"No," Vaillant said, holding her closer, perhaps in rebuke. "You can't have it that way."

The discussion had perhaps begun a long time back, the girl knew as the men went on with it now, the voice of the fisherman at the rudder loud and aggrieved, and the question so urgent that coming upon the Algerian's boat adrift had merely been interruption of the argument they wanted to settle now, tonight, before they got to shore. The place for drying the fishing-nets was before their doors, on the quayside cobbles, was what he said, and he cursed the mayor and the police and the town councilors for this new contrariety.

"*B'en*, you have nets," said the other one from his seat on the cross-board above the pulsing motor, his speech dogged and slow; "so you put them where the grandmother can sit in the doorway and mend them while she watches the soup. Isn't that true?" The beat of the motor came light as a tap-dancer's feet in the night, and the lantern swung with the fall and rise of the running boat. "France isn't young, and these things are established. They've always been true, so why should anyone change them now?" He watched the girl from under the visor of his cap, his eyes baleful, as if she, who came from a country of experiments, must take some share of the blame. "Those of us whose fathers were fishermen, and their fathers before them, we should know. The fishing-nets are stretched to dry where the grandmother sits before the door and watches the soup. It has to be that way."

"And now the mayor passes a law, and calls it obstructing traffic!" cried the fisherman at the rudder.

"Five generations of men with the same name as mine have stretched their nets on the quays," came the other man's slow, inflexible complaint. "That's more years than the mayor's held office. He hasn't held it a quarter of a century yet."

"Then what will you do, you fishermen?" said Vaillant. "It's your town, your nets, your mayor."

Some men were for defying the new law, the fisherman at the rudder answered, his voice coming closer to include them in the conspiracy. These men were for spreading the nets of the whole fleet from one end to the other of the quays, and for battling anyone who drove over them, or who tried to take them away.

"That could be revolution," Vaillant said.

"*B'en*, let it be revolution," said the fisherman on the cross-seat. "Maybe a king is what we need. They've got a king in England, except when something goes wrong like now, and then they get a queen instead"; and the man at the rudder went on saying that there were others who were for marching on the *mairie* and having a spokesman voice their protest to the mayor. "*B'en*, if you're more than three men walking down a street together this year, it's called a demonstration, and the police move in," said the man on the cross-seat, saying it slowly, so that each word seemed to hang between them, palpable on the air.

"There's another plan," said the fisherman behind them, and when the girl turned her head in the cool, fleeing wind, she saw "*Vive le roi*" written in frail white letters on the gunwale, near the stern. "There's been talk of destroying the casino, or what they've built of it. Every man, every woman, of Abelin, to take a stone of it at night, and throw it out into the sea. The mayor says the nets obstruct traffic, and the traffic he means is the trucks taking supplies out to build the casino that he can't get finished fast enough for the summer trade!"

"It's something for foreigners, the casino," said the fisherman on the cross-seat, and the motor pulsed quickly, lightly, between his legs. "We're with the Communists on that. It's something the mayor's putting up for the Americans who don't get their fill of gambling down the coast."

"The Americans, they've given me some of the worst moments of my life," said Vaillant, with the sound of humor in it as if he and the fishermen had the same familiar story to tell. "You remember the way it was in the Occupation, the bailed-out fliers hidden on farms, hidden in lofts, hidden in attics. They might have been archangels then, the Americans, the way the French risked their skins for them," he said. "Our job was to get French workingmen's clothes, workingmen's 'blues,' to them, and then to get them out. Sometimes I had four or five at a time, big boys from Texas, and maybe two hundred kilometers, or more, to go to get them into Normandy. And even if the pants stopped halfway up their legs and the coat sleeves came to their elbows, I'd start off pretty confident that we'd get by. But it was the crew-cuts, and the look of them, lanky as Lincoln, that made me sweat! No Frenchman ever walked the way they walked, loose-jointed and loitering, as if time was nothing and death nothing, even, when it came. We didn't always get through, not all of us," he said. "We had German patrols to dodge, and German check-points to pass, and sometimes we walked all night in the dark, month after month, Frenchmen and Americans walking together, talking together—"

The fisherman at the rudder was silent behind them, and the fisherman on the cross-seat listened, as the boat rode on toward the lights of Abelin glittering along the water and high on the hill, like a necklace and a queen's light crown.

"They got you too in the end, the Boches, didn't they?" said the fisherman on the cross-seat, perhaps wanting to hear the story again.

"Yes, they got me," said Vaillant. "But that's over now."

"And where did it get us, walking and talking with the Americans?" said the fisherman behind them, his voice not quite contemptuous, not quite nostalgic, but blended sadly of the two.

"Now they want to make France another state!" said the other man. "They'll take Frenchmen for their European defense, and they'll make the soil under us a vacation place, and the *chambre des députés* will sit in Washington!"

"The French'll be the infantrymen in the new European army, and the Boches the officers," said the voice from the rudder behind them. "That's what they're asking the French government to put its signature to!"

"Not the Americans I walked the roads with," Vaillant said. "They wouldn't have any use for a casino, and they'd give you a hand with the nets," he was saying, and the girl sat listening to him speak.

" 'And maybe in danger and darkness, when neither sees the other's face,' " she repeated softly in English when he was done. And now the thing came clear. "You wrote a letter to the newspaper. That's why I came to Abelin," she said.

"It was there in your passport, in your bag, thrown out with the debris around the bus," said Vaillant, and his eyes did not alter, but his lips brushed lightly, asking nothing, across her blowing hair.

As they passed into the harbor, a wave of warm air moved forward from the land, the residue of the hot hour of noon and the other hours of the long June day, coming to touch their faces, succor them, and the girl saw that the other fishing-boats were in, moored docilely in the angles of light and dark along the theater of the quays. Here everything was tamed, subdued, the wind having died in the same breath that the quick pulsing of the motor died, and the boat moved ever slower, drifting in liquid silence toward the land. This seemed the ending of an episode, the reaching of a conclusion whose value was not quite defined, and then the girl saw the people

109

who were crowded three-deep at the edge, and heard the sound of their voices rising, and her eyes ran the length of the waterfront, and back again, in fear.

"What is it? Who is the whole town waiting for?" she whispered to Vaillant.

There was Dr. Angelo, and Madame Marceau beside the proprietor of the hotel on the square, and the beard of the house-agent, with his underlip red in the hairs of it; there, the nameless women with bare shoulders, and the dark throats of the nameless men, and the murmur of voices rising. The lights of the quay shone on the colors of their faces and their clothes.

"The mayor is there. It looks official," said Vaillant, and he got to his feet in the scarcely moving boat. "Give me your hand," he said to the girl, and they stood together, facing the others, as the fisherman left the rudder to fling the uncoiled mooring-rope onto the stones.

VAILLANT WAS THE FIRST TO CLIMB
from the dipping boat onto the wharf, and
he turned and took the girl's hand and drew
her up, and the people gathered there stepped
back to clear a space for them, but merely
sufficient space that they might stand, like the
survivors of a shipwreck, with their hair still
wet from the blowing spray. The quayside
lights overhead gave the pigment of high
noon to the faces of the men and women in
the crowd and to the stones under their feet,
but the clock far beyond in the village church
tower struck midnight as the girl and Vaillant
looked at them waiting, intense and unpre-
dictable, in a wide, murmurous semi-circle
that might at any instant shift and close. In
this moment of indecision, with the breath
scarcely drawn before knowing how the wind
would blow, Madame Marceau stood allied
with the house-agent on his crutches, and the
doctor, and with the hotel-proprietor in his
ocher linen, but the fifth figure in the group
was a stranger to the girl. It was a figure of
unmistakable authority, wearing a formal
long-tailed coat, a broad-brimmed felt hat,
held upright by a Malacca cane; but a scarlet-
eyed, frail, ancient figure whose time of use
must have been long since passed, intact still
perhaps only because the frock coat was

padded to lend him a substance that was his no longer, expertly cut to hold his bones together as if he was buttoned into a glove. And Vaillant, with the girl's hand still in his, led her to this man.

"*Monsieur le maire*, this is Mary Farrant," he said, and the long dimples slashed his cheeks as he spoke, and it seemed just possible that he was about to laugh. But the murmuring of the people came ever more clearly, the words almost distinguishable, and the girl thought: *In another minute I'll be able to hear what it is they want to say.* She stood beside Vaillant, wearing the outsized windbreaker still, and with her feet bare, thinking that they might be gentle fathers, good sons, tender as mothers and tender as wives, these men and women who pressed close, but transformed now by the contagion of their multiplicity. And out of the composite murmuring that rose and subsided and rose, one woman's voice said, or seemed to say: "You could get yourself into trouble, Vaillant. The police have been looking for the girl!" But Vaillant went on saying to the mayor: "Mary Farrant went out in a boat, and the gas gave out, and she fell asleep and drifted five hours before we found her."

Because he did not speak of Marrakech, the girl turned her head quickly to the boat moored to the quay, but only the fishermen were there, sorting their slippery haul in the lantern-light, and the boat of Marrakech no longer tied to the stern, and the dark man slipped away.

"She has other claims to fame, monsieur," the old man said, his voice nasal, metallic, gone thin from constant wear. He had shifted the head of his cane from one hand to the other to take the girl's fingers in the jointed bones of his, and, standing before him, she saw that a net of veins flung out from the apple of each eye sought to hold the sagging eyeball in its place, and no flicker of pleasure, no welcome, altered his face that was webbed with the bitterness of his accumulated years. "When the fishing-fleet came in and said your boat had a derelict in tow, and that a girl was in it, we got out of our beds," he said, and he let her fingers fall from his as the murmuring of the people rose.

"Her picture was in the afternoon papers!" the voice of a man called the long way from the canopy of lights near the waterfront cafés, or else it was not this, but something different that he called. "She's American, the American who rode in the bus!" may have been the words that took shape, the sense lost before it was completely heard. It may even have been that the voices spoke of something else, the murmur of protest rising against the rents, and against the price of life, and the price of death, and one girl's face in the newsprint nothing to them who, merely because they had been born in a century they would never have chosen had they been asked, must bear daily witness to the dissolution of their country's unity.

"Mademoiselle Farrant is engaged to be married," the mayor said. "We talked with the young man by telephone today, an American official who will be driving down from Paris to take her back." From the corners of his acid mouth hung the empty saddlebags of his jowls, quivering a little from his speech, and his red-veined eyes watched Vaillant's face. "She has other claims to fame. So now we'll go, mademoiselle. You are my obligation until Monsieur Cornish comes," he said, his voice worn threadbare from the official uses it had served. (Oh, the speeches he must have made, the girl thought, not wanting to turn away from Vaillant to look into the pits and valleys of the old man's ravaged face. The speeches at graves, at weddings, at baptisms, at public functions through the years; one speech for the fishermen stretching their nets and another for the directors of the association of the wine-producers of all France, and still another for the masons on strike, and to the shipyard workers leaning in weariness on their handlebars. The speeches, she thought, to the German army when it came in, and the other speech when it went out, and the throat barely cleared of the sound of those words before the voice, like metal hammered thin, spoke in official welcome to the Americans and the English as their boats ground on the shore.) "Monsieur Cornish requested," he was trying to say, with his flesh hanging like a bloodhound's from his lower jaw, but the murmur of ire among the men and women rose.

"How many roulette tables will you put up in the casino when it's built, *monsieur le maire?*" a voice called out.

"Will the counters the tourists play with be silver dollars?" another voice asked in irony, and now the sound of composite outrage seemed palpable matter that moved toward them in a hot, swift tide.

But the girl turned to Vaillant, who no longer held her hand in his.

"Peter Cornish. I wanted to tell you about him, but there was never time," she said, and the English words, spoken in haste and guilt to him, set them apart from the others on the quay. "I wanted him to come down and talk with you, and now he's coming. He'll take my place."

"He'll be different," said Vaillant, and his eyes were grave. "He won't stand barefoot beside me with seaweed in his toes."

"But he can speak for America," the girl said softly, "and you can speak of France to him."

114

"I can't speak of France to everyone. It isn't that simple," Vaillant said, and now his wound was wide. "Your American," he said, his voice impatient, "I don't know if he'll turn out to be mine as well. When you were lying ill in Madame Marceau's house, I came for news of you every morning on my way to school, every afternoon on my way back. I might as well say it now to you before he comes," he said. "I brought you mint. I asked the maid to put it in your room, because it lives, and it stays strong. It isn't like flowers, all of them, that in the end decide to hang their heads and die."

And now the voices rose so loudly on the quay that the mayor moved one step forward on his cane and raised the withered emblem of his right hand, and it was clear that he was preparing to address the crowd.

"Don't ask them why they're here. That would give them the lead," counseled the house-agent in a low voice as he leaned forward on his crutches behind the mayor.

"The theme to keep uppermost is that it's the law-abiding citizen who reaps the rewards of universal respect," Dr. Angelo cautioned through his porcelain teeth. "Don't mention history."

"They're jumpy as horses smelling the mistral two hours before it begins to blow," said Madame Marceau sharply, and the mayor collected, in the gall and wormwood of his mouth, the words that he would say.

"Don't refer to the national holiday coming up next week," said the hotel proprietor hastily. "Anything national or international is a shot of cognac in their blood."

And now the mayor began. "*Messieurs, mesdames!*" he cried, the scabbard of his voice worn thin, but the edge of his will still sharp in it. "It is gratifying to see so many citizens of Abelin out here tonight, for the day has been

115

one of achievement, and heroism even, for this town. You storekeepers, villa-owners, artisans, fishermen, professional men, we have watched the *la joute* together, and some of you have taken part, and this year the games were played for the largest purse ever offered in our history!" The broad-brimmed felt hat, the padded jacket, the pointed patent-leather shoes, were the official paraphernalia of gentility, but the acid mouth, the red-veined, bloodhound eyes that sought for approbation were his own. As he talked, he held to the cane as if this was the divining-rod that would tell him, when all else had failed, where the fountainhead of their protest sprang beneath the stone. "This means that the future prosperity of Abelin should give us no concern, and that we must face indisputable fact before giving ear to those who would have us believe that the tills of this country would be empty were it not for foreign aid."

"Who's footing the bill for the slaughter in Indo-China?" a man's voice called across the quay, but the mayor's hand waved aside the sound of it.

"When will Vaillant get paid for winning *la joute?*" another voice cried. "We hear the tax-collector's getting a slice of it so he won't look into the rents of villas in Abelin!"

"Today we have seen a young tourist carried out to sea, and brought back by the brave lads of our fishing-fleet!" the mayor went on. "And I have learned tonight that the fish haul brought in by that same fishing-fleet a half an hour ago was one of the largest of the year! I have been given still another piece of excellent news. The wine-growers of the region say that this may prove a record year for the vine, and this means another contribution to the general prosperity. It is of national as well as interna—" he began saying, but, behind him, the hotel proprietor cleared his throat and hitched up his linen trousers nervously. Here stood the outnumbered group of them, almost at the edge, leaning on cane and crutches and parasol, and had the crowd of men and women before them advanced, not even in menace or anger, but moved forward however imperceptibly, these relics of what had once been the aristocracy of a continent would have been backed into the harbor waters that lay, breathing deeply, slowly, just below the stone. "This means," the mayor revised the sentiment, "that we should feel confident as we look into the future," and someone far in the crowd gave a measured, humorless laugh.

"How many more fines are the brave lads of the fishing-fleet going to be handed for drying their nets along the quays?" a voice called out in irony again, and now the murmuring of the men and women rose so loudly that the protest was almost decipherable in their mouths. "And the three-room houses with bath, and a place where a man can raise chickens to beat the cost of living—when are they going to be built in Abelin, *monsieur le maire?*" was the question they put him now, or "When are the rents of villas to be stabilized?" And the mayor struck with his cane at the cobbles for silence, but they did not heed him, for their patience seemed spent at last.

(That infinite patience of the French, the entire nation of them, the girl thought, the patience that bade them wait in queues at bus-stops, waiting not five minutes or ten, as an American waits, but waiting year after year with numbered tickets in their hands. And if the numbers they held failed to be called, still they would hold them, waiting for the count to return to zero and begin again, murmuring, perhaps even crying out in protest, but wait-

ing because there was no alternative offered but to wait.
The patience that accepted the indignity of class distinc-
tions in public conveyances, and the patience required to
stretch out and sleep on the wooden benches of third-
class railway carriages, with newspapers bearing the head-
lines of military disaster in the colonies instead of pillows
underneath their heads; the patience to accept plumbing
hacked out of, and befouling, the foundations of the houses
in which they lived; and to wait, in ever renewed hope,
holding the fifths or fourths or thirds of national lottery
tickets, for the wheel to spin and the winning numbers to
be called. The patience to wait eternally in line, even to
buy a postage stamp to wait, and, having reached the
post-office window at last, to see through the bars of it
the other weary, querulous, but still infinitely patient face,
waiting for a raise in the salary of public servants which
had not come yet and, if the past set any precedent, would
never come. The patience to accept forever the facilities
for heating one room only, winter after winter, and hot
water dependent on the untamed flames of a gas heater
hanging on a wall; the deeply enduring patience of France,
so poorly rewarded, so heedlessly abused, the girl thought,
and she looked at the people before her in grief and love.)

"When will you start asking the American tourist about
the bus going over?" a voice cried out, and a violent shud-
der of movement passed through the crowd, and it
seemed then that the decision of the people had been
made. "There were twenty-five people killed, killed by
her interference, American interference! There were witnesses!" they cried, and now they were coming, in their
bright summer clothes and their *espadrilles*, and no power
to stand between them and the group propped upright in
respectability. The mayor ceased to strike the cobbles with

his cane, and even the bitterness drained from his face, and his tongue ran quickly along his lip, and then Vaillant took the moment for his own.

"It is after midnight. It is now July the seventh, and the sun rises early in July," he said, and he stepped forward into the path of the men's and the women's advance. At the ring of his voice, the momentum of their protest ceased, and they paused as the musicians of an orchestra will briefly pause, their eyes on the conductor, their movement suspended until the next beat of his hand. "It's time the lights in the cafés went out, and that we went home to our beds. But first there are things that must be said!" he called out to the people, and they listened as if the answers would be given now to the questions they had asked. "You spoke of the bus," he said, and he drew himself taller, so that all who stood on the quay could see him, and with the fingers of both hands he combed back his damp black hair. "You spoke of the American who rode in the bus, saying she was responsible, although the facts have been known to many of us since the day the bus fell. So that no one is unjustly accused, everyone in Abelin should know these facts, and *monsieur le maire* may want to tell them to you now," he said, and he stepped back to give the cleared space on the cobbles to the mayor.

"Not here, not now," said the doctor, the command spoken in a low voice under the brim of the mayor's hat. The house-agent swung forward on his crutches with the unwieldy burden of his great white plaster leg.

"Tell them nothing, nothing!" he whispered, and his red lip trembled in his beard.

"It would be the end of the summer trade!" said the hotel proprietor, congestion swelling in his veins.

"Tell them anything!" Madame Marceau cawed out

like a wild blue-headed bird of prey. "Tell them anything if it exonerates the girl!"

The mayor laid the brittle bones of his fingers, one on the other, upon the handle of his cane, and he leaned, waiting for silence, a look now quizzical and now intense flickering like candlelight across the broken parchment of his face.

"You are assuming, Vaillant," he said then, "that there is something definite to tell."

"There is," said Vaillant, and he turned his back again on the group propped upright on their canes and crutches at the brink, and, moving flexibly, lightly, he flung his arms wide open to the others on the quay. The words that he spoke were the same as those he had spoken to the girl as they sat together at noon in the inner shade of the café, but his voice rang loudly now through the illuminated night. *The air tubes of the brakes were cut*, were the words he said; *severed partially, and when they were used again, they tore through.* "Don't blame that on the girl! She was in the bus!" he called out now. "It was sabotage, murder maybe, and if these are the wrong slogans to advertise a beach resort, still we've got to say them out!" So they took the truth, like the back of a hand across the face; and then they waited, hushed, for the rest that he would say. "We're told that we've never recovered from the revolution, we French!" he said. "They tell us we're victims of our history!" And whether or not he chose intentionally the words the mayor had feared to use, now that he spoke of revolution and murder and sabotage, and the violence of history, it was like a lullaby he sang them in the night. "Next week we'll put up the tricolor bunting and the tricolor lights, and we'll dance our feet off on the Fourteenth of July. But tonight we'll go home, and we'll get some sleep." And he might have been saying: *Be patient. Be patient a little longer. It is not tonight, but still the solution is near.* "The answer is that we've kept on fighting the daily battle for freedom, the way the Americans fight for it daily, and over and over, in their courts and their universities and their town halls. By going home now, we can prove the French no longer decide their political issues on a public square."

"In fact, the French no longer decide them!" a voice cried out, and, here and there in the crowd, the others laughed.

"Tomorrow there's school! I'm going home!" Vaillant called to them, and he himself seemed the confident, solid, the almost boisterous figure of all schoolboys, free of the classroom, his hair uncombed, his collar open, as he raised his hands in leave-taking to the crowd. "*Bon soir!*" he called, and, in voices replete with all the day had been, the others answered:

"*Bon soir, Michel! Bon soir!*" Only one isolate voice stated the matter in its simplest terms. "You'd better ask them for the money due you for winning *la joute*, Michel, before you go!"

Behind them, the town of Abelin climbed, light by light, from the cafés of the waterfront up the steep lanes, past the darkened villas, to the unseen vineyards in the open hills. And the dispersing people moved from the quay into the village streets, moving without haste, some with their arms around one another's shoulders, and others carrying their sleeping children curved, warm and soft, against their hearts. Some of them were singing, their voices tempered by weariness and the gentleness of the night, and Vaillant turned from the sight and sound of their exit to the group that stood around the mayor.

"I'll say good-night," Vaillant began, and then he was saying the other things, quickly, in English, to the girl. "Now you'll go home with Madame Marceau, and tomorrow your American will come, but we'll talk to each other again. It isn't going to end like this. I thought it was just as simple as that I needed you here and so you came. And so I've been stubborn about you. I'm still stubborn. Perhaps I don't know when I'm beaten," he said quickly. "Now sleep. You need sleep." He would have gone then, had not the three men in their dark, belted uniforms stood before him, police officers, agents of the law.

"*Mesdames, messieurs*," they said to the presence of Madame Marceau and the girl, and to the men, and they touched the beaks of their caps in greeting. The mayor nodded quietly, his power drawn close within him, the very core of his being waiting, as a spider waits in its web.

"*Salut*, Robert, Maurice, Pierre," said Vaillant, giving one his right hand, and one his left, and then his right hand released and given to the third man, as casually as friends shaking hands among themselves. And once more Vaillant would have turned and gone, had he not seen the revolvers in their belts. "Is there something serious on the calendar?" he said.

"*B'en*, it seems to be serious to some, and to others it doesn't make sense," said the last policeman of the three, and the girl looked at them, booted and belted and uniformed identically, but the one called Pierre a gentler, humbler man. A black mustache hung over his mouth, and his eyes, swollen like the eyes of a frog, perhaps from a heart condition, searched the faces before him for the answers that reason had mislaid. "*B'en*, Michel, I don't like the look of what's taking place here. I don't like to mix in it," he said. He took out from his jacket pocket a torn packet of cigarettes, and he shook the bent remains to Vaillant first, and then to the mayor, and last to the hotel proprietor, and then, at that moment, the girl perceived that the house-agent was no longer there.

This passing of cigarettes could mean nothing, the girl told herself as she watched the pack of them offered in the policeman's hand; and yet the mere taking or reject-ing of them had become a vocabulary as eloquent as a deaf-mute's fingering, saying: *Those who accept to smoke are Vaillant's men, and those who do not stand by the mayor.* Vaillant had straightened a cigarette out, and now he lit it on his lip, but the mayor's head moved slowly in negation as he waited, fragile and withered in his cunning web, the bead of his vigilance fixed bright and hard and cold. The other two officers hooked their thumbs in their belts and watched Pierre shake the crumpled pack before the doc-tor, who dismissed it with his hand. The hotel proprietor reflected a moment, and then, as he took one from the paper, his jaws held back a yawn.

"Excuse me," he said to the mayor, and he stood straightening the broken back of the cigarette under the quayside light, his forearms plump and shapely and threaded with long, black, silky hair. "I never refuse any-thing offered me by an officer of the law, not even a sum-mons!" he said, the cigarette Vaillant lit for him now perhaps insurance taken out against that time when he might have need of the police, even such an outmoded member of the force as this one, with his fumbling gestures of confraternity. "When the political battles they fight every night over my café tables get too hot, or the war in Indo-China gets too violent in the *boules* games on the square, I'll blow my whistle for you, Pierre!" he said, and he took a gulp of the smoke in.

123

They were men of another cut, Maurice and Robert, with their clean-shaven faces, their hard, small eyes, their stony jaws. They were for a country whose government feared its citizens might chance to speak their minds aloud, the girl thought, but not for France. They carried revolvers in their belts in warning, and their eyes served notice that it was their duty to question the motives of at least three quarters of humanity. *Do not make the mistake of being poor, or unsuccessful, or unorthodox,* they might have been saying, *or we shall have to correct you in public for it.* But the *agent* named Pierre spoke another language as he looked at Vaillant with his swollen eyes.

"*B'en*, they got out a warrant for your arrest, Michel!" he was saying, using the soft word "thine," as brother to brother in familiarity. "That's why we're here. They're setting Frenchmen against Frenchmen, as if that would save the country! Asking Frenchmen to take their brothers off to jail!"

"Pierre! A cigarette!" Madame Marceau called out, having had enough of holding her tongue, and she stepped free of the others and took one from his pack. "A light! A light!" she called, and Vaillant struck a match, and she leaned to his hand, her nose hanging, long and proud and fleshless, into the liquid of cupped light. "Taking him off to jail for what?" she said, drawing the first draft of smoke sharply in. "This is the first time I've done it in public. Perhaps it was time I did," she said.

"Done what, *madame la générale?*" Pierre asked, speaking with deference, but because of the years he had known her, speaking with a familiarity of all the things she was.

"Smoked! Smoked in public!" she snapped. "Arresting him for what?" she said again.

"I wouldn't call it 'arrested.' I wouldn't say that,"

Dr. Angelo said. "I believe there were a few questions the authorities—"

"An honest man has nothing to fear," the mayor said in pious bitterness.

"If they ask them quickly, I'll answer them," said Vaillant, and he flicked the dead match toward the sea. Then he called good-night, and he turned to go, but he did not go, for his eyes were on the girl. "Keep my jacket. I'll pick it up tomorrow after school," he said, as if already setting the hours, the minutes, quickly aside until he would see her face again. "Go home with Madame Marceau now, and sleep," he said.

He went with the two model officers walking on his right, and Pierre, with the cigarette hanging on his lip, on the other side, and he did not look back. And the group stood silent, watching him cross the deserted quay, seeing him, in his corduroys and his *espadrilles*, going as outlaw or gypsy might have gone, casual and reckless and without apology, between the minions of the law. The officers on his right walked with a little swagger in their gait, but Pierre's shoulders sloped in the uniform as if he was weary of this burden of discipline the others bore so well.

"Every evidence of order being kept is a welcome sign in France today," said the doctor pleasantly. "The sight of a well-cut piece of cloth and a good pair of boots, they'll do more to inspire public confidence than any amount of speech-making in the National Assembly."

And now Madame Marceau dropped her cigarette on the cobbles and ground its life out with her heel. She was through with the lot of them, she was impatient to be off, and she put her arm through the girl's arm, her voice shrill as a jay's as she told them, as if in reprimand, that France had lost every war since the army had laid aside its horizon blue. In the General's time they had won wars, they had put down revolt, they would never have counte- nanced disaster in Indo-China, she said, for the military had known how to keep the colonies in the hollow of its hand.

"Point that out to your Americans," she was saying wisely to the girl. In a minute, said the possession of her arm within the girl's, they would cross the quay together and leave the men to fumble their own lives, their own wars, into defeat, and she and the girl would climb in peace together up the dark, steep lane. "Tell your Ameri- cans that khaki's a color no Frenchman ever wore with pride. Tell Peter Cornish that tomorrow when he comes," she said.

They had talked to him by telephone, the doctor and the mayor, and the doctor said now they had learned with interest from the consulate that the young man's official function was to decide upon the merits of French institu- tions that were in need of aid. The mayor gave the girl a fierce, sad smile, and amended it that they understood only such institutions, either private or public, could apply for funds as were deeply rooted in French democracy. The hotel proprietor did not speak at once, but his manner conveyed the things that he could do: his establishment was equipped to serve formal lunches, even a wedding breakfast, if such were planned when the young man came, with a three-tier cake, and the prices fixed per tourist head.

As the little group made its way across the quay, the lights of the café terraces darkened, one by one, and the hotel proprietor spoke aloud in the night now of the three categories of delicacies served with the three menus: the best with medallions of Mediterranean lobster, the second with *coquilles St.-Jacques*, and the cheapest with local mussels in the regional wine. The card that he gave the girl had his name printed on it, and the name of his hotel on the square, this urgent message written not in French, or in English, but simply in gastronomy, entrusted to her to hand to Peter Cornish when he came. And then the house-agent was there with them again, swinging along beside them on the crutches' rubber toes. Would it interest her, he wanted to know, his smile red-lipped in the hairs of his beard, to look at a villa or two with Mr. Cornish, in the event that they wanted to spend the summer there? There might even be one of the doctor's villas vacant, and immediate occupancy assured, once the inventory was signed in triplicate, and a deposit equal to the first month's rent, in anticipation of breakage or a change of plans, and the first month's rent as well had been paid, said the eager trembling of his lips.

Just once, moving with the others across the darkened quay, the girl turned and looked back at the harbor, and as the beam of light from the semaphore swung rhythmically out across the sea, the line of the mole could be seen an instant, revealed, and then lost again, and then revealed. Upon it the scaffolding, which a town had taken as symbol of its protest, appeared in relief against the white, intermittent arm of light, its structure seen a moment, intricate and fragile on the long stone bulwark of the mole, and then wiped swiftly away. Then they had come to the avenue, where two cars waited beneath the street-lamp in the shadows cast by the plane trees edging the square.

"I shall see that Madame Marceau gets safely up the hill," the mayor had begun saying, and he stopped beside the first car and raised one fleshless hand to tap the shoulder of the driver who slept behind the wheel. "Mr. Cornish specified that you be kept under medical care," he said, giving the girl his tragic smile. "Dr. Angelo has made the proper preparations. He will take you to the *clinique* in his car."

"Ah, no, my friend, ah, no!" cried Madame Marceau. "Mary Farrant has been my responsibility!"

The driver had started the motor and switched on the headlights of the mayor's low gray sedan, and now he slipped from behind the wheel, uniformed and deferential, and stood holding the car door.

"No longer," the mayor said, the bone of his jaw tightening in the wrinkled, hanging skin. "You forfeited your claim to her. She will go with Dr. Angelo."

So they faced each other in ire in the shadows of the avenue, two old people who, having shared the same tradition all their lives, were committed to each other by more than nationality. They must have seen eye to eye on politics, on war and peace, morality, religion, on colonial rule, until the will of one struck like metal on the other's will, and so savagely that those who witnessed it now turned their heads away. At the sight of this schism in their own ranks, the house-agent and the hotel proprietor shook hands with each other, and then with the doctor and the girl, and said good-night, and then they were gone, and the mayor leaned motionless on his cane. And what was it that severed them, the old man with his bloodshot eyes that sought in the faces that were left for what he wanted and did not find; what was it that had driven between them like a wedge, the girl thought, between him and the blue-haired woman with her thin, arched nose? It was not only a stranger from Ohio, and the question of which direction she would go, but a deeper thing that had perhaps been a long time shaping in them and had found its argument at last.

"Forfeited nothing!" cried Madame Marceau. "Mary Farrant comes with me!"

"Madame," said the mayor, his eyes viscous in their eternal searching beneath the broad brim of his hat, "in your written statements about the young lady, you will remember there were irregularities. For the sake of your position in the community, I set them aside when I advised the police of Paris that we had found her here." Whatever it was that sucked breath into his nostrils and gave the nasal voice its power, it was some automatic reflex of life, not life itself, the girl thought, for the blood must have parched in his veins a long time since, and he seemed held upright by nothing more than the Malacca cane planted stubbornly against the stones. "So that is the end of it. There is nothing more to say," he said. But Madame Marceau was not through. If the mayor had already submitted to age as the certain harbinger of death, Madame Marceau had not, and her heart stamped in her flesh with bold vitality. She was stronger than doctor or mayor, richer, and warmer, more violent, thought the girl, and she would outtalk them, outdo them, outlive them in the end.

"I'm taking Mary Farrant up the hill with me. Make up your mind to that, *monsieur le maire*," she said; and, listening, the girl believed it was the Count, the young Count with white teeth and dark, blowing hair, who ran forever down the bright track of Madame Marceau's memory and warmed her heart with courage in his hands. *Ah, darling, darling, run on the beach with me now!* he may never have ceased calling to her, and maybe it was his loud, foolish laughter that she heard, fresher than daffodils

129

in the spring, instead of the mayor's words, as dry as dead leaves shifting across the dark. "Mary, you come with me," said Madame Marceau, but the doctor had already stepped behind the girl.

"This is a professional matter," he said, and his hands closed on her shoulders.

"Come!" said Madame Marceau, and she did not move, and now the mayor spoke, and the driver left his place by the open car door, and he stood, alert, between her and the girl. "Let her spend the last night in Abelin under my roof," Madame Marceau said then. She demanded nothing, asserted nothing, but, seeing the driver on guard between them, she asked clemency now of the doctor and the mayor. "She knows me, she needs me. Don't take her away," she said. "She's far from her own people, and out of her own country, so let her stay with me. I beg you, let me take her home," she said, and she turned in such urgency to the mayor that it might have been far more than the favor of just one night she asked of him, but the choice between life and death being offered, and the girl, whose life and death it was, not authorized to choose. *She is afraid*, the girl thought. *She is afraid for me. She is terribly afraid.* "During the years of my marriage, during all that time, almost a half a century, I wanted a daughter to protect from life as well as death, *monsieur le maire*. This girl—she was my daughter for a week or so," she said, standing revealed without shame before them, a weak woman pleading without subterfuge for one of her own kin.

"*Madame la générale*, my car is waiting for you," the mayor said.

It was not until she took a step toward the girl that the driver moved, and there was the sound of breathless protest, the slipping of feet, and Madame Marceau no longer stood in the deep shadows of the street. She and the mayor were in the car, and the door of it closed, and the driver behind the wheel, and the girl saw the gray sedan move from the curb and gather speed, the headlights of it making a golden tunnel of the street that mounted, narrow and steep, between the houses of the town. When the sound of its motor died on the hill, there was absolute silence on the avenue, the sleeping square, the quay.

"I have been asked from Paris to keep you under my supervision," the doctor said, and his hands moved slowly down from her shoulders, down her arms to her elbows, holding her fast. "Now, quiet, quiet," he said as she sought to pull herself free, and he propelled her before him toward his car. "Quiet, quiet, my little girl," he whispered, his voice wooing her as it might a young, recalcitrant animal, a young, stubborn, still unbroken horse that fought with its ungainly legs and its wild head. "Quiet, quiet," he said through his teeth, and now he had the back door of the car open, and with a strength that seemed colder and more calculated than an old man's abruptly summoned power, he lifted her in upon the seat and held her against him as he closed the door. "You have everything to gain," he whispered. "You have nothing to fear." And the girl felt a sudden weakness and helplessness wash through her blood, and the tears came down her face, and she cried beside him without any sound.

It was perhaps a quarter of an hour before he moved to the front seat and started the motor and began to drive, but while he sat beside her, holding her still, he talked of the American who would come, calling him Cornish, as if the name required no prefix, as Laniel, Churchill, Franco, Tito, required none.

"Cornish will arrive in Abelin tomorrow," he said, "so it was necessary to talk to you alone tonight, before he got into the hands of the wrong elements here. For the future of Abelin, I must make the situation clear to you without interference, and without the confusion of old wives' tales. It hangs in the balance, the fate of Abelin," he said in the darkness of the car, his voice as portentous as if speaking of the fate of an entire continent. "Stop crying. Listen to what I have to say," he said, his cold and powerful presence there beside her on the seat, his fingers closed as impersonally as handcuffs on her wrists, linking her to him in unbearable intimacy. "It is you who can save us, you who have so much to give that can be tabulated by a machine as well as by the heart. We are in the hands of the workingman in Abelin, the mason, the carpenter, the shipyard builder. You saw that tonight on the quay. We who have the responsibility on our shoulders, who direct the destiny of Abelin, we are on an island, surrounded by the strikes and the sabotage of the illiterate and the irresponsible. To be strong, it is essential that we build bridges to the mainland, establish points of contact with others who see things with balance and judgment throughout the world. Cornish arrives in Abelin tomorrow," he repeated, "and only you can tell him of the situation here."

And after that quarter of an hour had passed, and she sat submissive, holding the shuddering weakness of her crying in, he moved to the front seat, and gave her the final picture of it as he drove. The car followed the white cliff road that climbed high over the sea, moving southward toward the frontier of Italy, and she listened to him speak of a building so international that men and women would cross seas to come to it, talking many languages, coming by train, by boat, by car, people of substance and distinction, giving the town three times the population that it had. New houses would be built, villas to rent for the season, he said, and the hotel would be enlarged, and bathing-cabins stand the length of the beach. There was no reason at all, he said, why the rocks that encumbered the sands should not be hauled away. As the car climbed upward past gardens and olive groves, the headlights picked out a driveway that broke the curve of the low, winding wall, and the doctor drove through the open gates and let the motor die. He did not move at once from behind the wheel, but he turned in the seat and spoke with curious urgency, pressing the words singly and carefully upon her, seeking to persuade her of the life these nebulous others would bring to the fishing-town. Tourists would come from the East as well as from the West, he said, for France did not fear the East as the Americans feared it, French logic accepting the postulation of reality.

"Ten years ago Général de Gaulle signed a treaty with the Communists. That is the rational approach," he said. "The Eastern variety of Communist knows how to deal with the workingman. He puts out his eyes, and cuts out his tongue, and keeps him in his place. We could do with some of the Communist methods here," speaking in several ways of the building of international activity that must be constructed in Abelin before he finally pronounced its name. "We need help in the construction of it, American help. We need interest in the casino. You can get us this help. You can do this much for Abelin tomorrow when Cornish comes," he said.

When he got from the car, there was the splintering of gravel under his feet, and he moved to the gate and appeared to touch a switch there, and at once the gardens on either side of the driveway were lit by pools of light. In this illumination, palm trees stood leather-hided, silken-haired, unreal as stage props jerked into place when the scene had changed a few moments before and agitated still by the stagehands' haste. Behind these palms was the red sandstone of a house, with a labyrinth of vine-grown porticos confusing its side walls. The wind had risen, and the papery blades of the palm trees crossed like sabers, and uncrossed, but within the car the sound they made could not be heard. And then the girl too had opened the door, and stepped furtively down onto the drive, trembling as if with the cold now while the warm wind blew her dress and hair.

"No," said the doctor from the dark behind her. He put his arm through her arm and held her close again. "You can't get away yet. We'll have food and drink a little champagne together, before I drive you to the *clinique*. This is my villa. You're under my care. You need sleep," he said, and he drew her on with him, and she thought, without panic now, but in quiet, young conjecturing: *I haven't lived this long, come this far alone, to be frightened by a man whose hair is white and whose life is nearly through.* "I will take care of you," the doctor said in a low voice. "I have a man who cooks well, serves well, and who does not interfere." They had come past the palms, and come under the vines of the portico that rippled and rose and fell steadily, like running water in the wind, the vine leaves as green as shamrocks in the brimming pools of light. "I brought you here so that we could talk. I want you to understand about the plan for Abelin, so important to the mayor and me, who want to see the whole place prospering. We need order here, and discipline, self-discipline," he said, his fingers touching the skin of her wrist. "The town could be lost to agitators, so those who disrupt the peace are better under lock and key."

For an instant the girl seemed to recognize the implications of it, and then the recognition was gone, but the sense of it moved, wary with premonition, in her head.

"So Vaillant is put in prison. Is that part of it?" she heard her own voice say.

"Ah, Vaillant!" said the doctor, as if it were never Vaillant that he had spoken of. "I believe there are charges being brought against Vaillant. I believe things have come to light about the bus accident that were not known before."

And now they came from under the blowing vines, and from under the white beams of the portico, and they passed through the windy hallway of the terrace that stood high above the sea. Far, far below, the water must lie, the girl thought; the beach she had run on with Marrakech, and the savage rocks, and she listened for the far, hollow roar of the sea in the rushing presence of the wind. Here on the terrace with them there was only the doctor's sandstone house, as red as blood that has dried in the sun, suspended on the brink of space, with a row of cypress trees, their branches interlocked like arms, standing guard on the precarious edge.

"Charges?" the girl said. She repeated: "Charges?" In the wide inverted basin of light above the door was the movement of moths, and the drift of pale-green insects with gossamer wings, striking their infinite fragility against the stone ceiling overhead. "But what kind of charges?" she said.

"The police have been working on information given them," said the doctor, picking the words carefully. "They could not act before tonight. Tonight it seemed clear that the evidence led to just one man. It led to Vaillant. They want to question him."

"They think he may know who cut the brakes?" the girl said, and she watched the wind as it pressed against the wall of trees.

"Even more than that," said the doctor. "Unfortunately, much more."

"But there isn't any sense in it," the girl said, and she turned swiftly back to the frantic whirring of the moths and the drifting of the insects' pale, transparent wings. "Vaillant had nothing to do with it. That's absolutely absurd. If a man commits a crime, then there's got to be a motive, doesn't there?" she said.

"The motive," said the doctor, and his voice seemed touched now with regret; "Vaillant's motive is all too clear." And then, with the wind pressing hard against the cypress trees, the doctor recalled what had taken place here in 1943. "The Germans set up long-range guns the whole length of the terrace," he said. "They had no choice but to requisition every house that commanded a view of the sea. They put one gun here, and another here, and another here, and impossible to see them from the water because of the cypresses, which served as camouflage," and with the toe of his white canvas shoe he pointed out where the emplacements had been. "The Germans waited month after month all along the coast for the Americans and the British and the renegade French to come. You were a child then, so you could not remember that there were Frenchmen during the last war who mobilized on other soil to return and fight their countrymen, and that there were others who did their murderous jobs of sabotage here on French soil. That is why we cannot have full confidence in the Général de Gaulle. These men were in the pay of foreign powers, Great Britain, Russia, even your country," he said. "And Vaillant was one of them. A mercenary. And he, and the others like him, are still being paid."

"But paid by whom?" the girl cried out. "Vaillant believes in the Americans. Are we paying him for that?"

"How do we know what Vaillant believes?" Dr. Angelo said, and he held her arm so close in his that it was almost an embrace, her wrist between his palm and fingertips. "He tells the fishermen to continue obstructing traffic on the quays, and tells the men from the shipyards to clamor for new houses when they're incompetent to keep their old ones in repair. We know that when masons and carpenters climb down from the scaffoldings, Vaillant is with them. Every week he hands out leaflets along the port. Here, I have one in my pocket now," he said, and he felt in irritation in his jacket, and took out a square of yellow paper boldly lettered in black, and gave it to her under the light. "Oh, he's out after trouble, our schoolmaster," he said. "Strikes, sabotage, defiance of the authorities. I'm not surprised it has ended as it has."

"Tenants!" said the words on the shiny yellow page. "Remember that a garbage pail, like a water-heater, a boiler, a furnace, is the responsibility of your landlord! In two separate suits in Paris, in separate courts, decisions were given in favor of the tenants on the question of up-keep and replacement. Do the landlords of Abelin know the law?"

"He handed these out yesterday, after the *joute* games," the doctor said, "and the mayor takes so serious a view of this new attack on long-established principles that he will withhold payment of the purse until an investigation has been made. Once the tenants in the village here had read Vaillant's leaflet, not one replaced his garbage pail." The girl had begun to laugh, but when the doctor spoke again, the soft, hopeless sound of her laughter abruptly ceased. "From this kind of thing to the cutting of the brake-tubes was only a step," he said.

"And yet everyone speaks well of Vaillant," the girl began saying, and she thought back on the voices that had spoken with love of him, and the eyes that had looked at him with hope. "The waiter at the Café du Port, the people watching *la joute*, the fishermen in the boat with us, the people on the quay tonight—and there was a man who sat behind me in the bus, a man called Raffio," she said, and she heard the incoherent sound of protest in the doctor's throat.

"Why do you speak of Raffio?" he said. "The house-agent was a passenger as well, and the house-agent will be appointed our next mayor. There's Vaillant's motive! Come!" he said, his voice bright and false with energy. "We'll go inside, and forget the wind and the agitators of the coast!"

The room they entered was wide, low-ceilinged, and light as a section of the desert, the walls and carpet the color of sand, the low tables, the chairs cushioned in zebra-hide, the bookshelves of blond mahogany. The books were bound in tawny leather, and the light came through the parchment shades of lamps that stood, austere and isolate and metal-stemmed, on the bland, pallid surfaces of the wood. At the wide windows hung Venetian blinds, their slats drawn closed so that no eye could see from the porticos into the room, and their own eyes could not see the vine leaves or the white beams of the trellises or the cypress trees outside. There were no scattered ornaments, no litter of forgotten magazines, no indication of what the man who lived here or the habits of his life might be. Everything had been effaced, as fingerprints are wiped carefully from an instrument that has served its evil purpose, or from the handle of a door. Only three ebony heads which might have been African sculpture, but which were not, were placed, long-necked and polished, on table and shelf, making their statement of sauveness and prurience in the clinically sterile light.

"Sit down, sit down," said the doctor, and she sat down on the striped hide of the chair. Because of her pure skin, the smallness of her bones, the hair that kept its own shape despite the wind, she appeared well-coifed and neatly groomed in the windbreaker and blue dress that were not hers. "Let me order supper," the doctor said, and he touched a metal button in the paneling by the stairs. Then he stood beside her, his fingers on her wrist again in tentative embrace, and when he spoke of hunger and thirst he might have been speaking of the rapacious hunger of man's flesh, the parched thristing of age for the long, cool drafts of all that was still untouched, unsullied, by the handling of the years. "There are things I want to say to you before Cornish comes," he said, his voice cringing close beside her in the room. "I tell you Manet would graon with longing in his grave if he knew that the woman he painted lived in you again, walked the soil of France, and he not here to follow you from room to room and paint the cream of your skin, the long limbs, the russet hair." A servant stood in the doorway in a starched white linen coat, his pointed shoes and his neatly parted hair seemingly of identical strips of black patent leather, his small, insolent eyes commenting on what his ears had heard, and on what he saw before him now. "Lobster, Rhine wine, and a half-bottle of champagne served after the *crêpes*," the doctor said, straightening up from the girl's chair, the order sharp as a rebuke. "No coffee. My patient must get some sleep." The servant turned and went down the hall, the leather of his shoes crying sharply out, perhaps in protest at the lateness of the hour or the ornateness of the meal that he must serve. The doctor had opened a blond wood cabinet that stood against the wall, and he took two delicate glass goblets and a decanter of copper liquor out. "Keep your glass on this, my little princess," he said, and he set a metal tray on the low table before her. "I don't like rings marking the wood. It is sherry, very light and dry, more like a tonic than an intoxicant," he said, filling the glasses with exquisite care. Then he sat down facing her, the low table between them, and stretched his legs out in the trousers' finely woven silk. "Drink a little. Drink to the future of Abelin with me," he said, and he watched her lift the glass and scarcely wet her lips and then set the glass down. "Do you plan to meet Cornish barefoot and wearing another man's jacket?" he said, his teeth bared beneath his white mustache.

"He knows me. He knows what I am like," she said.

"But you should dress like a princess," said the doctor. "I want you to have handsome clothes."

His wife, he told her then, had never put on flesh, for he had insisted that she diet so as to keep the slender figure of a girl. But she had not remained a girl, she had got old, very old, he said, and it might have been that age was a disease she had contracted, a malignant growth that only death could cure. She had died suddenly, scarcely two years ago, he said, but he had kept her clothes hanging in the closets of her room, cleaned and in readiness.

"What wind is blowing?" the girl interrupted the sound

of his voice, suddenly fearing the power of the wind pushing hard against the house.

"The south wind, the sirocco from Sicily, with the evil eye of the Italians in it," said the doctor. He drank the rest of the sherry in his glass, and he leaned forward and took the decanter up and filled the delicately stemmed goblet again. "Drink, my princess, my barefoot princess," he said, and the girl drank a little, and she felt the warmth of the wine moving in her veins. "In readiness," the doctor repeated, returning to the clothes, "perhaps in readiness for another woman, or perhaps so that I could bargain for the life of Abelin." And the girl sat listening to him, her blood gone will-less in relaxation now, her eyes fixed, as if drugged, upon the doctor's face. "She was known for her elegance, my dead wife," said the doctor. "But everyone knew it was I who gave her the taste she had. I made her out of nothing, shaped her like wax from the time she was your age, younger even, the way any unspoiled young animal can be shaped by a man's will and an experienced hand. I met her in Paris, on the street one April evening, a little girl delivering hats, as thin as an alley cat, and as ignorant. I gave her life. She lived because I breathed into her nostrils, and she died daily, nightly, when I turned away. Drink, little princess, drink," he said, and the girl sat in the deep zebra-cushioned chair, her eyes fixed strangely on him, listening, and lifting her glass, and drinking obediently. "There's a drop of absinthe in it that makes the present far better than the past," he said, and he leaned forward and filled her glass again. "These clothes. You can see them hanging in her room upstairs. A fortune was spent on them. I want them to be your trousseau, one that any American bride would give a year of her life to own. So when you meet Cornish tomorrow you will be dressed as a woman should be who speaks for the French authorities."

"But I have agreed to nothing, nothing!" the girl cried out, and the room turned slowly, and the ebony heads quivered on their pedestals as if the invisible bodies below them had begun to writhe to the steady music of the sirocco's dance through the vine leaves and the cypress trees.

"But you will agree," the doctor said quietly. "Cornish will come, and you will show him the scaffolding out on the mole. You will tell him the building under construction has not been completed because the workingmen walked out on it. The casino," he said, leaning forward. "The casino. That is all you have to do. Whatever you meant to me here tonight, or meant to me when I listened for the beat of your heart day after day as you lay, knowing nothing, in your bed, I relinquish that now. I give you my dead wife's furs, her gowns, her lingerie, her silks, her shoes, asking nothing except that Cornish—" His voice did not finish it, and through the stupor of her mind and flesh the girl sensed the ferocity of the conflict he had fought within himself, the possessing of youth or else the possessing of currency, his craving for the first so keen that his voice had whined for it in this room, his fingers trembled for it on her wrist, defeated now by the other, even more implacable desire. "In terms of money," he said, and his palms seemed to itch for it as he rubbed them on the blond arms of the chair, "her clothes could not be bought for several million francs today. The materials are all of the finest, and the coats summer ermine and satin mink."

The girl thought then of an evening in Arizona, retrieving it from the haze of sleep or memory, a night in Arizona when she and her father had come back to the ranchhouse late, and her father had talked, giving each action of the day a definition as permanent as stone. And now she wanted the blunt midwestern statement of his voice to assess this climate, this land, this wind that blew, to give each man his exact measure of justice: Vaillant, Marrakech, the doctor, the house-agent, the mayor; their acts to be adjudged as if each act was a solitary statue set up on public view. She wanted the sight of his big-knuckled hands, the slabs of his knees in khaki cotton, to be there like familiar landmarks in the doctor's chair. "To know my worth," her father had said dryly at the end, "don't ask my colleagues. I never cured them of anything. You'll have to interview a cow." She began suddenly to laugh, remembering her father, laughing because of the sherry she had drunk, and thinking: *And after I've lived a lifetime, too, will there be nothing for me to say to my children except that to know my worth they'll have to interview a summer ermine or a mink?*

"But I couldn't take the clothes, Dr. Angelo! I could never do that!" she cried out softly through her laughter. "I would never need them, never! Don't you see how foolish it is?"

"Perhaps foolish," he said, "but I know no American woman would refuse them." He was smiling now, but in annoyance, and as he leaned across the table toward her, his eyes were as translucent as the marbles a boy plays with on the sidewalk in the spring. "And you, sitting here in my house tonight, have you any choice?" he said.

And then there was more than the movement of the wind on the terrace, and, like the three measured blows that are struck on the boards of a French stage before the curtain rises, three knocks sounded loudly on the panels of the door.

 AT THE SOUND OF THIS SUMMONS
on the door, the girl got to her feet in sudden
hope, and she held to the back of a chair with
both her hands as if steadying herself on a
boat against which the wind pushed hard.
She stood watching the doctor cross the sand-
colored rug, walking lightly, like a great, soft
cat, and pass under the archway into the hall,
recognizing the instant of hesitation in his
shoulders before he pulled the door open to
the wind. And then she saw the tall man
standing on the brink of light, his face gaunt,
and black, wiry hair growing back from the
two high promontories on his deeply lined
brow. Scientist, or philosopher, or poet, the
girl thought quickly, with gray marked at his
temples and a record of contemplation giving
power to his face. As he stepped across the
threshold, the wind came, hot as a blast of
noon, into the room with him, and she saw
that he wore the long, rusty habit of a priest,
and that he carried a carved wooden bird in
his right hand.

"Ah, so it's you, *mon père!*" cried the doctor,
speaking in bright, false welcome as he held
the door.

"Good evening, mademoiselle. Good evening, *monsieur le docteur*," the priest said, the
accent not meridional, but the voice, tough

as a dockhand's, coming incongruously from the reflective mask. Behind him, the doctor closed the door, using both hands to shut it against the pressure of the wind, and doing it impatiently, as if it was as well the priest's unwelcome interruption that he was closing out. "I found this on your doorstep," the priest said, and he laid the bird on the table under the cold, clinical light. It was carved from driftwood, and its head was lowered, its wings arched in flight, its body hard and beautiful and gray. "I used its beak to announce my visit so that you could hear me above the blowing of the wind. It's a gull, and handsomely made," he said, and his hand as he stroked the smooth wood of the bird was big-wristed, strong, and lashed with veins, not like a priest's or poet's, but more a laboring-man's hand.

"But it wasn't there when we came in," the girl said softly, and she looked at the subtle carving of the bird, with the single word *amour* written across its breast.

"Ah, it's Marrakech! He comes at night and leaves me these samples of his art. But this is the first time he's left a message of love," the doctor said, his voice sardonic. "He considers these masterpieces some kind of recompense for a favor I once rendered him. Once I treated his foot when infection had set in. He's never forgotten it."

"Perhaps he stood out there in the dark and watched you come in," the priest said, and he added quietly: "Perhaps this time the message of love is for the girl."

"Oh, I've got a cellarful of his offerings!" said the doctor in impatience. "They're useful in the winter in the fireplace."

"I'd burn these ebony heads instead," the priest said, speaking harshly, almost aggressively, but his forefinger gently stroking the smooth head of the gull. "They're some white man's imitation of native savagery. But we've talked of that before." And now, watching his face, the girl saw the singular eloquence in it, and the sense of the words he had not spoken seemed more urgent than the things he said aloud. She saw then that he was not an old man; he was perhaps not forty yet, she thought, and the iron hair at his temples, the stoop of his shoulders, were a part of the record of a life that had not been easy, and the labor of it had marked and aged his flesh. "I have trouble up at the Abbey School, *monsieur le docteur*. A man ill," he was saying. "That's why I'm here at this hour of night. I came on bicycle, but I'll leave my *vélo* here until to-morrow, and you can drive me up with you."

"I have a patient here," said the doctor, his hands in the pockets of his silk jacket, his mouth half smiling, his eyes as cold as glass.

"The man's in violent pain," the priest said, and now he looked up from the bird he held, glancing up at the doctor from under his heavy, dark brows, his gaze impelling, his face weary and strong.

"And this young woman here has been seriously ill," said the doctor, knowing the priest's words were as imperative as a command, but smiling still, still seeking a way out. "First concussion, and then half the night adrift in a boat, and now suffering from shock. Look at her. She can scarcely stand," he said, but the girl went quickly to the table where the priest stood, his face scarred with old trials, old griefs, that had not drawn his mouth with bitterness.

"I am well now," she said. "I would like to go with you."

"It must be at once," said the priest, his grave eyes on her for an instant. "We are not free men," he said then

146

to the doctor. "You as doctor, I as priest, we are committed to the people of this town. We are no more free than a man in jail," he added, and the doctor's smile abruptly died.

"I recognize my obligations," said the doctor, feeling his way with care, "but there is no need for Mademoiselle Farrant to go. She must stay here, have a sedative, some nourishment, get a night's rest."

"The night is almost through," the priest said. "She can sleep up at the school. My sick man is the *garçon* from the Café du Port—the old story of acute food poisoning, and acute human desperation too. Perhaps the fish he ate at dinner on the port, and the fury at seeing his countrymen divided still, ten years after the war is through. The fish is shipped over to the city fresh, but it's going bad by the time it gets shipped back to us. Another instance of logic subordinated to material gain that we're taking up with the mayor," he said, and this might have been the beginning of all that he intended to say, but he did not say it out.

"I saw him at noon today, the *garçon du café*. I was there with Vaillant," the girl said as if answering a question the priest had not yet asked of her, but his eyes were on her face.

"Is your bag in the car? Can we leave now?" he said to Dr. Angelo, and again the doctor touched the metal button in the paneling by the stairs.

"We will go. We will go," he said, his mind conniving still.

"Our *garçon* from the Café du Port, his time of pride and gratification was the war," the priest was saying, his head lowered as if to contemplate the wooden gull, but his eyes watching the girl. "He was a prisoner of war, and that

147

gave him a certain nobility, and when he escaped he became part of his country's determination. He went underground with the rest of us. He knew the drudgery and the honor of the Resistance, as Vaillant did, and as I did," he said, and the girl saw the explicit meaning in his eyes now, and she knew it was to speak of Vaillant that he had brought the story up at all. *Vaillant and I, we were on the same side then, we are on the same side now,* he might have been saying, and he did not look away from the girl. "It's the determination of a country that we're piecing together now, the courage of one man added to the next man's courage, until we are recognized as the substance of what France must be," he said, and the doctor gave a laugh.

"And now he has food poisoning, your *garçon* of the Café du Port!" he said, his porcelain smile frozen under his mustache. "So even exalted patriots are subject to intestinal infection now and then! You'll remember food poisoning has been my specialty. You might call it a specialty in death," he said to the priest, and he spoke of fish and mushroom poisoning, saying that sea-mussels could prove fatal if they had previously fastened on the copper cables of a ship, and the dead-men's-fingers found in a crab cause death at certain seasons of the year, speaking as if death by poisoning was a commonplace among those who fed on the products of the sea. "One cannot even be certain of sea-spider, delicate as they are, or shrimp," he was saying when the servant came in from the hall, his shoes crying out in protest still as he pushed before him a serving-wagon, two-tiered, and bright with chromium and glass. "Ah, here is our supper! I prepared the lobster myself," the doctor said.

"Gaston," said the priest in his tough, dockhand's voice, and he looked at the man in his white coat reflectively, "not priests, not doctors, but—in theory, anyway—domestic workers are subject to an eight-hour law."

"I'll bring a third glass for the wine, *monsieur le curé!*" the man called Gaston said.

"There isn't time tonight," said the priest, and he went quickly to the serving-wagon on which lay a scarlet lobster split in two and bedded on lettuce leaves, and a mold of butter, and olives stuffed with anchovies, and radishes, their rose hides cut like flower petals, and a long, crusted staff of bread. From a pail of ice on the lower tier craned the long neck of a bottle of white wine, its sloping shoulders covered with a pure white cloth. "If you will allow us, *monsieur le docteur,*" the priest said, standing there with his back bowed from the weight of all his life had been, "we will take the food along with us."

"After all, there are limits, *mon père!*" the doctor cried out, and he would have said more, but the priest went on instead:

"Oh, no, you are wrong, *monsieur le docteur.* For a long time there have been no limits, absolutely none. Perhaps the time is near when this will change—you with lobster and butter, and my people with hardly enough bread. Just open those serviettes out, Gaston. Just pack some ice around the butter so the sirocco won't melt it on the way. Mademoiselle can eat up there with the others," he said as he worked. "If there's more bread in the kitchen, let's have Gaston bring it so there'll be enough for breakfast for everyone," he said, and Gaston went running down the hall. The priest did not look up, but he knotted the four corners of the first serviette together, and then the four corners of the second, making knapsacks of them as he talked. "Take the bread, *monsieur le docteur,*" he said, when Gaston returned with the three long flutes of it, and the doctor opened his mouth to speak, but the priest went on: "There's nothing to fear for a country where every man speaks his own mind out. If we can keep the men who like the look of freedom out of jail, even at this late hour we may end by hearing France's voice speak out more clearly than any other on the continent."

Gaston had brought the black professional bag, and the doctor's fingers twitched with irritation as he took it in his hand. And then, as they moved to go, the girl reached out to take an olive from the silver plate, but before she had touched it, the priest's fingers caught her wrist.

"Do not eat. Not here, not now," he said so softly that for a moment she believed she had not heard him speak, and then as she looked into his dark, quiet eyes she knew it was this that he had said. He turned toward the door now, carrying the contrived knapsacks with care, and, passing the table, he saw the driftwood bird. "The gull, the gull, *monsieur le docteur!*" he said, and he pointed to it with his chin. "Allow us to take the gull with us to save it from the flames!"

"And what else? The chairs, the lamp, the silverware!" the doctor cried out, and the girl picked up the bird, seeming to feel the actual lift of flight in its powerfully arched wings.

The doctor took the driver's seat, so outraged, so rebuked, that it seemed he would not speak again, and the priest, his skirts flapping in the wind, set his bounty down against the wall that hemmed the lane. He opened the rear door and motioned the girl to enter, and then he set the burdened napkins carefully in. Once he had taken his place in the front seat by the doctor, the headlights bathed the palm trunks and the tough horns of the yucca with pale light, and the car backed from the drive. For the moment that the priest's speech lapsed, the furious silence of the doctor was louder than words within the car. He drove in cold, unarticulated anger, having yielded, and yet refusing still to yield, to this that profession and priest extorted from him, his fury like another presence with them, until the priest said suddenly:

"I've been to the jail tonight. I talked with Vaillant. I did not go as his spiritual adviser, for Vaillant is not of the Catholic faith, but I went as a comrade in solidarity. It was Madame Marceau who climbed the coast road to the Abbey School to tell me he was under arrest. She got there after midnight, running all the way."

"She's taking chances with her heart," the doctor said, tossing in irritation as he drove. "This spring I made her a business offer, based on her probable life-expectancy. I offered an investment that would bring her better returns than any life-insurance policy, inasmuch as the dividends would be paid while she was still alive. It's a system of financial protection for the aged that has been much in use in France since devaluation reduced the value of pensions by two thirds." Beyond the sound of his voice, the illumination of the headlights flooded the winding walls, and the silver of mimosa leaves was caught brightly in its current, and the passage of the wind running like water through the olive boughs. "I suggested that Madame Marceau deed her villa and grounds to me, while retaining the right to remain in residence for the duration of her life. In return, I was to pay her forty thousand francs per month, each month until her death. She may live ten years, she may live more, and I might very well have been the loser in the end. If she should live twenty years instead of the estimated ten, you can see that I would have got the thin end of the stick!"

"And what did Madame Marceau think of it?" the priest asked.

"She thought she was being cheated," said the doctor, stirring behind the wheel. "She's a stubborn woman to do business with."

"And Vaillant?" said the girl when the doctor had ceased to speak. "When will they let him go free?"

"Not until the American called Cornish comes and goes," the priest said. "The old men of Abelin are frightened. They're afraid that Vaillant may have a better story to tell America than the story without faith or promise that they have to tell." He had turned in the front seat, the convex brow, the long, brooding nose, the strong curve of his chin, seen in silhouette against the light that poured in a clear, pale channel down the hill. As they passed the square, the plane trees flowed toward the streetlights in the rushing tide of wind, and the car passed the torrent of them and climbed the narrow street between the houses that slept upright, climbed beyond the villas, leaving the garden walls and the cultivated boscage far below, moving on into the mysterious darkness of the vineyards, eventually to pass through the tilted slopes of them and come into the high, savage heathland of the *maquis*. And as they drove, the priest's curiously callous voice gave them in clear, swift, idiomatic speech the history of his and Vaillant's past five years, using the vigor of slang when it came easier, telling in not more than a dozen sentences the parallel histories of one man's love for man and another's love for God. He had known Vaillant first in Paris, he said; Vaillant, a student, and he a worker-priest, living in poverty identical with the poverty that half of Paris took as its lot and drank one more *pernod* at the corner *bistro* every night to take the taste of it away. "We met at a lecture at the Sorbonne, a lecture on political economy," he said, with the sound of irony in it, "two men who lived in poverty so absolute that a piece of bread was sometimes divided three ways, trying to find the answer in dialectics." He had done his eight hours of factory work a day, he said, and kept the loft of the storage-house where he slept open all night for those who did not have a bed. "At one end of the loft there was the altar where Mass was said for the men and women who believed in the ritual of it," he went on saying, "and said as well for those who believed that, among all the other swindles, religion was the biggest swindle of them all." As the French priest talked, saying these things without drama or emotion, the Frenchman called Angelo who drove became a figure that time had passed over and discarded in the simple course of history; for the priest spoke not of the dedication of priests or students to their beliefs, but simply of the accountability of man to other men. "We went on strike when the factory workers walked out on strike, and we marched to the Place de la République with them," the priest was saying, his tough, quiet voice effacing even the memory of what the doctor signified, or the things that he had said. "Like every workingman in France," the priest went on, "we learned that the working-class of the country is on one side and the police of the Fourth Republic on the other. We didn't learn it in a Sorbonne lecture-hall, Vaillant and I, but when the police sticks cracked down on our skulls. One night the Communists of the Quarter made their Party promises of better housing and better wages to the Algerians, who lived in squalor and illness among us worse than any we'd known. And that night the North Africans marched with the Communists, carrying the same placards they did, men like Marrakech, as gentle

153

as wild deer in a forest, ready to carry any sign that re-
deemed some part of the promise of what, ever since their
childhood, France was always going to be. And we were
there to fight for them, Michel and I, and we spent the
night in jail together, after the police had charged them
at the Place de la Bastille."

"And so you were removed from your parish, isn't that
true, *monsieur le curé?*" said the doctor, speaking pleasantly
as he drove. "Two years ago the church authorities accused you of spending your time with agitators. Isn't that
true, *monsieur le curé?* And then you came down here."

"No," said the priest, "the truth is more complex than
that. I had been working in the mines, the factories, since
'44. I was beginning to cough, and so they gave me a
country parish where I could breathe better air."

Now they were mounting the coast road, the swift car
climbing the steepest ledge of it, climbing toward what
might be, the girl saw suddenly, the first light thread of
day. But all sense of time and of locality was lost, and she
rode with the suave body of the seagull in her hands, not
knowing when they passed the broken wall where the bus
had fallen, because the priest was speaking of the men and
women who came to the Abbey School, and it was this
that came alive in the half-dark of the car. She touched
one strong wing of the bird, and her fingertips felt the
word of love written on its breast, as she listened to the
priest saying that those who came did not leave again, but
stayed to work in the house or in the vineyards, and some
became converts, and some did not, but, after a little,
they were different men and women, whatever they became.

"Even those who were Communists?" asked the doctor,
giving a pious sound to it.

"Yes," said the priest quietly, "for they will not be Communists again. At the Abbey School they tend the vineyards, pick the grapes, bottle the wine, side by side, the believers and the non-believers. If they work well, the proceeds will keep us going, and this will be their home, their platform, their activity."

"With the blessing on Communist and Catholic alike," said Dr. Angelo in irony.

"But Vaillant," the girl began, heeding the clamor of her own thoughts.

"When the police of a country begin working with the politicians," said the priest in answer, "then it's the end of liberty. It was Pierre who opened the jail door for me tonight and let me in. He said there has been a warrant sworn out against Michel. An eyewitness saw him tampering with the air-tubes of the brakes! If we live long enough, *monsieur le docteur*, we'll have seen everything!" said the priest, his profile as clear as if cut from black paper, but his head lowered in chagrin for the evil men devised.

"I have heard the story from the man who saw it happen," said the doctor, and he cleared his throat now as he drove. "We all believed it an accident at first, and then a man of the highest standing here put his reticence aside and told the police what he had seen. It was done, experts say, by a person of unusual intelligence—you must understand it, the air-tubes severed only halfway so that they held for the time the bus stopped at the Abbey School, and then they ripped entirely through when they were flung into sudden use."

"At the descent, when we came out of the tunnel," the girl said softly, and she held fast to the gull, not wanting to hear the sound of the voices crying out again. "The

155

tunnel! We're driving through it now!" she whispered, and there was the arch of the dripping stone roof flooded by the headlights, the walls darkly veined with wet, almost unbearable in their familiarity. "I saw Vaillant for the first time here, right on this road. He had his bicycle. I was on the bus." And then she cried out: "He didn't cut the air-tubes! I was there!"

"He was seen by the wheel. A half-dozen people saw him," said the doctor.

"He was helping Marrakech!" the girl cried out. "We can be witnesses, Madame Marceau, Marrakech, and me!"

Now they had come through the long cave of the tunnel, and the doctor drove close to the overhanging wall of land that stood above them, ashen in the beginning of the day.

"Marrakech would have to testify in silence," said the priest. "He would have to tell us, as he tells his stories, by the pictures that he draws in the sand." And then, as the car halted, the priest said half aloud the words that may have been in his mind when he came into the doctor's house with the pure, wild symbol of the seagull in his hands. "In the Quarter it was said that if Christ came back to earth again, he would come as an Algerian to France," he said in a low voice, and the doctor extinguished the headlights of the car. As the girl stepped through the open door, she saw that the twilight of dawn lay over the whole land.

She moved, half in sleep, with the men up the flight of stone steps cut through the *maquis*, and onto the path that led through the dense gray brush, the wind blowing steadily behind them the long way from the sea. Ahead, parched to kindling, mounted the stunted forest of the bush, and, step by step as they ascended, the shape of still farther, still lonelier mountains rose. When the girl turned to look back, the wind took the breath from her mouth and ran hot fingers through her hair, and she saw below them the hemisphere of water, its limits undefinable, an expanse without perspective, turning to luminous metal in the light.

"Come," said the priest, looking back as well, and his voice was gentle. "It is not far."

And they went on, with the doctor before them seeming to have no place in the absolute stillness, the professional bag he carried bearing remedies only for the flesh of man. As they rounded a shoulder of the bush, without warning the house was there before them, built of gray stone and turreted, and held as if cupped in the hollow of a hand. Behind it, a row of cypress trees stood as bulwark between the vineyards and the mistral in the path that it took from the heights, and these trees stirred in the south wind now, their delicate black spires trembling, their branches inter-meshed to protect the stairways of the vine. Behind the trees, the vineyards mounted, terrace on terrace of them, tilted like theater balconies toward where the sun would rise. The priest pushed open the heavy door of the house with his right shoulder, and set the two packed serviettes, which he had carried with care, down on a table in the shadows of the long gray entrance-hall.

"Come. We will go to Madame Marceau," he said in a low voice, and the girl put her hand in his square-palmed, work-hardened hand and went with him, like a sleep-walker, down the flagstones of the hall.

"But this sick man, the *garçon* of the Café du Port, where is he?" the doctor shouted after them, perhaps seeing as ruse now the priest's late visit to his house and the trip up the mountainside. "Which room is he in, *monsieur le curé?*"

157

he called in impatience after the dark, stoop-shouldered priest who had spoken of poverty as if there was an honor to it, and of liberty as if it was the heritage of every man.

But it was not the priest who answered, but Madame Marceau, whose voice and presence emerged simultaneously from the far end of the hall.

"Ah, he's gone, your patient, Dr. Angelo!" she cried out in grim triumph, hopping and limping and skipping forward, like a wounded bird. "When I told him what I'd seen on the quay—Michel Vaillant led off to jail!—he got out of bed, sick as he was, and jumped on his bicycle and went! He went doubled up like a jack-knife, Dr. Angelo, but he was going to ride from door to door and let the whole town know!" For a moment her eye went sharp with solicitude on the girl, and she said in a low voice: "Have you eaten anything?"

"It is morning," the priest said. "I won't forget you came tonight, *monsieur le docteur*. And now I'll walk down with you to the car."

"But the girl," said the doctor, the power and resource ebbed from his voice so that it was no more than the whisper of an old man in the cold gloom of the hall. But the priest put his arm through the doctor's arm and drew him away. "And the lobster, let me take the lobster down. They're high at this season," the doctor whimpered, but the door closed behind them, and Madame Marceau spoke quickly to the girl.

"At his house—did you eat at his house?" she said, and the girl shook her head in weariness.

"Marrakech," the girl said, standing motionless, having come to the end of even youth's endurance now. "We must find Marrakech. He can save Vaillant. He was

158

there. There isn't even time for sleep," she said, the wooden gull with the single word of love written on its breast still arched for flight in her hands.

And then, ten hours later, when she awoke, the other things were said. They sat in the shade of the terrace behind the Abbey School, the girl and Madame Marceau, and the rasping of the cicadas was high and sibilant and constant on the air. Beyond, on the staircases of the vineyards, worked the scattered, stooping figures of perhaps a dozen women and men. The air had been swept clear by the wind before it died, and in the lambency of afternoon the flagstones of the terrace, the dust of the soil, the lily-pads anchored in silence in the long, still pool, had the colors of French painting, purer and more astonishing than the colors of reality. The girl had eaten grapes and peaches, honey and bread, and goat cheese, and now the voices of the goats whose milk she had drunk called fragilely from the shed beyond the lily-pond as Madame Marceau talked. The elderly gentleman with the paunch, she was saying acidly, who wore the hat of crude pink straw and worked on the first terrace of the vines, he had been the editor-owner of a Communist daily in the ship-building town.

"Wait," the girl interrupted it. "Wait, please. First tell me this: did you too talk to Vaillant when he came here this morning, early this morning, before it was quite day?"

"He couldn't have come. He's locked up in jail," said Madame Marceau, her venomous eye on the man in the pink straw hat who worked, waist-deep, in the vine.

"Yes, he came," the girl said. "I tried to give him his jacket to take back with him, but he said I might need it still. He stood at the foot of my bed, and he talked of the curé Paul, and he told me the history of the Abbey School."

"It could have been nothing but a dream," said Madame Marceau from where she sat in the old wicker chair.

"No, never. He talked of his brother who is dead," the girl said, slowly reconstructing it. "I didn't know before that he had a brother who died. We talked about love," she said. "Oh, not about love between men and women, nothing like that, but love between brothers and whatever it is between people who feel the same way about things, about paintings, or about music, or politics. He likes Rousseau and Cézanne, and opera, any opera, too."

"Even Wagner?" said Madame Marceau in spite of herself.

"Just *Tristan and Isolde*. None of the others," the girl said. "He stood talking to me about these things from the foot of the bed, and I didn't want to sleep any more."

"Come, come, you must have been asleep all the time," said Madame Marceau in impatience, and she went on speaking of the man who had pushed his pink hat back on his head and stood mopping the sweat from his glistening jowls and brow. Up to the time of Stalin's death, she said, he had owned a Citroën and rented a villa every summer in Abelin, and his name was on every tongue. And then he had published a pen-and-ink likeness of the dead dictator which authorities thought had a peasant's slyness in the eyes, so Party officials had demanded a public apology. But he was too much of a friend to liquidate the artist, Madame Marceau said, and too much of a Frenchman to make an apology. "So no more funds from Moscow to keep the paper going, and he himself was purged and penniless, and his old friends turned their backs on him. That was enough for the curé Paul. He took him in," she said. The ex-editor had been known as a poet too, she went on saying, and his poems were printed on leaflets and handed out in the cafés at night. One of the last he had written was about the cyclist-workingman of France, extolling that portion of the population which cycled off to work at dawn, hands in camaraderie on one another's shoulders, and cycled back from work at night so tired that, had they not held to one another's shoulders for support, the lot of them would fall. "All I can say is that they managed to cycle to the nearest café for their *pastis* every night!" she said. This epic had been set to music, to the tune of the "Internationale," she said, and Vaillant had written a parody of it and printed it and handed his own leaflets out. A poem about cyclists, went Vaillant's parody, written by a poet who was chauffeured in a front-wheel-drive Citroën to his office every day! "But the curé let him enroll as a student here. A student of what, you may well ask!" Madame Marceau said, but the girl had asked nothing. It was hardly a seminary, the Abbey School; its history was that it had been left, ten years before, in the last will and testament of a recluse, to the curé of Abelin, to do what he wished with for the time that the parish was his. And, for better or worse, curé Paul had made a refuge for the damned of it, she said.

"They work on the vines, read books, play music," the girl said. "That is what Vaillant told me this morning when he came. And in the end they either find themselves again or find another self they didn't know was there."

And the house-agent and the mayor, said Madame Marceau, had fought the Will ten years ago, and fought it still, because of the value of the house and grounds as a season's rental, or a rental on long lease to anyone wanting to make it a hotel that overlooked, on one side, the vineyards hacked out of the rock and, on the other, the far, wide sweep of sea.

"The man with the soiled bandana on his head—over there, on the third tier up," said Madame Marceau, "he comes from the red belt of Paris, where the curé lived as a worker-priest, and they worked together on the same assembly line. The Party reprimanded our friend for lighting the candles on two occasions on the curé's altar in the loft. So he didn't wait to be expelled, but joined the curé here. A godless lot of believers!" she said, and then, with no change in her voice, but looking from under her hat's black brim across the trembling waves of heat, she said: "Dr. Angelo's wife died in 1952. The General died a year ago. Dr. Angelo was at their bedsides. They both died in agony. Dr. Angelo signed the death certificates, giving the cause of death as food poisoning, and I believed it then. I've changed my mind about it now."

"But what was it if not that? What illness, then?" the girl asked. She was thinking of Vaillant in prison still, and she stood up restlessly, wearing a pair of workman's blues and a man's yellow sport shirt with the sleeves rolled up which Madame Marceau had found in the school laundry among the freshly ironed clothes. "I've wasted so many hours of sleep," she said, standing there in the high, soft, meridional day, smooth-throated, copper-eyed, and tenderly young, with a reddish veil of light cast over her smooth hair.

"It would be simply that he had had enough of his wife. That kind of illness," Madame Marceau said, the words like acid in her mouth. "She was getting old. I had money, and she did not. When he spoke of marriage to me after she and the General were both dead, I began to understand. The General died in the doctor's villa one night, after dining alone with him. I was in Paris for a week, and he was dead before I got back. He had eaten mussels which the doctor had prepared." The girl stood looking down at Madame Marceau, the power of thought arrested for the moment, not hearing the voice that said these things, but hearing the doctor's whisper as if he stood close in the area of shade: *Sea-mussels even can prove fatal, and the dead-men's-fingers in a crab cause death at certain seasons . . . food poisoning, you'll remember, has been my specialty.* "For six months the question hasn't left my mind," said Madame Marceau, "and now I have to know."

"But if the doctor ate the same food they ate?" the girl said, not wanting death to have come that way. She looked down at the rope-soled *espadrilles* that were not hers, wondering how fast she could run in them, and wondering which student at the Abbey School had walked in them before.

"The doctor never touches seafood," said Madame Marceau, sitting hunched under her black straw hat like a high-beaked, grieving bird. "So when he took you home last night, I was afraid for you. I ran five kilometers to the Abbey School, and I'm lame from it still. It was one o'clock in the morning, and I came like a madwoman to tell *monsieur le curé* everything I feared."

"But me—the doctor would have no reason to get rid of me," the girl said, and she sat down again on the unsteady folding metal chair, her eyes on Madame Marceau's face.

"If he had asked something of you and you refused. If he had asked some favor of you," Madame Marceau said, and again the doctor's voice spoke insidiously. *Cornish will come, and you will show him the scaffolding out on the mole,* he was saying now as he had said it in the clinically chaste room. *The casino. You will tell him we need money for the casino. . . . That is all you have to do.* "There was a time when he was interested in the question of your income," said Madame Marceau. "I enlightened him on that. And he was amorously interested, too, at first, until he met your opposition there. So perhaps he and the mayor conceived another use for you. But whatever he asked of you last night, I doubt if it brought any credit on him, and he made his preparations—in the event that you refused—to wipe the record out. Or perhaps," said Madame Marceau in a low voice, "he had expected someone else to come and eat with him. Perhaps he had not prepared that supper last night for you."

"And the *garçon* of the Café du Port, was he here at the Abbey School last night?" the girl asked. "Or was he just a part of your plan?"

"Oh, he was here, and he was sick," said Madame Marceau, "but certainly not from anything but drink. He takes too much three nights a week, out of what *monsieur le curé* calls human desperation, a thing we've all had seizures of." Her voice was caustic still, but her glance no longer seemed a blade sharpened to scalp the hair in censure from whatever dared impinge upon her sight. It was as if the camera had trembled a moment in the hand, or the subject moved, and the features been thrown out of focus, so veiled they were now with uncertainty. "You were the reason *monsieur le curé* went for Dr. Angelo, the only reason. Marius, the *garçon*, served as excuse. I had begun to see the doctor for what he is, for this spring he went too far. In April he made me an offer, a business offer," said

Madame Marceau, and the camera steadied and the features of the face came sharp again. "He asked me to deed my villa and grounds to him, to be his at my death. In return, I might live on in my house, and he would see to the repairs, and pay the taxes on the property, and pay me, besides, a monthly sum of forty thousand francs until I died. I saw it then, in a flash," she said. "If I had agreed, I would have eaten mussels in white wine before the second month was through!"

"But it isn't sure. None of it's sure," the girl said slowly, and Madame Marceau leaned fiercely forward, her wild eyes seeming to merge into a single eye, her ringed hands gripping the split wicker of the chair-arms as the words came through her teeth.

"No, it isn't sure. Of course it isn't sure," she said in a sharp whisper, and the girl saw then that, flat on the crown of her black straw hat, two small stuffed birds were placed as trimming, one on either side, as hawks are nailed in warning on a barn door. "But there are twenty-five cats in the cellars of the Abbey School. Twenty-five of them," she repeated, and the birds on her hat, with their stiff, varnished wings and their yellow glass eyes, seemed to tremble as she spoke. "Last night I fed them the lobster that *monsieur le curé* had carried up from the doctor's house. I did it alone. I had to know. If I'd thought of it in time, I'd have fed it to the Communists out there instead of to the cats!" she said.

"And then?" said the girl, watching her face.

"At the last counting, there were still twenty-five," said Madame Marceau in chagrin. "But the day's not through."

The sense of urgency brought the girl to her feet again, and she knew they must follow the path at once, run down

165

the steps to the coast road, and go fast through the dripping cavern of the tunnel, and move quickly down the
open road. *Now, at once, we must find Marrakech*, she thought.
We must find him. He must go as witness with us to the jail.

"We must get down to Abelin and find Marrakech,"
she said to Madame Marceau. "Perhaps *monsieur le curé*
can show us a way down through the *maquis*."

"On foot in this heat!" said Madame Marceau. "I'm
lame from the climb up here last night! I can't hobble as
far as the vineyards, much as I'd like to ask the man in the
pink hat what political line he's going to take when he
graduates from here. *Monsieur le curé* left for Aix at noon,"
she went on saying. "He's picking up sixty children from
the slums of Paris to spend a month's vacation in the fresh
air, drinking wine, no doubt, and listening to the excom-
municated Party members air their woes!"

Beyond the sandy paths and the lily-pond, where drag-
onflies poised static in the high, soft light, the girl saw the
shed from which the voices of the goats spoke, and a
bicycle leaning against the gray, unpainted timber of its
door.

"We could go on bicycle," she said.

"Ho, on bicycle!" cried Madame Marceau in derision.
"The last time I rode a bicycle was twenty years ago!"

But the girl had already left the shade of the terrace
and crossed the sun-desiccated path, and Madame Marceau's voice cried out behind her still as she pushed the
bicycle aside and opened the shed door. The diluted dark
of the interior was traversed by slanting bars of sun, and
the goats raised their heads above these barriers of light,
and their chins shifted as they spoke their plea. But
whether it was food or water or liberty their quavering
voices asked of her, she did not know, and she stopped to

touch the short hair on their bony brows, and to look into their tilted golden eyes.

"Have you lost your father?" she said, speaking softly to them. "Has he gone so far that he cannot hear you calling his name?"

In the corner of the shed three ancient bicycles leaned, their handlebars interlocked like steer-horns in the shimmering bars of sun that fell through the window's broken glass. Behind the bicycles stood giant, dust-filmed demijohns, emptied of olive oil and long discarded, and broken-handled rakes, and twists of raffia, this agglomeration traced with spiderwebs whose threads shone singly in the avenues of light. It seemed to the girl then that the bicycles must have leaned there, awaiting this instant, for a hundred years, and as she pulled the first one free, and then the second, a shower of radiant dust rose on the sun-striped air. The first was a woman's bicycle, the second a man's, and the saddle and rear wheel of the third one were missing, but the other two were good enough to serve. She wheeled first one, and then the other, to the door, and she turned to seek an air-pump in the confusion of tools and debris on the window-sill. And then her hand ceased moving, and the breath stopped in her throat, for her fingers had nearly touched the body of a Maltese cat lying with its lips still fixed in the shape of agony.

For a long time, in which the thoughts in her head moved with deliberate care, she waited, and then she brought herself to stroke with her fingertip the dead cat's flank, in which the fluid of life was not yet cold. She moved the foreleg, the flexible silk paw that had dealt lingering death so evilly and often to the infinite delicacy of feathered wings and spine. In the distorted mask she read the record of convulsive pain, perhaps just assuaged, and when she

167

turned quickly to pull the door open to the sun, her heart was trembling in her breast. She returned twice, wheeling the bicycles out separately and setting them upright against an almond tree, and then she went back to close the faded timber door on death.

"Madame Marceau," she whispered, rehearsing the incredible words of it. "There's a dead cat in the goat-shed. A dead cat! Imagine that!" she whispered, but the fact of it made no sense at all.

She stood motionless then, looking blindly at the path, at the lily-pond, at the workers on the tilted terraces, the hats and handkerchiefs gaudy on their heads. Nothing had changed, and yet the balance of life and death had altered, so that whatever her eyes saw now was not the same. Madame Marceau was coming past the pond, having had enough of silence, coming stiff-legged, lame, her hatbrim nodding, and the girl drew her hand across her eyes to wipe the dazzlement away.

In a half-hour they were on the hot macadam of the road, pushing the bicycles beside them, saving their breath, it might be, for the long way ahead. Even passing the place where the bus had halted for the last time and where Vaillant had stooped beside the wheels, they did not speak, gave no sign of recognition, but they knew. And then the girl moved on ahead into the cool, dark throat of the tunnel, and they spoke only once in the journey under the roof of dripping stone.

"We'll find Marrakech. That's all we have to do," the girl said, and she did not turn her head.

"We'll try the square, the quays, the beach," said Madame Marceau, her voice grim.

After that they were silent, and there was only the echoing of their steps and the sound of the passage of the bicycle wheels on the macadam as they mounted toward the point of light ahead. And then they stood on the brink of the broad, dazzling world at the tunnel's open mouth, and they looked into each other's faces, searching each other's eyes almost in censure, as women will search the eyes of those they are committed to, for any sign of faltering or fear.

"Your brakes are good. You don't have to worry," the girl said, having seen the moment of uncertainty. "We'll take it slowly."

"If I don't survive," Madame Marceau began, but her pride put a stop to it, and then they were astride their bicycles, and the steep, circuitous descent was under way. It was half past four, but as the heat poured past their faces and throats, whined in their ears, it seemed the hottest hour. And now Madame Marceau made her final testament, made it aloud, thus voiding all previous wills and codicils to wills that had been drawn up in lawyers' offices, where she had sat, year after fiscal year, parceling out money and property, not knowing until now that there was anything else the dying had to give. On the saddle of a bicycle that might not hold together rounding the next turn, she cawed out the final disposition of imponderables, not giving them even now the names of loyalty and love. "If I were young still," she cried out behind the girl, "I wouldn't hesitate a moment! I can tell you that! If this is my last ride—" the words were shaken in violence from her mouth—"I can tell you, I'd stand by the curé and Michel Vaillant, whatever their faults and they're full of them! You and I and the others like us, we need men to speak to the working-people for us, because we don't know what to say to them ourselves! There wouldn't be any question—none—I'd—" The sound of it overtook and streamed fast past the girl, and she saw Madame Marceau career ahead, the lean, aristocratic figure as if frozen to the rust-scarred rattling frame. "I'd throw in my lot with them!" her voice cawed back, and as bicycle and rider leaned perilously to the turn, the hat was lifted from Madame Marceau's head, and the dead birds fastened to its crown sailed by, their gold glass eyes fixed without mercy on the girl in the instant that they passed.

"Wait, wait!" the girl cried out, gathering speed behind her, seeking to take the curve with her, perhaps even to succeed in resting one hand on her shoulder to check the impetus of her descent. But once they were racing side by side, she could only grip the handlebars harder to keep the wild wheels to the road. "Don't watch for the break in the wall where the bus went over," she admonished herself aloud through her jolting teeth. "Whichever direction you look when you're riding fast like this, that's the direction you go. Yes, yes!" she cried, outstripping the taut, grim figure of the Frenchwoman, who rode the torrent of heat curved like a jockey—knees high, head lowered, over the lean neck of her speeding mount. "Everyone else in Abelin has come to an end! Everyone except them! Squeeze the right handle! That's the front brake! Keep holding it steadily!"

"*Bien!*" cried Madame Marceau, her voice fainter on the fleeing air. "You must hear me out! Whatever their faults, they speak for others, not for themselves, and that's a scandal for the French! Vaillant and the curé, they speak as if they had hearts instead of cash registers under their ribs! The General!" she cried out, her chin nearly touching the handlebars as she shot past, her hair blowing in a square blue flag, and the gray curls wiped away. "Concussion this and concussion that, and all of it lies! It was just that he couldn't hold his drink!"

"Wait, Madame Marceau! Slow down, slow down!" the girl called after her in panic now.

"The years of making the truth look like something else!" the Frenchwoman's voice streamed back. "Do you know what it does to you? It gives you a shell like a turtle, it makes every word you speak turn bitter in your mouth!" The girl let her own bicycle go free, and she swung, wheel to Madame Marceau's wheel, in desperation down the blind white curve, and then clattered on ahead. "The Count—" came Madame Marceau's voice in wild pursuit. "I wouldn't have any hesitation now—I wouldn't have any regrets—"

And for the third time she passed the girl, but this time gathering such speed that the girl could not overtake her in the furious descent. She saw Madame Marceau's flapping skirt, the perilous slant of the bicycle as it took the final curve below, and then she was gone, the last words she had said left strident on the air. Following behind, the girl thought of her as a blue-haired swimmer who had fought her way in this final instant before the end up through the reeds and weeds of her life to the clear surface, breathing too late the air of franchise and making too late the simple choice of love.

Now vineyard country was opening on the land side of the road, and on the coast side the roofs of villas had begun to show between the olive and almond trees. Here were the hot stones of the ageless, winding walls, the dried ropes of wistaria, and horns of yucca spearing the heat, and this was the beginning of the town. *She will have missed the corner just ahead. I'll come upon her lying there*, the girl thought. *Everything that she was will be finished, and the thing she wanted to be in the end not quite begun.* But Madame Marceau was not around the next corner, or the next, and when the girl reached the summit of the tilted, narrow street, she swung herself from her bicycle, her legs unsteady under her with strain. And, walking, she held the rattletrap carcass of the bicycle back by its rusted antlers, and over her head appeared now the multicolored flags and banners of the eternally drying clothes. Here were the reaching arms of seamen's shirts, the bowed legs of their canvas trousers, the striped towels on which they dried their flesh, and the salmon-colored or blue rayon nightdresses their black-haired women wore. Here above her were the doll-sized skirts and trousers of the children they bore, and the checkered cloths on which they ate their fish and cheese and fruit and set their bottles of red wine, completing the circle of a people's intimacy. Under the canopy of clothes were stands of vegetables and fruit, and tables bearing glazed green pottery, and *espadrilles* in primary colors, and hay-soft hats laid one inside the other, their fringed brims ivory-white, or lilac, or turquoise, or flamingo pink.

"I must have been blind before I came to Abelin," the girl said, speaking half aloud in wonder. "I have never seen colors as pure as these before."

At the foot of the street, a fragment of the quays could be seen between the houses, and fishing-boats riding at their moorings, the colors of sky and sea clanging and bright, and the timber of the boats bleached paintless by the chloride of sun and brine. And Madame Marceau stood below in the alleyway of shade, combing her hair back in swift, sure jerks of movement from her temples and brow. The bicycle leaned against the wall, and Madame Marceau turned once and scrutinized the long, steep street, and waved her hand, and then returned to the quick, sure combing of her hair.

"My hat," she said when the girl stood by her. "You didn't manage to catch it as it went past? There's something going on out there on the quays, and my hair's a sight."

The girl set her own bicycle upright beside Madame Marceau's, and she was smiling, but in a moment tears might come into her eyes.

"I thought I would find you lying dead," she said, and they laid their arms around each other's waists, as schoolgirls do, or as mother and daughter who have breached the years between.

"It took me that long to work out the mechanics of the animal," said Madame Marceau in contempt for it as it leaned, rust-scarred and mule-eared, against the chalkwhite wall. "Why didn't you tell me to press the righthand handle of it? Once I found that out, I kept it under control. Stand over here and you can see the people on the quay," she said, and she drew the girl closer to the edge of shade, while her free hand jerked the comb through her hair. "It looks like revolution, and I'm not decently dressed," she said. Beyond the width of the cobbled quayside, the water, splintered with gold, was too hard and hot and glittering for beauty, and far to the left, above the restless people, the plane trees stood, heavy-leafed and windless, on the square.

"They've got the fishing-nets strung up. That's what they're doing," said Madame Marceau, her eyes halfclosed against the sun. And the girl saw then the deep red of the woven nets, the links on links of them, flexible, multiple, like the rusted links of a coat-of-mail, joining the people in an endless chain. "We'll leave the bicycles, and get out there, and try to make our way through," Madame Marceau said.

"Unless we find Marrakech among them," the girl said doggedly, as if saying it with conviction would make it true.

At the corner where the alley ended at the quay was a shop not marked by a show-window, but indicated by a rainbow-lacquered wooden sardine that hung over the door, tail down, sour-mouthed, cold-eyed, and mammoth, hooked by a wire through the mouth. Madame Marceau seized her bicycle by the horns and made for it quickly now, and the girl followed after, the bicycles rattling in their hands. In the front windows of the little house there had been crowded for display fishlines and reels and fishing-rods and trays of dark metal spinners flecked with silver, and others, vicious, intricate, double-hooked, and still others enameled like butterflies. There were blue rubber flippers, and periscope masks for underwater harpooning, and hand-nets on bamboo poles, and, lying among the coiled ropes of the marine harpoons, a Sears, Roebuck catalogue, as startling to the girl as if a voice had called out to her in the accents of home.

"An American catalogue!" she said, but it was nothing to Madame Marceau, fighting the beaded strings of the fly-curtain as she made her way through the door.

Above the confusion of the window display, the girl saw, framed in darkness, a woman's small, high-boned face, a living face, but so neatly done and so motionless that it might have been a portrait in oils hung on a wall. The title of it, the girl thought, could be "Fisherman's Wife," and the school Flemish, with every hair of the smoothly coifed brunette head, each tuck of the black

174

blouse, and the ivory skin faithfully portrayed. When they had passed through the swinging strings of the curtain, the woman stood up before them in the sudden dusk and coolness of the store.

"What's taking place down there on the quays?" Madame Marceau said in accusation, and she set her bicycle against the counter behind which the woman stood.

"The people of Abelin have had enough," said the woman, pronouncing "Abelin" as though a *g* were the final letter of the name. "I'm ashamed to be a shopkeeper, the way every honest man or woman in France must be ashamed, with prices going higher every day! Eight hundred and fifty francs for this net!" the woman said, having turned quickly and taken the net down to show the price-tag to them, and her small white nostrils, her tight-lipped mouth, were pinched as if by pain.

"Mademoiselle is American. It's nothing to her, the prices in France, my poor Madame Verre," said Madame Marceau.

"Ah, the Americans understand, all right! They understand if anyone does!" the little woman cried. She reached in over the masks and the harpoons in the window, and over the fish-baskets with the name "Abelin" embroidered on their straw, and she picked the American catalogue up. "Look at the things every American can buy!" she said, and she licked her thumb and turned the pages before them. "Blankets, saucepans, green or pink sheets, washing-machines! My daughter has all of them!" she said to the girl across the brightly colored illustrations of the untranslatable story of prosperity. "My daughter, a fisherman's daughter, she has a machine to beat her eggs for her! She married an American. He came in with the army of liberation. They live in Brooklyn now."

"I'm not going to shed tears for the fishermen's daughters of Abelin!" said Madame Marceau. "Their dowries alone could save the country economically! We'll leave our bicycles here, Madame Verre, and go down and have a look around the quays," she said, and she added: "When the Americans took their money out of the banks just once, they had a depression, so God knows what to do with a country like France, where nobody puts his money in a bank at all!"

"They're roping the mole and the casino off," the woman said, her face like a tightly closed small fist. "Marius took the day off from the Café du Port, and since dawn he's been going from door to door. In America," she said, turning to the girl again, "somebody would have to answer questions about the price of rents they're asking here. You wouldn't give roulette tables to a town when they wanted something else instead! In America they'd have it all out in the newspaper! That's what my daughter says! If Vaillant runs for mayor next spring—" she began, but she did not go on with it, the bitterness that warped her mouth bidding the hope die. "When anyone speaks out for us, he's put in jail," she said.

"When Vaillant runs for mayor, I'll vote for him," said Madame Marceau shortly, and her hand lifted the swinging beaded strings in the doorway and an angle of sun fell hot and bright on the floor.

"Then you've had a change of heart," said the woman, with the sound of enmity in her soft, meridional speech.

"I've kept my heart away from those who would cut it up for bait, that's all," said Madame Marceau. "I haven't made it public property."

But it was to the girl that the woman had urgent messages to give, to this line of communication suddenly es-

tablished between Brooklyn and the mainland, to this
newly harking ear.

"Here there isn't any newspaper or party to speak for
us," she said. "In 1946 we had the Communists. That was
the only time we've had a second party here. The mayor
put two of them in as councilmen, and once they started
getting their cuts on the rents, like the others, they didn't
say anything more about the rights of the people of
Abelin! Things don't happen that way in America. My
daughter says it's different over there. But we French,"
she said, and the girl thought then of the singular eloquence of these people, of the national logic that bade
them stretch their skins four ways and point with a scalpel
to the blemishes they saw. "For a long time now we French
have been badly governed, and now we've sickened with
discouragement. Live through two wars on nothing but
hope, and the supply begins running thin! I told the doctor that at noon when he came in looking for mussels,"
she said, and Madame Marceau let the beaded strings in
the doorway fall, and the angle of sun was abruptly wiped
away. "He hadn't found any in the fish-market, so he
came looking for them here," she said, the crescents cut
deeply around her mouth, and the pinched white nostril,
the hard eye, marring this face which the portrait-painter
of another time had sought to render as impassive as a
Flemish woman's face. She went on saying in explanation
to the girl that she sold fishing-bait, sandworms, and sea-
snails, and shellfish even, when the fishermen brought
them to her, all this, and the paraphernalia on display,
committing her to the sea. "I told him I'd sell him nothing, neither him nor the rest of them, with the evictions
they're putting through! Women and children moved out
in the streets by the police while the husband's at the ship-

yards, building ships for the national defense! Because the mayor and the lot of them are buying up real estate—"

"So the doctor," Madame Marceau interrupted it; "when he came in, was he alone?" And in the moment before she answered, Madame Marceau's eyes were sharp upon her face.

"Yes, alone," she said then, perhaps the protest of the people of Abelin the only thing she heard. "Except for the North African," she went on saying. "The one who has a fiddle, and who waltzes as he plays."

They went quickly, exchanging no words, leaving their bicycles behind them, the outline of what was taking place sharper than it had been before. And now the fishermen's houses on the waterfront were as if wakened from their somnolence, the people's faces drained from the windows and balconies, and the people themselves emerging as if from the deepest recesses of the pastel-tinted stones, moving into the endless labyrinths of the others on the quays. As they came, the wives, the grandmothers, the bare-legged young, they carried the great ropes of the nets like garlands with them, walking the hot cobbles on their strong, bare feet, with the russet nets slung over their shoulders or swinging in twisted ropes from hand to hand.

"Come help stretch out the nets!" they called after Madame Marceau and the girl, the sound of their mockery reserved for the tourists, and others like them, who sought to pass. "Come help us stretch out the nets to dry!" they cried in such guilessness, doing this thing that every fisherman on the coast had the long-established right to do. In the brilliance of a hot afternoon, they were merely stretching the nets to dry, and if all access to the mole was cut, and the streets winding down from the hills were closed, and the cliff-road severed, it was only because they had brought forth more nets than had been seen in Abelin before. Behind the barricade of them, the quays were isolated, and within their stronghold the determined milled, the port teeming with their complex activity. "Come help with the nets, Madame Marceau!" they cried in challenge after her, and after the girl.

"Why doesn't someone notify the police?" Madame Marceau cawed out, pushing her way among them.

"Ah, the police!" a man's voice said without ill-humor. "They'd need the police force of Paris to stop us, and the Bastille to hold us all! The *flics* aren't sticking their noses out today!"

"He comes from the shipyards, that one," said Madame Marceau under her breath. "God knows what his politics are! And there're men pulling there from the wine-growing properties, and two taxi-drivers, and the man who delivers the *Butagaz!* I could keep the fishermen in order, but I don't like the look of these others," she said, and she and the girl stood halted in the midst of them, no longer able to advance.

"If my father were here," the girl began.

"Well, what?" said Madame Marceau sharply, as if it were a man who had died the year before in Ohio who could tell them now what the answer might be.

"If my father were here, he would help with the nets," the girl said.

"I quite believe you!" snorted Madame Marceau. "That's an American's answer every time! Help with the work at hand, no matter if you don't know how to do it, and no matter what it commits you to! All right! I'll take his advice as far as the avenue. It's the quickest way of getting through. *Mon ami*," she said to the fisherman who pushed by them now, "you seem to need help. Give us

179

each a piece of your fishnet there," and her ringed, veined hands closed on the ropes, relinquishing in one gesture birthright, tradition, heritage. "And I'm doing this for an Algerian!" she said as she and the girl became a part of the russet chain. "Watch for the names of the fishing-towns woven in the mesh," Madame Marceau whispered. "I recognize some fishermen from Bandulu!"

And then the priest came through the density of people, speaking to those who spoke his name or stopped him to shake his hand, but his eyes, lying deep, like an ill man's, in the sockets of his skull, sought Madame Marceau out.

"What news?" he asked when he came beside her. "I got back from Aix and found both of you gone."

"Your cats. They got at the lobster. All right, I gave it to them, if that's your accusation," Madame Marceau said, and she and the girl were drawn on with the nets. "But now there's no more question. Now we know. We've been stopped from getting to the doctor's house by this tomfoolery!"

"I left my bicycle there last night. I'm on my way to get it now," the priest said, and he too put his hands to the nets, moving forward as the others moved. "I'll find Marrakech and bring him down. You go to the jail, see Vaillant, wait for us there. As for death by poisoning, there is more to say. There is a great deal more," he said, but he had begun to make a way for them through the people, and whatever he had to say was silenced now.

The two women followed the stoop of his shoulders in the shiny black of his habit, and the swing of his dusty skirt as he moved through the crowd. The nets were lowered to let him and the girl and Madame Marceau pass, and, standing outside the barricades, they watched him go, lean, muscular, his back curved as if beneath a burden, hastening past the hotel on the square where the *boules*-players played no longer, almost running on his soft black shoes, his helmet of hair, with the tonsure in the scalp, seen like a swimmer's head as he entered the deep pool of the plane trees' shade.

"We'll go up by the middle street. It's the steepest and quickest," Madame Marceau said then, as she had said it to the girl the day before. "The jail," she said, her breath coming fast from the climb, "it's just before we reach the church."

The cobbles of the street were interrupted once by a crescent of steps worn hollow by the passage of feet, and they mounted them quickly. And, higher, the way was broken again by a fountain that no vehicle could pass, its basin shaped like two open hands, with lines like the lines of life, and of fate, and of the heart marked in them, and the mouth of its bronze griffin dry. Just beyond, a long, black, suave-bodied car was halted. The hood was lowered, the cushions of its seats were red, and in this street where, below, no sign of life had stirred, barefooted children moved from one side to the other to view its beauty, and women in bright, full cotton skirts, holding their bare-armed infants on their hips, came out into the sun to look for a moment at this embodiment of speed and power and luxury, and then to walk away. They did not dwell in envy on the scarlet of its seats, its smooth black flanks, its streaming immobility, for it had no use or meaning in their lives, this silver-girded car. It might have come just then, that instant, the girl thought, off the assembly line, untouched by travel or by individual ownership; and then, even before she saw the license plates, she knew.

"That must be Peter's car," she said, and she laid her hand on the strong stone hands of the fountain.

 THEY CLIMBED PAST THE FOUN-
tain that had been so long dry that no water
mark darkened the stone, and mounted the
cobbles beyond it to the car, and when they
saw that only a pigskin glove lay on the red
leather of the seat, the girl looked for direction
to the children's faces.

"Where is the man who was driving it?"
she said.

"He couldn't get past the fountain," said
the boy, and his eyes were black, and his lips
the same brown as his skin. In the faded blue
of his singlet, his shoulder-blades were as
sharp as a young bird's wings. "He couldn't
turn the car, so he left it here. Perhaps he's
gone to the mechanic on the church square."

"The man gave him a hundred francs to
keep the rest of us from touching it," a little
girl said. She pointed respectfully to the boy,
and then she moved her finger over the reflection of her own face in the blade of polished
metal on the door.

"He couldn't speak French," the boy said,
the pale bill in his hand still. "But that is
what he meant to say."

The whites of the children's eyes were
stainless, and their arms and legs blackened
by the sun, and in the animal delicacy of their
bodies the girl saw the unexpected invitation

to run away. *We could run on the beach as fast as deer*, she thought. *I could lead them through the boulders to Marrakech's garden, and show them his seahorses, bridled and armored, in the basins of stone. I could run fast with them back into childhood, eat periwinkles all day on the beach with them. I could perhaps find my father again by turning my head and running fast.*

"Who taught you your classes today?" Madame Marceau was saying to the children, with her eye gone shrewd.

"The mayor read us about the national holidays of France," a tall boy said.

"We got out early," said the little girl, drawing her finger along the shining handle of the car door, and the smudged print of it showed for an instant on the metal, then faded away. "Monsieur Vaillant wasn't there."

The girl turned, then, seeking the actual avenue of escape, thinking to take their hands and run, for in a moment Peter Cornish might stand before her, and she would not know what words to say. But she saw fixed to the stone at the corner of one house, at the height of a man's shoulder, a bronze vase like those which hang on tombstones in French cemeteries, and she did not go. A bouquet of peonies was in it, white and red and mauve, hard-petaled, bright, and a spray of mint leaves, as fresh as spring, among the flowers. At first it was the mint that stopped her, and then she saw that, in the white drought of the street, the mint and the flowers were the only vegetation that lived, and that beneath the vase was a small marble plaque, rose-colored against the glare of the scaling plaster wall. On the plaque the names of four men were engraved, and their ages in numerals, and below the names and the ages was stated the manner in which they had died. Marcel Raffio, Étienne Angelo, Olivier Verre, and Yves Vaillant, the girl read from where she stood;

two of them sixteen, one eighteen, one twenty-two, and the legend merely: "Killed by the Germans against this wall, July 14, 1944."

"Those men?" the girl said, asking the question of Madame Marceau, her eyes on the plaque still, her voice low.

"Marcel was the son of the pharmacist. Dr. Angelo's nephew was Étienne, his sister's child. Madame Verre— the lady at the fishing-shop—Olivier was her son," said Madame Marceau, and the girl thought: *How can this be told to others who do not stand here and see it? How can it be put into any other tongue?* "Yves was Vaillant's brother, older than Michel. He was a schoolteacher too. I knew them all since they were like these others standing here," she said, and she jerked her chin at the children who touched the red leather cushions of the car, keeping emotion out of it. "They were brave, whatever their politics," she said.

"Does courage purify everything?" the girl asked, and she turned her head quickly to watch Madame Marceau's face.

"There's nothing else that men and women are re-membered for," said Madame Marceau, speaking almost bitterly.

"And when you are young, how do you know the thing you have in you is courage?" the girl said, and now noth-ing remained but the urgency to see Vaillant's face, to hear his voice and touch his hand. "Come quickly," she said, and she started up the cobbled street, with Madame Marceau following, lame, like a broken-winged, exotic bird. But the girl would have passed the prison door, not knowing the look of it, had not Madame Marceau cried out behind her. Except for the soiled ocher of its façade, it was like the other houses in the street, for the ground-floor windows of all the houses of Abelin were fitted with strong, ancient bars. "We must see Vaillant quickly," the girl said, and they went up the three stone steps together, and because the light of the sun was tempered now, their eyes were not blinded when they entered into the interior gloom.

There was one man, wearing a uniform, seated behind the center flat-topped desk, and he touched the beak of his cap in salute to them and smiled under the two black separate plumes of his mustache.

"*Entrez, mesdames!*" said Pierre, standing up from his chair, and his eyes protruded gravely, like a frog's eyes swelling in eloquence from its skull.

On the shelves that lined the room were accordion-like files, dog-eared and white with dust, their contents straining against the buckled canvas belts that sought to preserve in alphabetical order the disorderly facts of men's and women's lives. And there were reference volumes and yellowing columns of print that had been clipped from newspapers and tacked to the sagging wood for reasons that certainly no one could now recall.

"We have come about Vaillant, *mon cher ami*," said Madame Marceau, and she leaned on the desk that was littered with variously tinted papers and with cardboard folders so full that they could no longer hold the records of men's misdemeanors, but spewed their contents out on the table-tops and spilled them to the floor.

"*B'en*, the *chef's* up in conference with the mayor and the town council," Pierre said, "and Maurice is over in the city explaining to the school board that the school in Abelin needs a substitute while we've got the teacher in jail. Robert, he's down at the port, seeing which way the wind is blowing there. That makes me the village police

185

force," he said, reporting this to them slowly and scrupulously, as he had, slowly and patiently in this time of crisis, accepted the necessity of being several men.

"We want to make depositions as witnesses for Vaillant," Madame Marceau said.

"The shipyard men and the shopkeepers and the fishermen, they're doing what they can for him, stretching the fishnets right across the quays," Pierre said, his mouth smiling again as he took a pack of cigarettes from his pocket and looked at the contents of it with love. "They've sent a delegation up to the mayor, and this time maybe they'll get what they want. Will you have a cigarette, mesdames?" he said respectfully, and it was not a crumpled packet of French cigarettes that he held out, as it had been the night before.

"So, American cigarettes!" said Madame Marceau, and she took one. "And what are they demonstrating for, your population down on the quays?"

"*B'en*, they want new elections, and they want the man they'll vote for let out of jail," Pierre said, and he shook the cigarettes in their wrapper to count how many still remained. "An American gave them to me, just like that, just half an hour ago," he said.

"An American? The man who owns the car?" said Madame Marceau, and her hand with the cigarette in it stopped short of her mouth.

"I couldn't make out what he was talking about," Pierre said. He struck a sulphur match with the nail of his thumb, and waited a moment for the stench to go, and then he held the flame to Madame Marceau's cigarette. "So I took him down to Vaillant," he said. "In respect for the law, I locked him in, and the two of them are talking still."

"He's down there with Vaillant?" the girl said, hardly breathing it aloud.

Pierre nodded slowly, and he looked at the girl and Madame Marceau with his wide-set, froglike eyes as he slowly drew the first smoke in. Then he moved from the desk and opened the door into the hall, and when he switched on the light, they saw the descending spiral of stairs so old, so worn by time, that the ghostly figures of men seemed about to appear in silence on the stone: monks in dark gowns, with thonged sandals on their feet, who had perhaps just given succor to the condemned, or courtiers in silk, their hands tied behind their backs, their hair long and waved like the locks of movie-actresses, who, despite their silk and the jewels at their throats, were about to die. And Pierre was no longer the bungling, outdated officer of the law, but a museum guide who led them down, telling the life story of a monument with the proud gravity people bring to the recounting of their personal lives. He turned below them, belted and booted, giving the birth-date of the stairway to them, the words slow on his tongue as he tasted this tobacco that he loved.

"Men of the sixteenth century cut these stones and set them here," Pierre said, and he slapped the wall with his square palm. The cells below, he said, had held a distinguished company. Now there were only transients where once there had been poets, historians, murderers, he said. There had even been an admiral, who had fallen while attempting to escape and had been eaten by rats, and he spoke even of the rats of ancient Abelin with a cicerone's deep pride. "Men with royal blood in their veins and political prisoners sat chained for thirty or forty years in the cells you'll see below," he said, and these men seemed more living and more worthy to him than men who drew breath now. "Since two hundred years," he said, as if speaking of a fortnight, "local prisoners have been taken over to the city for trial, so nobody serves a long term here. That is finished," he said, the complaint in his voice saying the dignity of the place had gone with sentences of long duration. Housebreakers or pickpockets or men who stole cars didn't write lines of poetry, or draw astrological charts, or inscribe bars of music, or the names of women, on the walls, he told them, stopping on the worn, winding stairs to look back at the two women who followed him deeper and deeper into the dark heart of the stone. Only in the years of the Occupation, when the Germans had kept Resistance prisoners here, had something of the old tradition been revived, he said. "Men of the Resistance wrote their women's names, and the name of their country, and problems in trigonometry, the way a man of low principles and a short jail sentence wouldn't find the time to do," he said, and the past was so close, so vitally contemporaneous, that the girl knew suddenly that all she had witnessed in this country of pain and stress, all the voices that cried aloud in France, were a part of the breaking of these ancient ties.

They had reached the lower passage, and on the left side were the barred gates of the cells, each with a dusty-paned window set high against the ceiling of it, out of a man's reach, and chicken-wire tacked across the frame. They could hear the two men's voices ahead, and even Vaillant's laughter now, not loud or ringing, but a part of the quick murmuring of his speech. The other voice was Peter Cornish's; it was that of the prompter giving the cues, reading, it might be, the prescribed lines of the script for the benefit of the actor who held the stage. The afternoon light came in through the high windows in

the empty cells they passed, and now that the other, artificial light lay behind them in the deep well of the stairs, it
seemed to the girl that they approached reality, and she
was suddenly afraid.

They were together in the fourth cell, Peter seated on a
frame of iron springs hinged to the wall that folded down
as bed, and the chair on which Vaillant sat, with his back
to the bars, tipped back on its rear legs. And Vaillant,
with the current of mirth running through his voice, was
saying in English that "—the pants were never long
enough, and the jackets weren't made for anyone from
Texas. But it wasn't just that. It was the way they looked,
nearly all of them lanky as Lincoln, and the crew-cuts!
My God, I kept saying to myself when we were sweating
out the German patrols, why didn't someone, anyone, in
England, where they were based, tell them to get their
hair cut by Frenchmen and like Frenchmen. There were
enough Frenchmen who had been barbers once in exile
over there."

"I've brought you some visitors, Michel," Pierre said
through the bars to the heavy, black-maned man, and the
pronoun he used was "thee," and Vaillant turned and
saw them, and brought the front legs of the chair down on
the stone.

When Peter Cornish stood up, the frame of the springs
on which he had sat clapped closed against the wall, and
he stood, sandy-haired, nicely boned, withdrawn in hesitation, in one hand the mate to the pigskin glove which
had lain upon the red leather cushions of the car. He
might have been someone standing waiting to be intro-
duced at a cocktail party, not quite at ease now without
a glass as he gave the girl his civilized, wry smile. *Why
couldn't they have found someone stronger to speak for us?* she

thought in sudden impatience with those who had chosen him as representative of some portion of what the country and the people were. His flesh was so startlingly untouched by sun that he seemed a man of another race from Vaillant, as dolls she had owned as a child belonged to different sets and were not to be mingled even in play.

"Mary. This is insane, meeting again like this," he said, and his baffled eyes looked through the bars of the door at her.

"Yes, yes, I know," the girl whispered, and Pierre stepped before the two women, a wire key-ring in his hand, and he selected a key from the others on it, and fitted it to the lock of the door. But even when he swung the barred door back and nothing stood between her and the two men in the cell, the girl could not bring herself to lift her eyes and look toward Vaillant, knowing that if she turned her head to where he stood, the devout, shy recognition of all he was would fall like light upon her face. Instead, she looked at Cornish. "I will not run away any more," she said, in the voice of a stubborn, unrepentant child.

"Now, introduce me to your American," said Madame Marceau, and she moved with decision across the threshold of the cell.

The girl made an awkward gesture with her hands, and spoke their names, believing that in the terrible gravity of this moment such things as introductions need not be. *How can I introduce him?* she thought in strange confusion now. *I do not know who or what he is, and have never known, and yet I once agreed to marry him, perhaps only in order to introduce him to my own beliefs, or out of loneliness, or because my father loved his father and took us to a circus a long time ago.*

"So much has happened," she said, scarcely aloud.

190

"I've been through a private hell," Peter Cornish said, with his wry, slightly effete smile, so palpably the alien who had strayed in error onto this continent, the modern, profoundly baffled man come in error into the stone of this medieval cell to which he was not committed by history. Inside the open neck of his white shirt, a patterned silk scarf was folded, and his navy linen trousers were smartly belted and creased, and shoes of woven leather, like basketwork, were on his feet. "God knows how I've ever got my work done, but the men in the division were good. Now what about you?" he said, and his eyes moved carefully on her, perhaps trying to find some portion of the story in the man's shirt and the workman's blues she wore.

"I've found the kind of life I want to lead," the girl said, and now there seemed no possibility of ever looking at Vaillant's face, but only at his bare brown feet on the stone, with the cuffs of the corduroy trousers edged with dark from the sea-water of the night before. "I want to stay here in Abelin, perhaps a long while, perhaps until I'm too old to care about what happens to the people who live in a country, any country, or what happens to painting, because these are the things that matter most, at least to me—"

"If they'd pay you your *joute* purse, Michel, you could hire a lawyer and sue the lot of them," Madame Marceau interrupted the sound of it, the cigarette smoke coming through her nose.

"Ah, there are better things to do with money," said Vaillant, speaking French now, and he gave a laugh. "By this time the *joute* money has begun to smell. It has the strong odor of bribery," he said.

"Perhaps you'd like to listen, Mary, while this man gives you an account of himself," said Cornish then, and the girl looked up at him, suddenly aware that it was not the clothes he wore that gave him the incurable look of belonging to another place, and not his uneasy try at animation, but his own awareness of his official accountability. "He's got quite a history. He got American fliers out during the war. I had friends who bailed out over France, and so I knew our side of it, and now I walk up a street in the south of France, and into a jail, and this man completes the circle! As Henry Adams put it, we move in narrow valleys," he said. *And if you must account officially,* the girl thought in deep concern for him, *then the present and the future are both lost. It is safe to speak in terms of the past, but not to acknowledge the present, never to foresee.* "He got a friend of mine out, a man called Pemberton. You've heard me speak of him. Pemberton came from Alabama, roomed with me at Yale. After the war I saw a lot of him in Washington, and he never could tell me enough about that time, the parachuting over France, and the men who got them out," said Cornish, and he looked at Vaillant in manifest male pride.

"I have listened to him," the girl said. She turned quickly, humbly, to Vaillant then, seeking the courage to meet his eyes for a strange, troubled instant, not remembering that once she had looked at him she could not look away. The others seemed to have withdrawn then from the room, and there was only Vaillant, alive with a quick, electric power, his shirt unbuttoned on the brown skin of his neck, and the sleeves rolled back on his forearms; but it was the extravagantly heroic head, the portrait, hot with color, of spirit and vigor and perhaps senseless bravery, that held her with the promises it made. "Your jacket," she said in a low voice, "I didn't bring it. It's up at the Abbey School. I'm sure it's safe there," but these were not the things she had wanted to say.

Vaillant's dark, bold eyes had an almost unbearable look of humor in them, and the deep marks of the dimples came in his cheeks, and went, and then scarred his cheeks again, but he did not laugh. *He isn't just a man who helped Americans out of France. He's something for the future*, was one of the things she wanted to say in explanation of him. *He's buried history, and the men that he speaks to come together and try to find a common language, a European tongue.* And then she saw that Vaillant was keeping himself from laughing, and she felt the color rise across her throat and stain her cheeks and temples and brow. *He thinks I am funny*, she thought in sudden, quivering pain.

"An old windbreaker that never had any value until you gave it value," he said, and whatever might have followed was halted by the sound of a bell whirring in the stairs.

At once Pierre stepped back into the passage, and closed the barred door on the four of them, and turned the key.

"That may be the *chef*. In respect for the law, I'm locking Vaillant's door," he said. "You'll be all right for five minutes in there with him. The *chef* doesn't want us letting visitors in. I'll be down, I'll be back," he was saying, and now that a higher echelon of authority was under the same roof, he was no longer the cicerone of history. He went with the key-ring in his hand, his frog eyes looking over his shoulder in consternation at the physical presence of the irreparable mistakes that he had made.

Madame Marceau had stood silent long enough, and she dropped the end of her cigarette on the stone and tapped out its fire with the toe of her white canvas shoe.

"If you've been telling Monsieur Cornish about Abelin, Michel, then don't leave anything in doubt," she said. "The mayor and the doctor, they've made their plans, and they'll give him the picture cut to fit. Last night when I was escorted home by force, the mayor told me they'd made reservations at Antoinetti's on the square for Monsieur Cornish, the official spokesman of America. Ho, ho, ha, ha, and the official spokesman behind bars! It makes me laugh," she said grimly, but she did not laugh. "They're organizing a reception committee for him, and there'll be a *dîner d'honneur* which he'll end by paying for through the nose, and speeches about making Abelin the center for this and the center of that, and the resurrection of France through wine! Oh, I can see the whole charade!" And then she turned, fierce with impatience, on the American, whose baffled eyes asked for interpretation of what was taking place. "French! Can't you understand French?" she cried out. "We've got to get Vaillant out of jail! Can't you understand that much? Jail!" she cried wildly, and her hands gripped the air before her in indication of bars before her face, and she herself the blue-haired monkey glaring between. "It's gone beyond party politics here, oh, far beyond! They're putting honest men under lock and key, and they're sprinkling poison on the food they ask you to their homes to eat!"

And Cornish stood shaking his head slowly, declining in helplessness this story in which he had recognized three words: the name of the country on whose soil he stood, and the name of that country's beverage, and the name of the first Frenchman he had met with whom he felt at ease.

"What a grand old countrywoman you have, Vaillant!" he said. "One of those irate ladies of the European aristocracy!"—these things that he said, the girl knew, the barrier set between himself and whatever human came too close. "We have them at home, in New England," he said. "I have a family of aunts myself who take one look at a man and make up their minds like *that!*" he said, snapping his second finger against the cushion of his thumb, the barrier of phrases made quickly, uneasily, before anyone should come too near.

"I wanted to get to the south, far south, and meet your women there," said Vaillant. "Next time it will be Louisiana," he said, the murmur of laughter in his voice still, but the quality of light, swift veracity altered now that he tried to play the same game of evasion that Cornish played.

"Women should never be assigned to diplomatic posts," said Cornish, pleased that he and Vaillant understood each other so well. "Let them be doctors and surgeons and criminal lawyers, for if anything goes wrong, it's only the life of a man that's lost by their miscalculations. But it's the good name of a government if an error is made in diplomacy."

"And a man's life, Peter—" the girl began, and she thought in troubled concern for him still: *He needs someone to breathe warmth on his heart, perhaps a Spanish dancer, a Carmen moving her soft hips as she turns before him; or an Italian woman holding her pliable, voluptuous hands out to him, asking him to swing in the tarantella with his arms around her, with everything wiped out except the heat of love.*

"Yes, yes, I know," said Peter, the frail charm of his perplexity drawn like a veil across the features of his face. "Ask Vaillant what value he puts on a man's life. He's dealt more than any of us in that currency," and now it was clear that between him and Vaillant a kinship had been established, a brotherhood based on the valor of all heroes, or on the identity of one called Pemberton, whom they both knew, and that women were banished from this terrain where they met.

"And yet look at the names of women carved here by men!" said Vaillant, and he motioned toward the walls of the cell.

"But not as diplomats!" said Cornish with his wry grin. In a minute he might say, sociably and smiling still: "For God's sake, Vaillant, let's have a drink somewhere together! Can't we get out of here?"

But Madame Marceau hobbled to the empty chair, her eye on Vaillant as she began to talk.

"*Monsieur le curé* carried a boiled lobster up from the doctor's house last night," she said. "The cats got at it. At least one of them is dead," and Vaillant listened with no humor in his eyes.

"He stopped here to see me on his way to Angelo's. That was one o'clock this morning, before the business with the cat; and he suspected Angelo then," said Vaillant. "He had reasons of his own for that. One man had told him what he feared three months before he died."

"Someone had known, suspected?" said Madame Marceau, barely whispering it.

"He wanted something better than supposition to go on, the curé," Vaillant said, "and perhaps he has it now."

Footsteps sounded on the spiral stairs at the far end of the passage, and the girl stood listening to them come. Because of the excitement trembling in her, she could only believe that the men of other centuries and the men of the Resistance who had been imprisoned here were in the cell with them now, waiting, as they had waited in other years, harking to the sound of feet, those of their executioners, or their deliverers, or merely of those who came at intervals to bring them water and bread. She turned quickly to Cornish, thinking that this, just this sound of feet coming down the stone stairs and into the passage, could bring him into the incommunicable lives and deaths of people who were foreigners to him still.

"Listen to the footsteps coming, Peter," she said in a low voice, and her hand was trembling as she touched his arm. If he could hear the footsteps as prisoners heard them, she thought, and, having listened as the imprisoned listened, in uncertainty and hope, and in hopelessness and fear, then he might give ear to all the rest. "When you hear them, your own identity goes away," she said, thinking: *I'm every prisoner who ever stood here waiting, Peter. I'm the ones who died, and the ones who survived, and I'm frightened. I'm Vaillant, and I'm his brother whom they took out and shot against a wall.*

"Men can't, or anyway don't, shed their identities with the same readiness as women," said Cornish, and he looked at Vaillant. "Is that what is meant by stamina?" he said affably. The girl saw his untanned hand with the pigskin glove in the fingers of it, and she thought that if a curtain had fallen to their wrists, dropped just this far, and the hands of the four people in the cell appeared like dancers just below the hem, their qualities, their weaknesses, their capacities and incapacities, with nothing deleted, would all be there. "It's probably the froggy-eyed man with the ring of keys," said Cornish, listening to the footsteps come, saying this merely that the sound of his voice might stand between them and whatever lay within his heart.

One Sunday in the spring, the girl remembered, they had driven out from Paris and stopped on the outskirts of a village on the Marne to pick the first dark violets, and the men and boys of the village, in their good clothes, had gathered around the long black car. It had stood there contained within a realm of wonder, ringed by the faces, an achievement beyond politics or nationality. How fast would it go, and how many liters of gas could it carry? the men asked, and the girl had translated the words to him, and Cornish moved with gentle alacrity to show them, his white-nailed finger touching the numerals on the face of the speedometer, his eyes filled with pleasure at the male astonishment encircling them. It might have been that he had come this long way from America merely to stand in the springtime sun of France and press the button which made the top of the incredible car rise, complexly ribbed as a bat's wing, and settle with un-erring perfection into place, and then, at another touch of the button, fold back upon itself again.

"Tell them this," he had said to the girl, his eagerness requesting that they accept him as simply as they had the car, in interpretation for him who had no adequate lan-guage of his own. And they listened in wonder as she told of two sets of shock-absorbers, a spare set that shifted into use when the road was rough, and front seats that could be transformed, at the flick of a lever, into full-length beds. "Tell them there's an automatic gear-shift," he said, and he might have been saying to them: "Because of these things, accept me, believe in me!"

"I would marry him just for his car!" Madame Mar-ceau said now, seeing the girl's hand on his arm, but the girl heard the mockery in her voice, and cried out in his defense.

"It's because of the things he's owned all his life!" she cried almost in grief for this man who was her countryman.

198

"He's never been empty-handed the way Michel Vaillant and the way the men who died out there against the wall have been. He's always had something to put between himself and what other men are. Perhaps that's why he chose the kind of work he did, where the decisions need never be his, putting official America between himself and his own—"

But before she could finish it, the priest stood in the passage, hollow-eyed, stoop-shouldered, in his rusty black, and beside him Pierre, with the key already in his hand. As Pierre opened the barred door, the priest's dark, eloquent eyes opened other doors with the same calm urgency. He followed this man, miscast as an agent of law and order, into the cell, and bowed in brief salutation to the stranger there, and even before he spoke, his eyes pronounced their own self-depreciation as he looked at Vaillant's face.

"I was a half-hour late. Marrakech and the doctor had already gone," he said.

"Gone where?" said Madame Marceau sharply.

"Only Gaston was there," the priest said. "He had packed the food for them to take. They've gone out to trawl and set out lobster traps. They'll cook out on the island tonight."

"So we've lost!" said Madame Marceau. She had doubled her thin-boned hands into fists, and now they beat slowly at her knees. "Mary, could we have cycled down faster than we did, not talked so long to Madame Verre, taken a knife and slashed our way through the fishing-nets? We must have moved like snails! And now it's over. Marrakech is dead!"

"If it was murder that Angelo committed last year, and

the year before that, I can see the motivation," said Vaillant. "But why should it be Marrakech he's after now?"

"Because Marrakech is the third witness!" Madame Marceau cried out in impatience with the incurable slowness of man.

"Take it further back," said Vaillant, the words explicit, but spoken fast. "Because I'm against the coalition of mayor, house-agent, and doctor, a warrant is sworn out for my arrest, just to keep me from doing the things I want to do. Is that how you've worked it out?" he said. "They want to see me convicted of sabotage, and out of the political race, and so they've planted the cutting of the brakes on me. Is that the way it goes? And at least one of them will murder any witness whose evidence will clear my name, not only because he wants me out of the way, but because he's done murder before. Is that how you see it?" he said.

"Yes, like that, like that!" cried Madame Marceau, one fist still beating in slow desperation at her knee.

"And he waited three weeks after the bus fell before making up his mind?" said Vaillant, watching her face. "No, no. There's something wrong with it."

"Perhaps because at first the blame was mine," the girl said. "I had made the bus-driver angry, and in his anger he had driven too fast. Dr. Angelo said I would be questioned about that."

"*B'en*, they tried to keep it quiet about the air-tubes being cut," Pierre said. "For three weeks the story's been running from tongue to tongue, but they didn't want it to come out. They tried putting the blame one place, and then another, and the mayor put on the *joute* games early this year, but last night they couldn't keep it quiet any longer after Michel stood there saying the whole thing out. So, all right," he said, speaking slowly, as if truth were a thing so deeply rooted that it took time and labor to free it of its soil. "So if it was sabotage, then they had to find the saboteur, and Michel looked as good as any-one around, because what they wanted to do was to get him out of the way. So once the people had started home for bed last night, the house-agent came along with his complaint, and they served a warrant on Michel."

"And now that there are three witnesses to speak for me—" Vaillant began.

"Ah, no, Michel," the priest said quickly, wondering even that Vaillant had not seen it as it was. "Angelo wants to get rid of Marrakech, but not because of any disputable piece of evidence Marrakech might give. As long as Marrakech was his, and functioned as part of him, he had nothing to fear. Can't you see how it might have been?" he said, saying "thou" in tender familiarity. "Marrakech, the outcast, the lost, committed by one man only to hu-manity, by the doctor who had dressed his foot and saved him from tetanus and death? Every night he passed by Angelo's door, to give the silent reverence of good-night upon his step. I have come across him more than once in the past two years, late at night, moving, with no more substance than a shadow, along the wall. Angelo could trust him as he could his own right arm, and Marrakech left offerings for him to seal this trust, things he had fashioned with his own hands in love. That is, he could trust him until yesterday, when Marrakech went off in his boat with a young woman, merely by that act dispensing with all that Angelo had been. Gaston told me this after-noon that when Marrakech stopped by at night, they would give him a plate of food," said the priest. "Last

night Angelo had prepared lobster for him. Gaston told
me, knowing nothing except that Angelo had cooked the
lobster separately, and that Marrakech had not come and
stood waiting in homage at the door. After that, I think
the doctor got a little desperate. It was three weeks after
the bus had fallen, but it was only just public knowledge
that the air-tubes had been cut deliberately. It was late in
the day, but not too late. Marrakech had gone off in a
boat with a young woman, and it might be that he was
wavering in his loyalty. But if Angelo acted quickly, he
could put an end to what Marrakech might tell."

"But what? Tell what?" said Madame Marceau in
irritation with the stubborn deviousness of man.

"What he himself—Marrakech—had been doing under
the bus," the priest said.

"But it wouldn't make sense, that poor benighted little
man," Madame Marceau said, but her fist lay suddenly
quiet on her knee. There was silence in the cell for a moment, and the girl and Vaillant looked at each other's
faces and shook their heads as if shaking the possibility of it
off like guilt, making the identical gesture that swimmers
make when they shake the sea-water from their eyes.

"There'll be a boat down at the port that we can use,"
said Vaillant, speaking quickly. Now he watched the priest
with a bright, easy alertness, like a racer waiting for the
flag to drop, believing that the final edict of freedom would
come from him, and not from an officer of the law.

"We rode back on bicycle together, the chief of police
and I," the priest said. "He told me that the decision
reached by the mayor, the town council, and the delegation from the quays is that you're to deal with the people at
the port. They paid him the money you won in *la joute*, to

be held against your freedom as security." He gave a jerk of laughter at the irony of it. "There's not a lawyer on the coast who would fight that part of it for you, because he would know that a deal put over by the authorities of Abelin would be of a kind that would slip through every loophole of the law."

"The *chef's* up at the desk now, waiting to see you, Michel," Pierre said, and he made a motion with the key-ring toward the open door. "Michel," he said, and he did not smile under the two long black plumes of his mustaches, "you won't mention to him that I let you out for an hour this morning, will you, Michel? He wouldn't like the idea of it."

"I'm not certain it happened," said Vaillant. "I'm not certain it wasn't a dream you had, Pierre."

"Your belt and *espadrilles*, they're in the top drawer of my desk, the righthand drawer, Michel," Pierre said, his mouth gone soft.

"So he's free. Is that it?" said Madame Marceau, but Vaillant did not go.

"How free are they allowing me to be, Pierre?" he said.

"*B'en*, out under surveillance. The *chef* and the mayor made the deal with the delegation," Pierre said, naming slowly, and with emphasis, these three separate authorities. "You're to get the people into order down there, but no public speeches, no leaflets handed out. Tomorrow at ten o'clock they'll meet again to take up the questions of new elections. That's what they've agreed. But now, tonight, they don't want the tourists packing up and leaving and giving a bad name to the place. They're expecting an American official to turn up, so they want everything quiet, picturesque, like on the postcards, and no signs of trouble anywhere. You're just to go down there, Michel, and send the fishermen and the others home to eat their soup, but you're not free."

"They needn't worry about the official. You've got him here in jail," said Vaillant.

"*B'en*," said Pierre, and under the visor of his cap his eyes protruded grievously. "I didn't know this would be the one. I haven't said anything to the *chef*. He doesn't know the lot of them are here."

"Then let them go out the other way," said Vaillant, and he turned quickly to the priest. "Take them down through the old passage to the port," he said, using the small, intimate word "thee." "I'll talk to the *chef*, and then we'll meet down on the mole. I'll pick up a boat and get it to you." Then he had passed quickly from the cell, passing them all, his bare feet making no sound. But, once in the passage, he halted. "Cornish, I'll need you down there," he said in English, looking back, and there was more that he still wanted to say.

"I've lost the sense of it all," said Cornish, flicking the pigskin glove in agitation against his trouser-leg.

"I need you to walk with me down there, just that, nothing more," said Vaillant, speaking quickly, but with emotion, as if the words had been waiting a long time in his heart. "You have the revolutionary process digested in you, assimilated since generations in your blood, the way we French have it, for we are your counterpart on the continent. We have always been your counterpart here, and if we have been badly served by those who represent us, then perhaps the same can be said of you. That we, as nations, belong to the same tradition is something that does not alter overnight. We, you and I, Cornish, we are among the educated, moral men," he said, with the sound of humor in it. "By profession, we're doomed to function among the intellectuals, but perhaps we haven't the right any more, or the right at this moment in our lives, to let it end there. With one quarter of my country voting Communist and the other three quarters split in a dozen ways, I have to speak, I have to act. I have to believe that it's me —the good European—and you—the good American— who together will find the energy and honesty to build our own defense."

"Our own?" repeated Cornish, his eyes baffled and humorless. "I'm afraid that isn't the role an American over here—at least, not an American at my level—is authorized to take." But whether that level was too high or too low could not be known from the halted features of his face.

"The men down there on the quays, they see Americans either as members of a ground-crew, or as fliers, always as men in uniform," said Vaillant. "So that if you walked down there with me, shook hands with them, drank the *apéritif* with two or three of them, merely as man, it would be something they had not known about before. If you listened to what they have to say about the government, local or national, about German rearmament not only dividing Frenchmen among themselves but, worse, within themselves, you would be getting closer to what they are. You see how it is," he said, "the army, any army, and now your army here, mingles with the people, gets drunk in public, picks up girls, while the official civilians that come do not participate. The people of the country and the army have come to know each other well, but the people and the foreign service have yet to speak. We, you and I, whatever we experience, we have our compensations, Cornish. As intellectuals, we may be as poor as the workingman is poor," he said, the scars slashing his cheeks, "but

we are indemnified both by our knowledge of what we
are, and by the high regard of other men. But the others
whose part I wish to take have no compensations, none. If
you would meet me down on the port," he said, "we might
begin to talk together—"

"Yes," said Cornish, and the glove flicked nervously at
his trouser-leg. "I'd be interested. I'd like to see what
they're up to," perhaps accepting to go merely because he
and this one Frenchman out of all the rest were committed
to each other by the valor of heroes in the name of one who
had, ten years before, walked all night toward freedom
with Vaillant through the dark.

THEY SHOOK HANDS WITH PIERRE before they left, he standing at the opening in the righthand wall of the prison passageway as the president of the republic might have stood at a more formal door, shaking hands with a distinguished departing company. The priest went first, stooping to pass under the arch of the opening, and Madame Marceau followed, coming, lame, behind the priest, and then the girl, and Cornish last. They had scarcely stepped into the rocky passage, and were not yet engulfed in its obscurity, when Pierre called after them, keeping the sound of it low, saying that after the first turn in the dark there would be daylight through the gutter-gratings all the way. He held the square iron panel of the door open long enough for them to distinguish the smooth stones of the incline under foot, and then he called good-by down the echoing corridor, and behind them the weight and metal of the door rang closed.

The priest began speaking at once, the tough, unsanctified voice magnified in volume by the surrounding rock, telling them the story of what had taken place that afternoon. On the way back from Aix, he said, he and the sixty children from Paris and the two novices who had accompanied them that far had an hour to wait between buses in the shipbuilding town. In that hour's wait in the heat, he had left the children and the novices, with the sixty small cardboard suitcases or string-tied bundles that held their change of clothes, on benches in the shade of the plane trees on the square, and he himself had walked up one street and down another in search of a piece of information that might prove or disprove what the doctor was. He had walked into first one pharmacy and then another, asking the same question of whatever figure stood in authority in a white chemist's blouse behind the cases of nylon brushes and combs, or glass-stoppered perfume bottles, or sponge-bags of bright rubberized silk, or variously tinted baby-scales. He had asked them simply if it was here that prescriptions were filled for Dr. Angelo of Abelin.

"And what were you after, *mon père?*" said Madame Marceau, impatient with the stiffness of her legs and the roughness of the way.

It might have been a scene upon a dimly lighted operatic stage that was played now, with the contralto and the baritone, the second parts, developing the plot in musical exchange, while the soprano and the tenor sang their own troubled duet imperviously. The four of them in the underground passage, the way they took lit only by the pale laths of day between the iron gutter-gratings of the steep streets overhead, sang the parts of their own dramas as if they followed separate scores, the tenor, named Cornish, speaking of the spring in Paris when he and the girl had walked in the rose-gardens of the Bagatelle, of the scented presence that had lingered on the paths and lawns, the phantom of a woman called Marie-Antoinette, of the boat they had drifted in across the waters of the Bois, pursued by swans, while the willows wept in silence along the shore. While the baritone, who might have been poet, or scientist, or philosopher, but happened to be priest, with an indomitable power in his voice, and a vision in his eyes so clear that others could almost see the depth and fervor of his hope, spoke in a rapid undertone to the contralto of his search through the pharmacies of the ship-building town.

"There are perhaps two dozen in all, but not more than five in the neighborhood of the square," he said. "I wanted to cover at least those five in the hour I had. It was to be the beginning. That was all."

"But you must have had some reason to believe, or else suspect," warbled the contralto, who was Madame Marceau, hitting the notes a little high and querulously.

"Three months ago Raffio came to see me at the Abbey School one afternoon," the baritone declaimed. "That was in April. He told me then that he knew Angelo had tried once to do away with him, and had failed, and he believed that he would try again."

"Raffio, too! Oh, poor old garlic-breath!" sang Madame Marceau to the intermittent dark.

And now the soprano answered the tenor's complaint, asserting with poignant sweetness that love was not love that lived only in memory, the emotion he had felt for her and she for him perhaps never been love, for it had never stirred the blood, but moved quiescently as a swan's breast across the lake. It had perhaps been tender recognition of the eternal setting for love, or had sprung alive in them because the heart was broken by loneliness, or else torn wide by spring.

"All May you were Marie-Antoinette to me!" the tenor

sang accusingly. "Even to putting your fingers around
your throat and saying: 'They tell me the executioner's
blade is very sharp, and my neck is very small!' "

"That was because I fell in love with all the women of
France's history!" the soprano's voice rang musically
against the stone. "I was in love with Massenet's *Manon*
and his *Thaïs*, but not with you! I was the *Dame aux
Camélias*, Peter, and Puccini's *Tosca*, and all the dead
young queens! I played them for you, and you liked the
acting and the score, but now it's through!"

"Oh, Mary, Mary, what role are you playing here?"
the tenor sang. "Paris is there still, waiting for your reper-
toire! The stage is clear!"

"Twice in two years," came the baritone's part confi-
dentially, "Raffio told me, Angelo had bought arsenic
from him. You know a man for twenty years, peacetime
and wartime, was what he said, and even if you don't like
his business methods or his politics or the cold grin on his
face, when he says he has rats in his cellar you take it at
that. The other thing didn't come to Raffio's mind until
Angelo asked a third time for arsenic. That was this spring;
and then it struck Raffio suddenly, the way in which first
Madame Angelo and then the General died. He heard
himself giving the doctor a mad excuse: that there'd been
an inspector down from Lyon, and, because of abuses, he
wasn't authorized to sell arsenic any more. It was meaningless, and Raffio knew it. He might just as well have
said: 'I've been thinking over your past history.' "

"That was the time when Angelo made his business
proposition to me. Mid-April," the contralto stated
grimly. "It would be only good, hard logic to connect the
two."

And "Ah, Paris, Paris," came the soprano's voice, rising tender and warm against the stone. "It was not a place, but an intermission between childhood and maturity. So that is through, and the women I loved returned without me to history and literature, and I have altered. I will stay here, Peter, and you must not care. I will work out the next act here, playing it straight, as my father would have played it, trying to find his kind of humor too. But I remember van Gogh cutting off his ear, and nothing seems funny after that, because every artist who remains an artist to the end cuts out his heart and submits it, hoping it will do. When I came down through France, I could see from the windows of the train the printed warnings of hoof-and-mouth disease nailed to the trees, and I knew that my father would have picked up his bag that held just what sufficed him always, nothing more, and pulled the emergency brake and got out there. Because that would have been the place where he was needed, and so he would have stayed. I too, I too," sang the soprano, "must make my choice, and now it's made! I must stay here!"

"Your choice!" soared the tenor's voice, and when the girl turned back to him, she saw in his eyes a hard, cold bead of unrelenting rebuke, and she thought suddenly: *It is there forever. It will never die.* "You have lost," went the aria of his reproach, perhaps meaning to specify "your equilibrium" or say "lost dignity, lost caste, or lost your senses," and he looked at her, halted before him, not merely a girl with a skin like silk and a warm mouth and dream-drugged eyes, but a woman who sat in judgment on him, an American dressed up in a Frenchman's clothes. "I'm going to take you home, and home is not Paris. Home

211

is the interval between assignments, three thousand miles away. I'll have to find someone of your family, even though distantly related, someone to—"

"There is no one left," the sweet, grave voice sang. "My relatives are here," and whatever conflict there had been between them now tapered to the past, for the present was the tough, dedicated figure in a dusty dress who moved before them down the passageway. "I will tell you everything he says," the girl whispered, setting the operatic role aside. "I will translate what he is saying now."

"So there it was," the priest told Madame Marceau as they walked. "Raffio had refused to sell him poison, and so, a week later, Angelo asked him to come up one afternoon for tea. Raffio took this as the doctor's way of making peace with him, and went, and both of them drank tea and ate the chocolate cake the doctor cut. Raffio didn't know then that the doctor's soul was cold with calculation and with terror too, not knowing how much Raffio suspected in the deaths of the General and Madame Angelo. It may have been that day in the pharmacy in Abelin, when Raffio said he couldn't sell arsenic any more, that Angelo made his decision. Before that, there was no reason why Raffio should go. But after that tea-party," said the priest, his voice, by the mere fact of its virility, mocking the elegance of the occasion on which the doctor and the owner of the pharmacy had sat at a nicely appointed table on the terrace, against the backdrop of cypress trees, and one had eaten poison and one had not; "after that, Raffio knew that the doctor had got what he wanted somewhere else," the priest said. "He knew it because he was sick all night, violently sick, and his wife, knowing nothing, called Dr. Angelo. That was a moment, poor Raffio said, to look up from your pillow in what might be your final agony, and see your executioner standing, smiling, by the bed! 'Murderer!' he howled out, and Angelo laid a hand on his brow and felt for the pulse that raced in his blood, while Raffio tried to fight himself free. 'Delirious,' Angelo said to Raffio's wife, and he stayed all night, and somehow saved him, perhaps out of foresight, but anyway saved him. Perhaps for no other reason but to be able to say to the men of the jury, provided every calculation he had made went wrong: 'Look here, gentlemen, I saved Octave Raffio's life. That is on the record. So the state's case doesn't hold up that various individuals succumbed to violent death immediately after I had purchased arsenic, and immediately after they had eaten a meal with me. Food poisoning is a common occurrence here in the south if things aren't kept under refrigeration or handled as hygienically as we medical men know they should be. Perhaps my man, Gaston, was careless. I've lectured him for years on keeping food fresh, but if you're dealing with ignorance, ignorance in a white jacket probably worse than the unostentatious variety! . . . And see here!' he could always add, 'I ate the same chocolate cake as Raffio, and nothing happened to me!' Raffio came up to the Abbey School one night in April and told me all this," the priest said, and he walked with his eager, hurrying step before them, his hair like a metal helmet, with the tonsure glinting in the bars of light that fell, with the rhythm of his step, across the gloom. "He told me all this, and that in his pain he had cried out to Angelo: 'You ate from the other half of the cake! I saw that! You didn't eat from the same half I did, Angelo!' "

"Oh, the fool!" said Madame Marceau, stumbling on.

The story returned now to the fourth pharmacy the priest had walked into that afternoon in his search in the

213

shipbuilding town. There he had put the same question to the man behind the counter that he had put to the three other white-bloused men.

"Is it here that prescriptions are filled for Dr. Angelo of Abelin?" he said. And this time the answer was different. This time it was yes; and so the priest put the second question to him. "Has Dr. Angelo ever bought arsenic here?" he asked, and either because of the priest's frock he wore, or the vision of something that men believed in, whatever their belief, that was there, unblemished, in his face, the chemist said he would look up the records and let him know. Several minutes of that hour between buses passed while he waited, said the priest, and then the chemist came back with the information that a prescription of Dr. Angelo's for arsenic had been filled on the fourteenth of April that same year, specifying for the purpose of killing rats in the cellar of Dr. Angelo's house. "So I did not have to look any farther," the priest said. "Come over to the right," he said now to Madame Marceau. "The sea-water seeps up through the stones at this level. "We're directly under the quays."

"How much did that answer make clear to you, *mon père?*" said Madame Marceau, and she leaned on his arm in unaccustomed weariness.

"That Angelo had bought arsenic two days before he invited Raffio up to tea," the priest said, "and, this being true, it could mean that there was no question of food poisoning at all. If Raffio did not die, it could have been merely that he had not eaten enough of the cake. So, having failed once, it might be that Angelo decided he would have to move with care. He couldn't risk a second miscalculation, so he hit upon another way."

"But what way?" Madame Marceau began, and then,

shocked into silence by her own obtuseness, she ceased to speak, and she halted on the stones that were threaded now with dark, bright veins of water from the sea.

"The bus," the girl whispered behind her. "The bus, the bus. Oh, no!"

Now they had come abruptly to the end, and the priest forced up the rusted iron bar that held the heavy door, and he and Cornish pulled at it together, and its hinges cried as it swung in. And there, at once, in the clarity of the outdoor world, as sharp as if transmuted through a magic-lantern's glass, the semaphore stood in the charmed light of the dying afternoon, and they stepped into the air from which the sun ebbed gently, without haste. Beyond the semaphore opened the wide, motionless sea, the far horizon already marked with the dark-blue edge of night. If only it was this that they could face forever, the girl thought, for the sea and the sky were like cool lids laid on the eyes, and the scars were wiped from the priest's brow as he stood beside her, looking away from land. The movement of people on the distant quays, and their voices, were far behind, and they could refuse the sight of them, the girl thought, refuse their inference, and accept, as painters did, only the far, high cliffs and the water and the clear shell of the sky. But the scaffolding of the casino tapped at the shoulder like a hand, and the girl turned quickly, seeing the waterfront of Abelin behind it, with the curve of the houses that were lilac and rose and green, like an arm in a multicolored sleeve. The priest turned too, and he looked at Cornish, examining him from under his thick, mobile brows as if seeing him for the first time here in this pellucid light.

"That which you see, that is the casino for which they desire money," he said, speaking abruptly and painfully in

English to him. "They desire money to complete it, but the men here will not work on it. When they have money, they will bring in other men to work."

"They could hire Algerian labor for it. They tell me the North Africans will work for a loaf of bread and a liter of wine a day!" said Cornish, but the priest, whose eyes were on him still, did not seem to hear him speak.

"I too desire money, but I would put it to a different use," he said.

"For his school, for the Abbey School," the girl said to Cornish, and she said it in French for the priest then. "For your school."

"To make trust funds for the ex-Communists of the south of France," said Madame Marceau, sitting down below them on the rocks, but the venom of her tongue had lost its edge, and the look of censure gone weary in her eye.

"My school lives well," said the priest, pronouncing the English words painstakingly. "The people there pick the grapes for the wine, and they make the wine, and they bottle it, and they ship it away. We ship it away as far as Australia," he said, with difficulty, and then he spoke in French to the girl. "Tell him this: tell him they not only make the wine, but they drink it themselves, with the soup and bread and cheese at night, and they go to bed a little drunk some nights. That is the recompense, that and work, for the things that they have failed to be. And after a while some kind of meaning evolves. They work, and they eat, and they drink the wine they have grown themselves, and they know they are necessary to the land and the vine, and they do not need help, or charity, or a political party, or a church. The truth is just that, not being afraid to see one's own reality. But in Paris, in Paris— Tell him

216

this," he said, the voice even more urgent now, and he motioned toward the complex scaffolding, and Cornish looked too in the direction of the frail edifice of boards. "Tell him it could serve in Paris as kindling for a great fire that would burn all winter to warm those who sleep and die on the sidewalks in the cold. It could be begun by this, and be nourished by Christmas trees, not even stripped of their ornaments, but carried from every house on Christmas day and piled onto the blaze. Tell him," he said, and now, beyond the pale wood of the scaffolding, they could see on the harbor waters a swan-white yacht pulling gently at its moorings, and a half-dozen delicate-bodied sloops riding lightly at anchor, their flanks like alabaster in this long hour before dusk, and a single fishing-boat, its motor pulsing, coming now across the water toward the lonely stone mole, "tell him that Vaillant and I speak now for France," but he said it with humility. "Vaillant fights for man, for his garbage pails and his nets on the quays, and I fight for God, and perhaps the two things are the same thing in the end."

"We offer God, man, and everything we have to the French, and they take it," said Cornish in sudden irritation, once the girl had translated the priest's words, "except for the one thing that the free world wants them to take! Ask him why his men and women, who do not need charity or a political party or a church, won't give up their ancient animosities? Probably even Vaillant has his objections to mutual defense."

But the girl did not need to interpret the words, for the priest had understood.

"He says men do not believe any more that victory by arms is final," she said when the priest had spoken again.

217

"He says Frenchmen have accepted the American dream of a world without war. He says it is something else, not arms, that wins."

"I'm not sure I know what he means," said Cornish in irony, his eyes in accusation on them all. "Walk through any sleeping, lazy little town in France to the American airfield on the outskirts of it. Do that, and you'll know you're walking through a world that has died into the live world of reality. Do that just once, and you'll know that France—no, even more—the Latin countries are old dogs dozing in the sun, and they stir a little when the hunt goes through, bugles sounding, the pack baying, and then go back to sleep again. The Latins resent us, as they resent the Germans, but not for the reasons they like to give. It's because when they see young, healthy, rich men, they know how sick and old and bankrupt they are, and their hearts turn green. Vaillant should get out of the place, get over to America. He's got too much vitality. Having known men like Pemberton once, and having gone to an American university, he isn't just a Frenchman any more. Perhaps Pemberton could get him a job. I'd say a word for him if I could, but the French Resistance as background, that has its drawbacks from the official point of view. If he had the luck to get an immigration visa, he could always give French lessons in America, pick up a living like that, or else driving a car."

"No. We need him here," said the priest. He spoke in French, looking at the girl. "No matter how much the Americans may need him to teach them French," he said, with no malice in it, "we need him here as mayor of Abelin, a constructive, coherent man."

And now the single boat that moved on the water came closer, the throb of its motor soft on the air for an instant longer and then expiring as it drifted toward the wall. Vaillant sat on the cross-board of its seat, and one fisherman behind him at the rudder, and another by the motor in the prow.

"Cornish, it's our show now," said Vaillant, while the boat moved still, his voice startlingly clear across the narrowing stretch of dark, shallow sea. "Paul, you and the men here will get out to the island after Marrakech, if you see it that way," he said to the priest. He had stepped from the boat onto the mole, his hand laid on the hump of the priest's shoulder for the moment that he spoke. "The ladies had better make their way back to Antoinetti's and wait there until the people have cleared off from the quays. Cornish and I will see them home later, when we're through."

"Wait, Vaillant, wait," the girl said in a low voice when he turned to go, and she slipped the Indian bracelet from her wrist. "This is the strongest one," she said, as she had said it before to him, and Vaillant stood there, more alive than any man had ever been, and something already determined in him seemed to hesitate, and then he shook his vivid, heavy head.

"This time it isn't a game," he said, his eyes filled with elation, dark and stirring and incalculably rich, like the eyes of a man in love. "It isn't romance. Cornish came at the right moment. Yesterday it had not quite begun, and tomorrow it will be established, but today the process is taking shape." He said it in English, with the banter not quite gone from his voice, his bright, lively eyes, the language he spoke, including Cornish in the information he gave. "They're asking for what they want, and only coincidentally asking for the instrument that may serve to put it through. For I'm nothing to them but the schoolmaster who coerced them into town meetings year after year when they wanted to sleep, and printed leaflets and made them read them and hand them out, and talked of a sewer system when they wanted to order a drink instead. And now we're not even waiting for next week and the Fourteenth of July to come, Cornish, but we're putting on the fireworks ahead of time for you! Come, and we'll have a glass of wine with them and send them home—"

"Yes, a glass of wine," said Cornish, and he gave Vaillant his wry, dubious smile. Then he went with him, the bafflement and disbelief there in his face, drawn, without choice or commitment, by nothing more than the power of Vaillant's refusal to let him stand aside.

The girl paused on the cement-seamed rocks of the mole watching them go, even her breath in abeyance, her fingers closed on the bracelet, thinking: *So this is the way it is to end, like this, and the rest of it nothing. His lips on my hair, his arm around my shoulders, his voice saying 'It's the right color for hair to be,' all of it nothing at all.* She could see them going back to the people, hurrying along the sea-wall, two men alone together, as she had once thought that it might be. *And perhaps this is the answer,* she thought; *perhaps this, just bringing them together. Perhaps this is the reason I came to Abelin.* The priest was moving toward the boat in which the fishermen sat, and she turned quickly.

"*Monsieur le curé,* I'm going with you out to the island," she said.

And Madame Marceau got stiffly to her feet and followed. She sat on the cross-board at the center, where Vaillant had sat, and the girl beside her, and the priest and the fishermen behind them took the rudder-seat. The second man crouched by the motor, in his hand the end of rope to flay it into action, bare-armed, bare-shouldered, in his faded singlet and blues. And then they swung out of the harbor to the pulse of the motor, passed the white cone of the semaphore, and for a long time she did not turn her head toward land, but rode with her mind on Marrakech, and the air blowing fresh upon her face and hair. When she looked back to shore, Abelin was gone in the beginning of dusk, and the mainland on which it had stood stretched long and dim, seemingly the whole length of a shadowy continent lying against the sky. The priest and the fisher-man at the rudder may have spoken together, or Madame Marceau have leaned forward to caw out her condemna-tion of man, but the girl did not hear their voices or the words they said. As the wide, strong fishing-boat moved swiftly on, rising and falling, rising and falling, borne on swells already dark with the coming night, she saw this as their concentrated universe, this boat, and they the sole survivors of humanity in the vast, uncharted space of sea and sky. But then the island took shape, seen first like a derelict golden-sailed ship, having kept the light longer than the mainland had; and then, as they approached, swell by long, rolling swell, it became castle or cathedral, and the turrets of its rock began to rise. None of them in the boat spoke as the island took on height and beauty in the sea ahead, and the girl watched in wonder the island's soaring columns of blond stone. It was as if they ap-proached a cathedral whose steps and spires had been deeply eroded by time, an edifice standing tall and intri-cate, its shafts rising like stalks of iris from the water, and the summits and ledges grown with tenacious, wind-stunted pine.

"But there's no way of landing," the girl said, half aloud. They, who had seemed so powerful in isolation in the steadily advancing boat, were dwarfed and defenseless now beneath the island's perpendicular flank, and the boat itself become as frail as a leaf upon the waters from which the island rose.

"The beach is in the cove on the south side," said the priest.

When they had half girdled the island, they saw the other boat drawn up on the small fan-shaped beach, Marrakech's boat, its boards streaked with the thin wash of azure paint. In the fading light, the boat, the beach, and the wild island that soared above were touched with a poignancy and loneliness, as if the human life that had once been their concern was stilled.

"It is hopelessly big," the girl said, looking up into the great stone nave that was laced with galleries, broken by delicate staircases of rock. Whoever survived perhaps waited within the cathedral's ruined walls, she thought, and watched them now as they drifted toward the sand.

"Only parts of it are accessible, so it is smaller than it seems," said the priest. The motor was silent now, and the water murmured musically against the prow, and, before them, the island was contained in that echoing quiet which is the climate of a church between the hours at which Mass is said. "You can see the path to the left," said the priest, but he looked instead at the high, arched facsimiles of windows in the soaring stone, perhaps seeking to discern movement there. "Marrakech puts his lobster pots out by the rocks at the fall of night. It's just around the cliff," he said.

Once the boat drifted close to land, the fishermen, who had been without identity to the girl, became men in their own right, and the first one rolled his trousers to his knees and stepped over the side into the water, the bronzed arm, in which the muscle moved with sinuous life, guiding the nose of it to shore. The other man sat by the rudder still, fat-cheeked, and the skin that held his weight of flesh not cleansed by sun and brine, as if rendered immune not only to tenderness and generosity but also to the elements. The soiled end of the cigarette hung on his lip, and the beads of his sight bypassed the women and halted on the man whose feet were planted in the damp, unblemished sand.

"*B'en*, we didn't come to any arrangement with Michel," said the man on the beach. He shifted the blue cap back and forth, forefinger and thumb closed on the cracked leather visor that came low on his brows. "He said to go over to the island with you. That's all he said. He didn't say anything about waiting, or coming back for you, or about ladies being on the trip. He didn't take the time to specify," he told the priest, who stood up in the boat in his black dress.

"We're looking for Dr. Angelo and Marrakech," said the priest, but it was not that, but another uncertainty, that gnawed like vermin at their hearts.

"Michel didn't say who would pay for the gas," the fisherman at the rudder said, the thin lips seeming barely to move, but the cigarette jerking as he talked. "If this is a kind of church excursion, then maybe the church would pay."

"*B'en*, there's a price for tourists who take a trip out to the island," said the fisherman who stood on the beach, maneuvering the blue cotton cap up and down on his head. "There's a daylight tariff. I don't know what the tariff is after dark, but it's higher, and now it'll be getting dark fast."

"It could be double," said the fisherman at the rudder, the cigarette jerking. "There's the kerosene that goes into

223

your lamp, and you can put a value on the sleep you're losing."

"And the price of the fish you might be bringing in if it happened to be the time of the haul," said the fisherman on the sand. "The last time I brought a party out to the island, it was afternoon, and I got two thousand francs and the *apéritif*."

"It's not surprising that none of you wear socks," said Madame Marceau as abruptly as if coming awake. "The toes of them too full, oh, much too full! How the *louis d'or* would rattle when you walked!"

The priest had lifted the hem of his dress, ready to step from the boat onto the damp, firm sand, and he looked at the fishermen's faces in the fading light.

"Stay here with the ladies while I find Angelo and Marrakech," he said. He stood on the sloping, fan-shaped beach, his eyes on them in grief so fierce that it seemed almost anger as he turned away. *Oh, Frenchmen, poor Frenchmen, we have spoken of other things in louder voices in the course of history,* said his fervent silence. *We have given the world a light called freedom that is not to be assessed in francs, and not to be bought or rented or sold. We have, merely by being Frenchmen, accepted an obligation in identity, so that no two priests, and no two policemen, are alike, and one fisherman so different from the other that they might be of different substance, no party, religion, no currency, ever having succeeded in making us conform, or in stamping us with its trade-mark, or in branding us indelibly. Oh, Frenchmen, Frenchmen, this haggling here may have cost a man's life!* his haste might have been saying to them as he went quickly, his shoulders bowed under the weight of their guilt, almost running in his flexible black shoes up the triangle of sand.

"*B'en*, the Americans, they've done so much damage to

224

the country," said the fisherman on the beach, watching the priest go, "tearing up farmland for their airfields, razing houses, and laying pastures and orchards waste, that if they paid for three generations it wouldn't be enough. I was reading about it yesterday." Then he glanced, a little craftily, from under the cracked leather of his visor at the girl. "So maybe *mademoiselle l'Américaine* would pay for the gas used coming out here, and pay for the time, and the kerosene—"

"Now, how much would you say a man's life is worth?" Madame Marceau interrupted, as if having divined the things the priest had not said. "A North African's would not be the same tariff as a royalist's, naturally, and probably the rates go up on Sundays and holidays and after dark. But would you estimate that the life of a twisted man with a blue-black skin, who stands about as high as your hip, would be worth a few liters of gas?"

"The General himself belonged to the royalist party," said the man at the rudder, his eyes hard, and the cigarette jerking on his lip, and Madame Marceau spoke then the final repudiation of all the General had been.

"General Marceau and I never saw eye to eye on anything," she said, *or heart to heart, or lip to lip.* "When you get home tonight, slit open your mattresses and take the coins out, gentlemen!" she said to them, almost savagely.

"Are you going to stand there and listen to this kind of talk?" said the fisherman at the rudder, his thin lips barely moving as he spoke.

"Come on out now, and we'll catch up with the *curé!*" the other called in answer from the beach, and he tightened the belt of his faded blues.

"Your money," Madame Marceau was saying to them still, "it could save lives, black men's, old people's, lives.

225

Your money, mine. The *curé* told me last week that every four hours in France an old person kills himself because he has been hungry so long that he can't bear being hungry any more. Every four hours," she repeated, but the fishermen were gone, and she sat silent now, looking straight before her in fixed and speechless pain as if into a mirror that the priest's words had hung, cruel, ruthless, inescapable, before her face.

The two women sat alone in the boat, and above them rose the intricate façade of rock, and the girl watched it until the tall columns seemed to stir with the half-seen fluttering of wings, and the planes of shadow and pallor to shift place, like the furtive shifting of scenery on a darkened stage. But she knew the semblance of movement was a phantasmagoria of the twilight, and for a long while after she had deciphered a dark, jerking, gargoyle-like head high in the stone, she took it as part of the ghostly, agitated flux, and she did not speak. And then, as she watched, the head solidified and floated clear of the weaving rock, and she saw the gesticulation of a hand.

"I see Marrakech, quite high up there. Can you see him?" she said in a quiet voice.

"I can see nothing," the Frenchwoman said, straining her eyes.

"Yes, Marrakech," the girl said quickly, and she stood up from the cross-board seat. "I'm going up to him," she said.

"Don't move until *monsieur le curé* comes back!" cried Madame Marceau, but the girl was out of the boat and running up the slope of sand. "Don't go, Mary, oh, do not go!" Madame Marceau cried into the vast, still tide of evening, and she stood up lamely, and the knees refused to straighten, the legs declined her weight, and she sat down suddenly again.

The cliff opened in varied ways before the girl, honeycombing into archways and steep flights of stairs, perhaps worn in the rock by the feet of goats, and into hollow corridors winding upward through the stone. She mounted quickly, taking the stairways and the narrow chimneys while looking down into the great cathedral's nave, seeing the ruined altars that lay below, glancing back through the windows in which was the stained glass of the dusk, and the far picture of the two boats drawn up on the shore. Madame Marceau sat, blue-headed, like a lonely vulture on its perch, and the velvet of night moved in across the sea.

"Marrakech, Marrakech, how far are you?" the girl called out softly, stopping to listen for the sound of life. "Marrakech, are you there?" she called, climbing higher in the honeycomb of stone. The third time that she halted and called out she heard movement in the rocks above her, and she reached up her hand. "Come down, Marrakech. Come down to the beach," she said, and she knew from the pliancy, and the length of the bones that closed on hers, that this was Marrakech's hand. "Come down to the boat," she whispered to the dark, but the hand drew her gently, and she climbed the few steps to where he was.

Standing beside him under the open sky, the first faint diamonds of stars over their heads, the girl saw they were clear of the lower gallery of rocks. A wash of artificial light stained the surface of the darkness here, for on this, which was less terrace than a high, oval plateau, a cautious fire had been built far back against the last proscenium of soaring stone. Marrakech held her hand in his still, and he drew her, like a bride to be given in some ancient ritual of sacrifice and lust, toward the bright, covert nest of flame. He moved, singleminded as a child on his warped legs, wild devotion transfiguring his face, his hand trembling as he drew her through the stunted bush of the vegetation back, back, to where the fire burned below the cliff that rose like the pipes of a great organ to the clear shell of the sky. The man who sat beside this fire had drawn up his knees, and his arms hung over them, and one hand held a smooth-stalked stick with which he touched the ash.

"You have come just in time," he said, looking up at the girl, and the porcelain of his teeth caught the firelight. "You must sit down and eat with us," he said, indicating the covered iron pot held by a fork of driftwood above the heat.

"No, ah, no!" whispered the girl. "No, Dr. Angelo," she said, still holding fast to Marrakech's hand.

"Because you are afraid?" said the doctor, speaking gently to her as she stood motionless on the edge of the flickering, imperfect light. "You have heard stories about food poisoning here in Abelin, so now you are afraid to eat?"

"Yes, perhaps it is that," the girl said quickly, and she thought: *They can't be long in coming. They will climb faster than I climbed.* "Yes, the *garçon* of the Café du Port," she said, feeling her tongue and throat gone dry, "and the others—there were others—"

"Sit down, mademoiselle. Sit down, Marrakech," said the doctor, and Marrakech moved at once, in devout obedience, and sat down, cross-legged, on the stony soil. But the girl stood stubbornly watching the doctor across the steaming pot and the low, hot heart of flame. "I saw you come with Madame Marceau and the *curé* and the

228

two strong men of the fishing-fleet, François and Jean. I cannot believe that it is just to see how our lobster traps are doing that all of you came this far. You have reason to be concerned, good reasons, I too have my suspicions," he said. "Gaston, my man, he's not at all voluble, and he has no relatives, no apparent life of his own. A man might lose his sanity, living in introspection as he does. I see him eighteen hours a day, but still I don't know what goes on under the white jacket he wears."

As he talked, the girl's thoughts moved in cold, blind panic, and she saw herself and Marrakech as captive here with him between the last, tall arcade of rock and the steep drop to the beach below, contained in the faint but impenetrable nimbus of the firelight, and cut off from all escape by height.

"I must go. I must go with Marrakech," she whispered. "I must go."

"There will be a little time to wait for the others," the doctor said, as a kind man might have said it, and he leaned forward to lay two horns of driftwood on the fire, setting them carefully in beneath the flame. "The *curé* and his companions were cut off by a fall of rock. I saw it go, and I called to them, but they couldn't hear my voice above the sound of the sea. The wind is rising. It's already on the water, I'm hoping the three of them were already safely past when the rocks went down," he said, and the girl felt a hand close sickly on her heart. "You're cold. Come nearer, mademoiselle," the doctor said, but she stood motionless, the fire between them, and the covered pot, with the odor of cooking fish tainting the air.

Fire, she thought, watching the doctor; it touched a man or a room with its light and made other things of them; it took wood and, in consuming it, gave it another shape, and she watched the doctor altered now by the quick, subtle fingers of flame. Fire had every trick and every character in its flux, she thought as she stood there, halted by her fear, remembering other fires, as if to give her courage now, seeing again the mystery of the changing wood. One summer a fireplace under the stars had served as stage, and her father had been the narrator, and it was Wagner's *Ring* that was played out in the burning logs, Siegfried, with the Nordic blood gone molten in his veins, and the Lorelei playing their golden lyres, their harps, in the wood that was endlessly transformed by the deep, soft, eroding flame. And now the doctor was transfigured in the firelight, his face become a mask so evil that it no longer seemed the assembled features of one human face, but a mask designed for all conniving, voracious men to wear. The fire had worked unceasingly until there was nothing left to lend it resemblance or familiarity. *He is not a man*, the girl thought, standing motionless; *he is power, merely power, power that waits like iron for the weak to fail, the monstrous figure and mask of that*. At her feet, Marrakech had begun to sway back and forth, back and forth, like a pendulum swinging and marking the instants of passing time, back and forth, in a frenzy of homage to this power, with the lids fallen over his eyes.

"For two years now," the doctor was saying, and the fire worked feverishly, so that now he seemed to grin, and now he did not, and now his tongue seemed to dart along his lip, forked like a serpent's tongue; "for two years, Gaston has been talking of rats, rats in the cellar of my villa, and I swear I've never seen any signs of them. In April he asked me to write out a prescription for arsenic, even. He wanted to sprinkle arsenic in the cellar, he said, and I didn't want him to think I questioned his judgment or his sanity, so I wrote the prescription out." The doctor reached for an antlered length of driftwood, then, and stirred the ash. "The lobster last night—I prepared it myself, the lobster the *curé* took up to the Abbey School. But a claw of it was left in the pot, and Gaston wouldn't eat it, he wouldn't touch it, and, in the end, I saw him throw it out. I don't mean to say that anything was done to the lobster between the time I took it out of the boiling water and the time it was brought in on the serving-tray last night," he said, "but with lobster at the price it is currently, nobody in his senses would throw a claw of it away. And I didn't like the man's face when he stood there refusing to eat it for his lunch, defying me. It's been on my mind as to who ate it up at the Abbey School," he said, and the red of the fire touched his teeth, and there seemed to be first a look of shrewdness and then a look of guile-lessness flickering in pantomime across the cold marble of his eyes. "I'm not suggesting anything. I'm merely thinking back over the deaths of other people through the years. I suppose you don't know if the lobster the *curé* took up to the Abbey School was—"

"Yes," said the girl, her voice barely audible. "Eaten by the cats. At least one of them had died by afternoon."

"Sit down, mademoiselle," said the doctor, a look of singular brutality around his mouth now. "Perhaps we have a criminal case on our hands. Who knows? Mary Farrant, this is a land of suspicion, and talking out openly may help to clear the air of the misgivings I have. There is one sinner among us whom all of us see as capable of any-thing, a man with a thin, foxlike face and a beard as red as that foul beast's brush—a man you know. I am speaking of the house-agent, who rode in the bus with you, and who maneuvered Vaillant's arrest last night. If the proper approaches were made to him, he could be made to withdraw his charge," he said. "The wind is rising. You can see by the clarity of the distance if you turn your head, and the sharpness of the stars, that the mistral will soon be blowing hard. Come near to the fire, Mary Farrant, and I'll tell you the story about the house-agent and the woman he loved, if you like that word, a woman nearly as young as you"; and, at her feet, Marrakech swayed in a ritual of worship of this man, this marble god of power, who possessed the secrets of medicine, and of finance, and who would speak now of the intimacies of love. "Fifteen years ago a young man came down from Lyon with his wife. They were on their honeymoon," said the doctor, "and he'd brought a little money that he'd saved, with the idea of putting it into some kind of business on the coast. His wife was a girl still, and she had the same untouched and tender quality that you have, Mary Farrant, like the heart of a rose cut out and offered that becomes an agony to man," he said, the brutal look still on his mouth. "When she walked down the streets of Abelin, the sane thoughts of husbands, fathers, brothers, died and other things came alive in them, the way it happens when you walk past. And the house-agent, who'd never wanted anything but money before she came to Abelin, set about getting her in his own way. Everything he does is done as slyly as a fox— slipping out through the crowd last night to let the police know that Vaillant was there, and how much else that none of us yet know? So fifteen years ago he advanced the young man from Lyon money, a great deal of money, to set up a restaurant in Bandulu. It was a down payment as well on another man's wife, on this woman who looked like you, Mary Farrant, and who obsessed him night and day. Whenever he'd sign a lease or put his name to a contract, the house-agent would groan aloud. We knew this about him, and knew he would groan like a man in ecstasy when money was paid into his hand. And then he began to do it whenever the girl came down the street, the young wife on her honeymoon, and groaned all night in his bed, his *bonne* told Gaston, perhaps at the thought of having her one day with him there. She was like you," said the doctor, and he looked up from the fire at the girl, and his eyes moved slowly on her. "A little older, a little more subtle, but the mouth, the skin, the long legs the same," he said, and the girl stood frozen there. And then he laid the stick of driftwood carefully down, and got without effort to his feet, while Marrakech swayed below the girl in his frenzy of love. "At the end of a year, before the decorating of the restaurant and the new installations had been paid, the house-agent asked for his money back, every centime of it," the doctor said. "He had planned it like that. And the young man from Lyon could blow out his brains, as long as he couldn't pay his creditors, or else give the house-agent his wife. That was the offer the house-agent made. I was there when he made it, not in so many words, but the meaning was clear. If the young man gave him his wife and left the coast, his debts would be taken care of," he said, and the firelight painted a grin on his mouth, and then took it away.

"And what did the man from Lyon do?" the girl asked through her stiff, dry lips, her heart trembling now as if the answer that came would be the final choice of all men between the value of money and the value of love.

"He did both," the doctor said pleasantly. "His wife was the one who had the sense. She knew by then exactly how much the house-agent had, and she wanted it, and she wanted the kind of scheming, obsessed love he had to

give. So she left her husband for the wily fox, and he
married her once the young man from Lyon had put
himself out of the way. Our red-bearded sinner doesn't
enjoy being reminded of that deal, or of other deals that
he's put through. It disturbs his sanctimoniousness. But I
would remind him with a certain degree of pleasure, if it
brought any satisfaction to you. If it made him withdraw
his charges against Vaillant, if it resulted in Vaillant going
free—" He came slowly around the fire then, moving
softly, like a great lax cat, and below them the rhythm of
Marrakech's swaying seemed to falter, as if something
within him sharpened with awareness, and came to a
pause. "I would do it for you. Do you understand?" said
the doctor. He had come close to her now, and the girl
stood motionless as he took her bare wrists in his fingers
and drew them up against his face, his mouth seeking as if
in hunger the pulse that quivered in the skin. "I am offering you life, I am asking you to consent to live," he whispered. "Not here, not in Abelin, but traveling together,
seeing Spain, and Italy, and Greece, you my young wife,
and I would kneel at your feet, asking nothing, nothing,
accepting whatever you wanted to give. If Vaillant's crime
is sabotage, murder, I still could get him off. I could do it,"
the doctor whispered, and in the instant before she moved,
the girl saw that Marrakech was leaning to the bleached
strip of soil that lay between him and the fire, drawing the
picture with the charred end of the stick that the doctor
had laid aside. It was a seagull that he drew, its head
lowered, its wings arched in flight; it was the wooden seagull that he drew, like a direction repeated, an explanation
given again, and, having drawn it, he turned his an-
guished, wounded eyes up to her face.

In the same moment that she recognized the gull, she

jerked her wrists free, and then she stooped to Marrakech, and seized his hand, and drew him upright, and as the doctor sprang toward them, she began running toward the cliff that dropped in darkness to the sea.

"Run, Marrakech, run, oh, faster, faster!" she sobbed through her teeth. "Oh, Marrakech, run!" she cried, and the twisted little man came dancing and leaping behind her on the bent springs of his legs. "The mussels—the last supper you were to eat—that's why he brought you here!" she whispered fiercely, and now they were nearly at the edge, with the sheer arches of stone dropping unseen below. The intricate honeycomb of escape was there at their feet, but Marrakech fought her desperately now, fighting for his blind, frenzied belief in all that Angelo had been to him, and was still, and perhaps would have been until the end if the girl had not cried her prayers aloud. "Help us to get away, Marrakech! Oh, help us! Help us to get down the cliff now, and once in the boat I will tell you what I know! We can row hard, you and I, oh, Marrakech!" she sobbed. "For our lives, for Vaillant, for the stars, and the days and nights to come, oh, help me, help me, Marrakech!"

But he fought still for the years given in fealty to Dr. Angelo, for in renouncing him, every act performed for him would have to be abjured, and the dancing, the fiddling, the thieving, the whole of his existence become meaningless, the interpretation garbled, and the final act of triumph turned to felony. They were there at the cliff, and she strove to drag him into the galleries of the descent, but the doctor was on them now, heavy, soft-limbed, and panting, and the thing was done. With no word spoken and nothing heard but the crying of their breath, the doctor wrenched Marrakech from the girl's two hands, seizing him perhaps by the throat, perhaps by the wiry wig of hair, and by one leg, and then came the rush of sound beyond them, into space. For an instant she saw as clearly as if the scene had been illuminated by a flash of light, the rocks, the sea, the violent death, and at once, turned sly by need, she moved in silence into the façade and descended backward, step by carefully muted step. She clung with her fingers to the stone, feeling the blood coming wet upon the tips of them, mumbling the inaudible prayers like an old woman, toothless and demented, taking shallow gulps of breath into her mouth so that no sound of terror would give him the clue. And above her the doctor moved back and forth along the edge, stopped by the dark as a soft-footed jungle cat is stopped by the bars of its cage.

The descent was long, and she had done little more than half of it when she saw through the stone mullions of the windows of the cliff three lighted lanterns swaying between the water and the sand. They were lanterns hanging in the prows of boats, she thought, nodding in regular formation with the movement of the waves under the wind: Marrakech's boat, and the boat that had brought them here, and the third boat unknown. *Why three? Why three?* she asked the dark, but nothing faltered in her until she sensed that someone was climbing toward her from below, climbing steadily and fast.

"And what if it was my father?" she said half aloud, and now the courage disintegrated in her heart. "What if it was my father, allowed to return for this one moment out of all eternity, allowed to come merely to let me touch his face for an instant and then to go back. I would be good, I would be good," she whispered, moving backward down the staircases of stone into the cathedral's lonely nave. "I would not ask him to stay," she said, but the tears were already on her face. And then the man who climbed below her spoke her name.

"Mary?" he said in inquiry to the night, and it was Vaillant's voice, and his hands reached up to her, and because of the weakness in her veins, she released her hold upon the stone. Clinging to nothing now, she slid between him and the honeycombing of the wall, turning without will and without intent, as the bodies of the drowned turn in the tide. So now she slid facing him down the stone, passing so close that their cheeks and lips brushed, until her feet in the *espadrilles* rested on his, and he held her hard against him, and it was almost like sobbing now when he began to laugh. There was the smell of sea on his flesh and his clothes, and the taste of sea on his mouth as he fiercely kissed her mouth. "This is the beginning," he said, after a moment, and his voice was shaken by love. "There has never been anything else," he said, and then they were lost in the swooning touch of each other again. But, abruptly, and as if by force, he drew himself away. "This is the thing I wasn't going to do," he said, holding her shoulders hard in his hands. "I went to find you at the hotel, and you weren't there, hadn't been there, they said, so I knew you must have come out here. I wanted to know you were safe. That was all. I was going to keep my teeth closed on any talk but this," he said.

"Vaillant, I want to stay in Abelin. I want to stay with you," the girl said to the roughness of his open shirt, and to the warm flesh of his breast, and the smell of brine.

"It isn't just between you and me," said Vaillant, and *my love, my love, my love*, whispered his lips across her hair. "We'll have to ask Cornish what we're to do."

"Vaillant—Michel," the girl said to him, speaking

237

slowly and carefully in the dark. "I always wanted to be there at a country's beginning. I wanted to be a pioneer's daughter, or a pioneer's wife, but I came too late. I wanted to help give a shape to the things that weren't quite started yet, the way he tried to and perhaps did—the man whose child I am. For in the end, you do not shape things, but they give you their shape, and I wanted that. This year, this moment, as you hold my shoulders, Vaillant, I believe that France is just beginning, that this is the new frontier, and everything to be won yet, to be discovered. I want to be a part of it."

"The Indians not yet dead," he said, and he did not laugh, but his open hands moved down her arms and cradled her elbows in his palms. "The wilderness before us, and I '*la longue Carrabine*,' journeying by the moss on the beaches," he said, and not to kiss each other's mouths again was more than they could bear. "The champagne was already uncorked when we got to the hotel," he said after a long moment, "and the reception committee was there. Cornish stayed. He wanted to see both sides, both theirs and mine, and I wanted that too. But he'll come to see it as Abelin does, and he'll want to take part. We had a *coupe* together, and he didn't know when I walked out. The mayor and the house-agent were officiating, and only Angelo missing, disposing of Marrakech out here."

"I tried to save Marrakech. I tried, but I did it the wrong way," the girl said quickly.

"Madame Marceau reached him before I did," Vaillant said then. "I was halfway up the cliff, and I dropped down again, not knowing who had fallen until she called his name. He was dead, dead at once; and if anyone had told her then that this was the statue that should stand on the coast here, facing across the water to North Africa, she, the *haute bourgeoisie* of France, with the broken body of a colonial native held against her breast, she would have had nothing but scorn for it."

The rest of it was said in the descent, jerked out without sequence as they climbed down from balcony to balcony, holding to the carved stone pilasters, Vaillant below the girl, guiding her with shoulder and arm and hand. The *curé* and the two fishermen had been cut off by a fall of rock, he said, and they were not harmed, but were marooned there still, and he had talked across the boulders to them. The *curé* had said he had seen Angelo's face watching above just after the rocks fell, and he had asked Vaillant at once what word there was of Marrakech; but the fishermen had asked about no man, living or dead, or even if the mistral was blowing hard on the north side yet. They had asked, calling it across the mass of fallen rock, who would pay for the gas and the kerosene when they got back to Abelin.

"I said then I'd pay it out of my *joute* purse, my bail," said Vaillant, jerking the words out as he climbed below her in the dark, saying: "I told Cornish I'd asked for an American to come, and that you had answered by mistake, and that it wouldn't do. You were the wheatfields of Ohio, and the apple trees, I said, and I didn't know what to do with them here. I had wanted someone who knew the American constitution, and its amendments, and campaign procedure in the states. I asked him to take you quickly away," he said, his hands still guiding her down.

"And what did Peter say?" said the girl, and she halted a moment in the descent.

"He said he could see what had happened to me," said Vaillant, and she could feel the beating of his heart, and the beating of her own, like the footsteps of two people walking on together. *And if I cannot go on with him like this,* she thought, *where will I find the courage to walk on alone?*

He did not tell her then about the casino, although he knew. It was a long time after that, after the fishermen and the *curé* had come at last across the rockfall and climbed the cliff with Vaillant again and brought the doctor down. It was nearly two hours later, as the boats came in under the swinging arm of the semaphore, the boat that led, with Vaillant at the motor and the fisherman called François at the rudder and the women on the cross-board of the middle seat. The second one carried the priest and the doctor and the fisherman called Jean; and the third boat was Marrakech's, bearing the dark, lonely body under the tarpaulin, towed in the wake of those who lived. The boats had ridden a cold, horned sea, for the mistral was strong now, and as they entered the waters of the harbor Vaillant spoke with the sound of mirth in his voice again.

"Have a look out on the mole," he said, and the girl and Madame Marceau turned to look at the sea-wall. They could see the stones of it well, for the streetlights shone with uncanny brilliance through the mistral-scoured air, and from the light of those hanging clear of the plane trees, whose foliage was slapped upright by the wind, they saw that the casino was gone. "Perhaps while they stretched the nets this afternoon. Every stick and stone of it. Don't ask me how. The mayor," said Vaillant, and he cut the motor now, and the rhythmic pulsing died, "he wanted to take Peter Cornish out to look at it, maybe subsidize it," he said, and then he began to laugh. "But it wasn't there—"

* * *

It took a little time for the thing to become clear. It was nearly a week before it could be seen that there was no case against Dr. Angelo. His dead wife and the General were both under the ground, and Raffio, who might have told one chapter of the story, was dead as well. Although twelve cats had died up at the Abbey School and traces of arsenic been found in their viscera, there was no certain proof that all of them had eaten the doctor's lobster, or that it was the doctor, and not Gaston, who had put the arsenic in. Gaston maintained that the doctor had written the prescription of his own accord and sent him with it to the pharmacy in town, and the doctor said this was a lie. After Gaston gave notice and left the doctor's employ and left Abelin, it was believed that he would eventually have testimony of value to give. But the police of the shipbuilding town picked him up and returned him for further questioning, and it was apparent he had nothing more to tell.

As for the murder of Marrakech, not even the girl had been a witness to it. It had been dark outside the radius of fire, and whatever had happened had not been seen; it was merely what she supposed had taken place. The doctor said that he and Marrakech had struggled at the edge after the little Algerian ("Oh, the lustful little man!" the doctor said) had sought to restrain the girl from joining Madame Marceau on the beach below, and Marrakech had missed his footing and fallen to the sea. ("What point would there have been to it? What reason for it?" said the doctor, and he spread his hands, smiling at the story the girl told.) It was the doctor who ordered the tombstone for Marrakech's grave, and he who petitioned the church, through the *curé*, for the right to bury the black man in hallowed ground. But, a negative answer having come from the archbishop of the diocese, Marrakech had been buried in the garden of the Abbey School, at the foot of a tall, straight cypress tree.

On the eve of the Fourteenth of July it had been agreed that elections would take place on the first of September, once the tourist season had come to a close. In return, there would be no demonstrations on Bastille Day, no chairs carried off the café terraces and flung into the harbor, as had been done one year, and no singing of the "Internationale." The merry-go-rounds would turn on the square, and there would be fireworks at night, as if the people of Abelin were children still. But even with elections in September, Vaillant could not be a candidate until he was cleared of guilt, and now, in the early afternoon of the holiday, the girl turned to the wooden seagull, asking it to speak to her as she smoothed its lowered head. She sat in a blue dress in the shade of Madame Marceau's garden, touching the letters of the word *amour* carved on the seagull's breast, seeking the meaning of the arched bird in her hands. Marrakech had left it like a sign on the step the night of Vaillant's arrest and had drawn its likeness on the ground, in protest as eloquent as argument, when the doctor spoke by the fire of Vaillant's crime. And then, abruptly, she saw the difference in its head. It was as though it had turned to eye her, the suave, beaked cranium now cocked askew.

"You see! The head comes off!" she said half aloud. She stood up quickly, the two separate pieces of it in her hand, and then she hastened across the garden to the house. "There's a paper inside the seagull, some kind of document," she said, standing by Madame Marceau's desk in the twilight of the room, and Madame Marceau put down her pen.

242

"Well, take it out," she said.

The girl drew from the hollow body of the bird a long, fine roll of paper, slightly crumpled, delicate as silk, and as she did this neither woman spoke. But Madame Marceau closed her account book on the page across which the printed heading ran: "Items for the Day," and placed it and its dependent papers in a lower drawer, making space for the girl to open the document out. She spread it on the leather-cornered blotting-pad of billiard-table green, smoothing the creases from its texture with her fingers and thumbs until it lay, twice the size of an open newspaper, before them on the desk. Then they bent over it together, seeing first the sensitivity of the drawing, the painstaking inked design, aware of the workmanship of this macabre comic strip before coming to the meaning of its speech.

In the upper lefthand corner, where the story began, was a date of the preceding year, and there, in the first picture, a stunted black man danced, a violin under his chin. In the next picture he did not dance, and the violin was lowered, for blood gushed from his foot; and in the next a white man knelt before him in a doctor's blouse, and in unlikely humility, and dressed his wound. The pictures were limned with such adulation that nobility was given to the hands nursing the black foot, and the face of the stooping man given such beauty that it seemed a mask, not of power, but of infinite enlightenment. It had the continuity of a frieze, this message from a man now dead, and it was neither confession nor apology, but merely the exposition of his deathless love.

"There's one picture missing," said Madame Marceau grimly as she looked at the one of the doctor's hands on a taut, curved rod bent to the waves; and, next, the boat—

Marrakech's boat—in which the black man and the white man rode as equal men, depicted filled with lobster, with mussels in ebony shells, and the highlights done carefully. "It's the picture of the doctor's hands closing on his throat that isn't there," she said.

"Ah, don't," whispered the girl.

A second date marked the following chapter, a day in spring, when the doctor led the dwarfed but sensitive figure out of jail, and the police, in savage caricature, pointed in accusation with their nightsticks to pilfered grapes and oranges and plums, done with such succulence that one could taste their flesh upon the tongue.

"Could it be that the doctor," the girl said in a low voice, "just for Marrakech, for no one else—"

"Felt charity? Was moved by love? Ah, never!" Madame Marceau cried. "If all sinister men are lonely men, then maybe he craved a human to whom he could turn. But I don't believe it. It was all for a purpose. Angelo was kind only when he had a plan in mind."

Then came the final sequence: the doctor's hand, life-sized and bold, guiding the Algerian's tentative hand, the white fingers placing the surgeon's scalpel at the required angle in the dark, quiescent fingers, placing it over and over in picture that followed varying picture until the black hand manipulated the scalpel alone; until, at the end, the blade was made to sever the tubes beneath a mammoth rubber-tired wheel, severing them as the same hand would have turned traitor on itself and severed its own viens had the doctor specified it should be done. And then the last design: that of the dwarfed figure fiddling and waltzing away in the frenzied triumph of its dance.

"He was proud that he did it. Do you see?" the girl said in a low voice of grief. "He was proud. He didn't want anyone else to be given the honor of it. This was something he had worked a long time on, this record, and he brought it up in haste that night, after they took Vaillant away."

"In homage," said Madame Marceau, and she seemed to shiver in the room. "In homage to Angelo," she said. "It makes the blood run cold."

"Or perhaps thinking I would find the secret of the gull, and find this history, and let the truth be known," the girl said. "He wanted the acclaim for it—"

"And now?" said Madame Marceau, and she sat back bleakly in her chair.

"But it's evidence! Don't you see it's evidence?" the girl said. As she folded the paper carefully over again, her hands were trembling, and she put the fine silk of it down the seagull's gaping throat, and the wood cried out when she twisted the bird's head into place again. "This is the evidence that will clear Vaillant and put Dr. Angelo under arrest," she said.

"With the kind of men who decide our fate in Abelin, I'm not sure that it will," said Madame Marceau. "It might convince them that Angelo should be appointed director of the surgical wing of the Foundlings' Hospital of Toulon, in recognition of his ingenuity."

"No, this time it's different. This year it's different. This time the world's beginning again. I'm going down to the police. We've solved a crime, Madame Marceau," she said in a voice that was faint with awe.

The girl went quickly down the lane, and into the village street that was stripped of its banners of drying clothes in respect for the meaning of the day. And from the port below came the sound of music, high, sweet, insouciant, the calliope-like piping, and the tune like the music pumped out by a merry-go-round at a country fair, the strains of it pounding the time for the rise and fall of the wooden horses; music that wove between silver-winged airplanes, child-sized, and miniature buses, and gondolas that dipped and rose as they revolved. Through this music the laughter of men and women rang, as if echoing against a swimming-pool's four walls. "Ha-ha-ha, ha-ha-ha!" came the laughter, and for a moment the girl thought the people must be dancing, the whole village of them dancing hand in hand as the calliope played. But when she had come past the houses that stood on the waterfront, she saw that people filled the terraces of the cafés, and rode the merry-go-rounds that turned between the plane trees on the square; that they stood upright in swings that turned the swingers over in mid-air, and drove the waltzing electric cars that, in clanging fury, spun nose to nose.

As she crossed the quays, carrying the arched gull in her hands, she could see that *la joute*, which had been played with such passion a week before, was now being played again, and she made her way, wondering at this, through the crowd of people to the edge. There were the two advancing boats, and the two players, wearing their shirts of luminous red and their white trousers, with the stocking-caps on their heads, riding high on the platforms, the gilded shields on their left arms, the lances in their raised right hands. But this time no crew of other players waited their turns below. Only after the two boats had glided past each other, each with a fisherman at the motor in the boat's deep trough, and after the two lances had struck, and both men fallen the long way to the glittering needles of the sea, did she recognize the players who swam toward each other, Vaillant, shaking the water from his eyes, and the other, and for a moment she did not believe it could be true.

"You're good! You're excellent!" Vaillant was calling out, the English words coming across the fluid distance with startling clarity. She remembered Vaillant telling her, then, that when both players fell, they must swim to each other and kiss each other's cheeks, the meaning being that man was committed to man, victor to vanquished, and now they did this. Vaillant was laughing, with the stocking-cap slipped back on his black hair. "It's two to nothing, in your favor," he said. "We'll try it again."

"He's new at the game, the *type* who's panting hard out there," said a voice beside her, and the girl saw that it was Marius, wiping the palms of his hands dry on his *garçon's* apron as he watched the swimmers with a jaundiced eye. "Michel's given him a handicap, but he can't win. They don't play this game where he comes from. It seems they're doing it for a woman, Michel and the American," he said. From the square behind them came the *ping* of the shooting-gallery guns and the clash of the electric cars. "That's what the game was for once, not done for money, or for the tourist trade, but done for a woman. Maybe that gives it a kind of honor again." He stood watching the two men swim to their boats, and he added bitterly: "Perhaps that's what the lot of us are looking for."

A NOTE ON THE TYPE

The text of this book was set on the Monotype in a face called Baskerville, named for John Baskerville (1706–75), of Birmingham, England, who was a writing-master with a special renown for cutting inscriptions in stone. About 1750 he began experimenting with punch-cutting and making typographical material, which led, in 1757, to the publication of his first work, a Virgil in royal quarto, with great primer letters, in which the types throughout had been designed by him. This was followed by his famous editions of Milton, the Bible, the Book of Common Prayer, and several Latin classic authors. His types foreshadowed what we know today as the "modern" group of type faces, and these and his printing became greatly admired. After his death Baskerville's widow sold all his punches and matrices to the SOCIÉTÉ PHILOSOPHIQUE, LITTÉRAIRE ET TYPOGRAPHIQUE (totally embodied in the person of Beaumarchais, author of THE MARRIAGE OF FIGARO and THE BARBER OF SEVILLE), which used some of the types to print the seventy-volume edition, at Kehl, of Voltaire's works. After a checkered career on the Continent, where they dropped out of sight for some years, the punches and matrices finally came into the possession of the distinguished Paris type-founders, Deberney & Peignot, who, in singularly generous fashion, returned them to the Cambridge University Press in 1953.

Composed, printed, and bound by KINGSPORT PRESS, INC., Kingsport, Tennessee. Paper manufactured by S. D. WARREN COMPANY, Boston, Massachusetts. Designed by HARRY FORD.